CHRISTINA RICH

The Negotiated Marriage

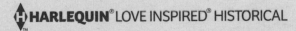

Recycling programs
for this product may
not exist in your area.

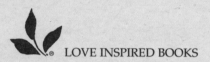

LOVE INSPIRED BOOKS

ISBN-13: 978-0-373-28385-9

The Negotiated Marriage

Copyright © 2016 by Christina Rich

www.Harlequin.com

Printed in U.S.A.

Then Peter opened his mouth, and said,
"Of a truth I perceive that God is no respecter of
persons: But in every nation he that feareth him,
and worketh righteousness, is accepted with him."
—*Acts* 10:34–35

Mom and Dad, thank you for being some of my biggest fans. Thank you for believing in me.
Love,
Chris

Chapter One

Rusa Valley, Kansas
Spring 1867

"Hold it right there!" Camy Sims drew a bead on the man lying down at the bank of the creek, his feet dipped in the water. She eased the bucket to the ground. How dare anyone trespass on their land? *Her* land, given that Uncle Hamish disappeared with the wind and her sisters Ellie and Mara seemed to have other things in mind like carriage rides and frilly dresses. Not Camy. She didn't have aspirations for anything other than staying right here on Sim's Creek and enjoying the solitude of country life. A solitude sorely interrupted by a man who refused to acknowledge her presence. "I said, don't move."

He didn't. Not a single muscle. Tilting her head away from the rifle resting against her shoulder, Camy squinted through the dappling of grey morning light filtering through the thick canopy of leaves until the man came into focus. His bare feet ebbed and flowed with the current of the river. Perhaps he'd fallen asleep.

She couldn't blame him for succumbing to the beauty here. Wisps of smoke rose from the charred firewood, telling her he'd camped the night in her favorite place of solitude, a place away from Mara's continuous chatter of prospective husbands and Ellie's melancholy, a state she'd been in since she returned home last August after months with a distant cousin. Anger sparked and burned through her veins at the intrusion.

After all the railroad's attempts at acquiring their land before the winter, Camy should have known they'd come creeping through the woods once the weather warmed. She only wished she knew why they wanted the Simses' land. It was far from ideal, at least to her way of thinking. There were places closer to town where the land lay flat and the banks were more even, places where the river wouldn't wash the railroad's bridge downstream. If only this man were a simple passerby who had been lured by the languorous song of the water trickling over the rocks and the serenade of the birds. Given that a wayward stranger hadn't passed by here since she could remember, his presence meant one thing: he was trying to gain access to her land. And that just wouldn't do. Did he come expecting their gratefulness at a measly offer, or did he come ready to make threats and burn their home down?

She intended to find out even though her sisters would complain at her dallying too long as Mara, no doubt, would be anxious to complete morning chores so they could go to town. Camy's younger sister loved the social blur of town life, whereas Ellie and Camy only wanted to discreetly discover details about any strangers who might be a threat to them. The latest gossip from Mrs. Smith, Rusa Valley's socialite, was about a man. Tall, handsome and more important, according to Mara, richer than King Solomon. As if those things were all that mattered in a prospective husband.

But from the looks of this man, he wasn't rich or handsome, at least not in the sense her sisters claimed. No doubt they'd thank her for taking the time to scoot the scallywag right off their land once they got over their anger at her dealing with him on her own. Besides, if Ellie knew about the stranger, she'd demand they all move into town as she'd threatened to do after the last incident with a group of ruffians. No amount of money, bluff and bluster could entice Camy to leave her home.

Picking up the water bucket, Camy crept down the well-worn path, focused on the still figure. After all, it wouldn't do for her to be caught unaware. Why, what if the man was only playing possum? Her sisters would think her silly, as no man in his right mind would play dead in his bare feet. Not around here leastways. There were too many thorns ready to pierce clear to the bone, and she should know given that Ellie had doctored her feet plenty of times. As she got closer to the stranger, she knew that no man would played possum with his feet in the icy water and the rest of his body at an odd angle with his arms strung out. His lip bloodied.

Camy skidded to a halt. Clumps of dirt rolled down the path until they splashed into the water. Was he dead?

She couldn't very well leave him there, dead or alive. If he was alive she'd give him a swift kick to his backside, and if he wasn't, well, she'd just have Ellie fetch the Drs. Northrop, all three of them. Of course, if he was already dead, she could just roll him into the water. The river would wash him past Sims Ferry and on down to Doc Northrop's Landing where the old doctor most likely dipped his pole in the water. The man would be the doctors' problem, not hers.

Camy shoved her spectacles back onto the bridge of her nose and shifted her gaze over the still body, looking for any hint of life. She drew in a fortifying breath and eased down the rest of the path until she was only a few feet from his body. Waves of chestnut locks blanketed his brow, covering his eyes. Her fingers itched to brush the strands away for her to see if his lashes were as thick and dark as she imagined. Even with the bloodied lip and shadow of a beard, handsome didn't even come close to describing the chiseled jaw and aquiline nose. He was beautiful.

Her gaze roamed toward his chest. The tension holding her shoulders taut released at the steady rise and fall. She took note of its wide berth, the way his shirt stretched tight. Corded forearms, visible from his rolled sleeves. He no longer seemed like a stranger, but like a man who belonged in the country. A man who belonged here. In her place. Her secret place, and that just wouldn't do at all.

She took a few steps closer and jabbed him with the barrel of her rifle. "Mister, are you hard of hearing? Or daft?"

He groaned. As he turned his head, his dark locks fell, revealing thick, dark lashes and mossy green eyes hooded by thick, dark eyebrows. He clasped his hand to his head.

"You need to be getting out of here, mister."

He groaned again as he eased into a sitting position. He pulled his feet out of the water and his knees into his chest and then buried his face into his hands. Blood stained the rock near where his head had been. Crimson-matted clumps of hair stuck out at odd angles from the back of his head. Someone obviously took a strong disliking to him to leave him here like this. She wanted to help, to inspect his wounds as her sister Ellie would do, but after all the schemes the railroad had pulled last year, she wouldn't put this one beyond them too.

"Mister, you can't sit here all day. More than likely the sky is about to unleash a torrent and this here river will flood. If you don't want to be going for a swim downriver, I suggest you get moving."

He lifted his head and squinted at her through a swollen and blackening eye as if she'd lost her wits. His gazed roamed over her from head to toe and back again until he settled on her face. "Where am I? Where's my horse?"

Camy glanced around the trees. "I don't know anything about your horse, mister. This here's Sims Creek. At least here in this little bend. Upriver it's Northrop River and downriver the same. But right here, it's Sims Creek."

His brow furrowed. "Hamish Sims?"

A sickening thud dropped into Camy's stomach. Had her uncle turned yellow-bellied and befriended the enemy? Most certainly not. He'd made a promise, and a Sims always kept a promise. Excepting her da. This was just another ploy. Camy moved back a few paces and motioned toward his coat with the rifle. "Get your stuff and get off my land."

He massaged the back of his neck and then unfolded to his full height. He narrowed his eyes and gave her a glare that begged for a fight. Gold-flecked daggers flashed from his eyes, causing a shiver of caution to race down her spine. Perhaps she should agree to leave her home and take her sisters to town where they'd be happier and much safer.

He thrust his hands on his hips. "Your land?"

"That's right, mister." Camy rooted her feet in place. It wasn't exactly hers alone, but Hamish had promised it to her and she wouldn't allow this stranger's height to intimidate her and make her give up her fight so easily.

He swayed toward her, one corner of his mouth curving upward as if he knew something she didn't, and then held out his hand. "Duncan Murray."

The earthy scent emanating from him assaulted her senses, catching her off guard. The name suited his towering height and brawny muscles. If she pulled on her memories, she could hear tales spun by her mother and could almost imagine him brandishing a sword in the plaid buried in the bottom of her mother's trunk. His name was strong and true to his heritage. However, the way he stifled his accent indicated he was not so proud to be a Scotsman. If there was one thing both her parents taught her and her sisters, it was to never be ashamed of their heritage. Never.

"I dinnae care who you are, Mr. Murray." She allowed her own accent, faded through the years, to thicken as she straightened her spine and propped the butt of the rifle against her shoulder. "I do not want to shoot you, but I will if I must."

"And I have no wish to be shot."

Before she knew what he was about, he closed the distance between them and removed the rifle from her hands. Losing her footing, she slid down the bank and sucked in a sharp breath as the icy water soaked through her clothing. The current tugged at her legs, rocking her. She held her arms out to gain balance and then wrapped them around her midsection. He laid the rifle on the bank and offered her a hand. She stared at the calloused palm and started to reach for it until she recalled the last encounter with a hired thug claiming to be with the railroad. Not only had they promised to burn their home if they didn't accept an offer soon, but they had threatened to dump her and her sisters in the river.

"I'll get out myself, thank you."

"Very well, then." Mr. Murray plucked his coat from the ground. The man took the liberty of filling the bucket with water, grabbed her rifle and started up the path.

"Where are you going?"

"To find that scoundrel Hamish."

He didn't even have the decency to look at her, or persist in offering her aid to safety. She found herself at a further disadvantage, as Mr. Murray had all of her belongings, heading straight for her sisters. He might not be blond and blue-eyed, but Mara would no doubt swoon and then fawn over his every whim. Ellie, on the other hand, would be packing their trunks and moving them into the safety of town with the likes of folks who were more apt to sip tea in their stuffy parlor rooms than take a walk along the river.

Over her freezing limbs. "You cannot very well walk around without your shoes."

Never mind that detail had not bothered her a moment ago when she told him he had to leave. She eased through the turbulent water sucking at her skirts, careful not to lose balance, and grabbed hold of a root protruding out of the bank. She tested its strength and then, using her foot as leverage against the bank, tried to pull herself up the side. She slid right back into the water, her fingers white-knuckled around the root as the water tugged at her. She wasn't about to give up. She'd seen him first. And she'd see him gone before Mara laid eyes on him. Before Ellie moved them from their home.

"Which is one reason why I intend to find Hamish."

Little chance of that. She hadn't seen her uncle since before the leaves fell from their moorings, and that had been months ago, but she wasn't about to tell Mr. Duncan Murray such truths lest he take it in his head to steal their land.

"And what is the other, Mr. Murray?"

He halted halfway up the path and faced her. A lopsided grin appeared, forcing a dimple in his cheek. That field of butterflies fluttered with the force of her clothes hanging out on the line in a southerly Kansas wind. His swollen eye and bloodied lip did nothing to lessen the effect. "To find my horse."

She almost let loose a sigh of relief. Nobody could blame a man for searching for his horse. If that was the only reason he was here.

"And to negotiate the purchase of this land, *after* I meet Cameron Sims."

"What did you say?"

Duncan hadn't meant for those words to spill out of his mouth, but she'd been so insistent that he get off her land, land they both very well knew wasn't hers, that he couldn't help goading her. All he wanted to do was inspect the land Hamish had offered him at a measly sum, a piece of property his friend had claimed rivaled the beauty of Duncan's beloved Highlands. The fact that it was only miles from Rusa Valley where he could oversee his investment in the railroad as it clanked through town made Hamish's offer more appealing. Calvin Weston, a member of the railroad committee and the man who had approached Duncan about providing funds for iron and labor for the railroad, wouldn't be too happy about Duncan keeping a close watch on how his money was spent.

All he had to do was hand Hamish the bills in his pocket and sign his name on the deed and the land would be his. Of course, there was the little matter about his future bride, a minute detail Hamish had forgotten to mention until they'd made camp. A detail that had Duncan gathering his belongings and heading back to Topeka. That was until Hamish had caught him off guard and rammed the butt of his rifle into Duncan's face. Obviously his friend was intent on Duncan purchasing the land *and* marrying a lass. The next thing he knew his ribs were being poked by a wild-haired, wild-eyed beauty.

Staring at the woman in the water, he was more than grateful she wasn't the woman Hamish thought to pawn on him. At least he hoped not, as she was far from the description Hamish had given him. Much prettier and full of vinegar with her pink, bow-shaped mouth Not the meek wallflower Hamish had told him about. Not to mention that she looked nothing like his friend and could be of no relation.

He shrugged. He didn't need any female luring him into a real marriage. "I'm here to purchase this land."

"It's not for sale." Her lips flattened into a thin line. Her spectacles magnified the arrows shooting from her frigid eyes, piercing his black heart. As if her aversion toward him wasn't enough to spark his competitive nature, the mass of dark curls springing from the knot at the nape of her neck tempted him further. Her enticing accent stirred long-forgotten memories of warm hearths and heather-covered fields. Her resolve to do things herself, the strength in her hands as she held on to the root, the mud speckling her gown and the dusting of freckles draped over her button nose, reminded him of all the reasons Hamish Sims's proposition had held some appeal. Miles from city life promised a reprieve from social gatherings and the matchmaking mamas hoping to pawn their daughters onto his bank account. Besides, Hamish had argued, what better way to halt the incessant schemes than to marry a homely sort of lass? Duncan never expected a man he'd considered a friend to join ranks with scheming mothers. Hamish knew how he felt about marriage, but now Duncan wondered if the old man hadn't spoken with some wisdom. Perhaps a marriage in name only could be beneficial.

"I have it on good authority that it is." Duncan stretched his jaw, testing the damage left by Hamish, and then rubbed the back of his head where he'd landed on a rock.

"I don't know what sort of sham you're trying to pull, Mr. Murray. This land is not for sale." The light sprinkling of rain turned to fat drops. She lifted her face to the rain. The droplets of mud washed away, leaving a soft glow bathing her cheeks. The corners of her mouth curved into a slight smile, as if she enjoyed the feel of nature's kiss on her skin. For a small space of time he traveled back to his beloved Highlands, and if he allowed himself the pleasure of lingering she'd soon be twirling about like a wee child, wrapping strands of her hair around his finger, crumbling the hardened brick and mortar encasing his heart.

No wonder she was hidden out here in the woods— she was a danger to society. Most ladies of his acquaintance ran indoors at the first sight of a rain cloud, not to mention suffering from the vapors at a dunking in the river. She seemed to delight in it.

She dropped her gaze back to his. A deep scowl appeared before she resumed her efforts to get out of the river. "Hamish will never sell this land. I'd guarantee a month's worth of cooking and cleaning on that."

Too bad he couldn't take her up on the cooking. It'd been a long time since he'd eaten anything other than beans. He had the funds to eat at Calhoun's whenever he chose, but no sooner had he settled his napkin on his lap than a gaggle of females congregated at his table full of giggles, batting eyelashes and dinner invitations. Once the matchmaking mamas discovered he had no intention of courting their daughters, they rescinded their offers of dinner. Hot stew, fresh biscuits and homemade apple pie sure set his mouth to watering.

No matter, it had been a small price to pay to retain his bachelorhood and save the world from the likes of him. He'd seen what happened to women who became slaves to marriage and their husband's fists, to the children born of such unions. He'd been one of them, and he wasn't about to make the same mistakes as his father, which meant he had to convince Hamish that any marriage he considered could be nothing more than words spoken before a minister. A marriage in name only.

She finally pulled herself out of the water and onto the bank. She held her skirt up as if to examine the damage. The curve of her calf clad in wool stockings waved at him. He caught his jaw slacking and he snapped it shut as he shifted his gaze to the sun-kissed freckles gracing the curve of her cheeks. He grunted, disgusted with himself. He focused on a dark freckle above her nondescript wire-rimmed spectacles. He couldn't afford the distraction of her natural beauty.

Duncan shook his head. He needed to focus on his current task, and it wasn't her.

Although Hamish had it in him to knock Duncan in the head when he wasn't looking, he more than likely hadn't the heart to rid this place of squatters, not when they looked like her, doe-eyed and hapless. He was no old man with a soft heart; his heart had hardened years ago. He wouldn't fall for her womanly charm, not that she meant to exude it. Obviously she didn't, else she'd hold his gaze and bat her lashes like so many of the ladies in town.

Nope. He wasn't going to give her the chance. Once he hunted down Hamish, paid the measly amount of cash, signed the deed and hired the minister, he'd boot her right off *his* land. She shivered, as if she heard his thoughts, her arms tightening around her waist to ward off the tepid spring breeze.

"You're going to catch a cold standing there all day in wet clothes." He started toward her with the intention of moving her away from the edge of the bank, but stopped himself. No doubt, if he touched her he'd catch the illness that had plagued his father.

"I don't sicken so easily."

He imagined not. Just as well. She was none of his concern, even though he wished she would move farther away from the edge. One slip and she'd be back in the water. He hadn't had the urge to rescue a damsel in a long time, and he'd do well to pay heed to the dinner bells clanging in his head. He couldn't allow the urge to take root. Wouldn't. The rain quickened its pace. Turning from her, he headed up the path, away from the strings drawing him back toward her, away from the gleam in her milk-laden, coffee-colored eyes that he couldn't quite comprehend.

"Why are you looking for Cameron Sims?"

He didn't need to turn around and see the glare in her eyes, not when fire singed the back of his neck.

"Mr. Murray, I demand you stop, right this minute."

Demand? Thankful she was definitely not the woman Hamish intended him to marry, he felt the knot of uncertainty that had been balled up in his gut release. She was neither biddable nor undemanding.

"Mr. Murray, I'm warning you."

He had never been partial to brown eyes, but hers stirred emotions buried deep beneath a thick layer of mistrust, and if he wasn't careful he'd find himself legshackled at the altar with a beautiful lady and a gun pressed against his spine. He flinched at the memory. "To marry her," he muttered beneath his breath.

"Mr. Murray!"

Before he could shake off the memory, he found

his foot lassoed and his body jerked upside down. The bucket and the rifle flew from his hands, hitting the ground. A loud crack split the air.

Chapter Two

Her scream punched Duncan in the gut as the smell of gunpowder wafted around him. He twisted his upper body around to search for her. A plethora of green and brown clouded his vision as he fought against his spinning and throbbing head. He squeezed his eyes shut and opened them, hoping to gain his bearings, but no one object came into focus. "Miss? Miss!"

Nothing. Inhaling a deep breath, he wrapped his free leg around the one caught in the trap and spread his arms out wide until his swinging, upside-down body slowed. Careful not to start the movement all over again, he craned his neck until he spied the spot where she'd been standing.

She was gone.

He muttered beneath his breath as the mound of yellow fabric bobbed downstream and around the bend. The report must have startled her, causing her to lose her footing and fall back into the river. He should have insisted she move away from the edge. He should have pulled her out of the water and held on to her until her feet were on firmer ground.

Why wasn't she hollering for help?

Unless she couldn't.

He jammed his hand into his pocket and pulled out his penknife. Swinging his body upward, he tried to grab hold of the rope above his foot and ended up renewing the back-and-forth motion. He tried again, and again. The sky, declaring war on his situation, began pouring buckets of rain, stinging his eyes. The rope bit into his ankle. If he were a praying man, he'd ask for a bit of mercy, but he'd discovered long ago that God, mercy and Duncan Murray had nothing to do with each other.

Perhaps the good Lord would listen for the lady. "God, if you're willing to bend your ear to a black-hearted Murray like me, not for me, for her." The line attached to his leg jerked him upward, and then dropping, he started swinging again. "That woman needs some h—"

The trap released from its mooring without him even making a jab at the rope. Like a wounded bird falling from the sky, Duncan fell, hitting the ground with a hard thud. His breath rushed out of him and he laid there stunned.

A toothless, gray-bearded Hamish, in an oversize patched coat, hunched over him. Had the old man come to bash him in the head again?

"Ye messed that one up, ye did." Hamish squinted as he glanced toward the river. "Best go get her, as I ain't none too good at swimmin'."

"You have some answering to do, my friend," Duncan said as he rolled to his feet and ran down the path. He dove into the river, icy water engulfing him. He pushed through the water several paces until the current began to quicken and swirl around his legs, seeking to drag him under the surface. Unless she knew how to swim, it would be impossible for her to navigate the waters with her small stature, especially with yards of sodden fabric weighing her down. He dove beneath the murky water and swam toward the last place he'd seen her yellow dress.

The current thrust him around the bend where the banks of the creek widened near the place he'd crossed with Hamish on his ferry only the day before. Spying a heap of yellow lying on the wooden raft, Duncan cut through the water. He grabbed hold of a corner post to keep from being sent farther downriver. Resting his forehead against the hewn wood, he drew in a few calming breaths, and then he glanced at the lady.

She lay on her back, her hand across her midsection. If it weren't for the rapid rise and fall of her chest, he'd assume she enjoyed resting on her perch much like the water turtles who gathered on rocks to sunbathe. However, the sun remained hidden far behind the clouds and the heavy rain.

Duncan swiped the water from his eyes and pushed himself onto the anchored ferry. The back of his head pounded with the fierce clang of a hammer hitting a rail tie. Leaning on his elbows, he circled his neck, stretching the tense muscles, trying to relieve the thundering in his skull. However, if he was to be honest with himself, which he made a point to do—after all, if a man couldn't tell himself the truth, he wasn't worth a fleck of dust—he hoped to settle the fright right out of his bones. He'd known the woman less than a quarter of an hour, and already she'd torn more emotion out of him than any lady of his acquaintance since he'd left Scotland, ten years ago at the young age of seventeen. She'd made him care about her well-being *and* play the knight.

He could hear her laughter in his mind before he'd even completed the thought. If it hadn't been for him, she'd still be standing on the bank, hands on hips, commanding him to halt. Her ability to navigate the creek, in a gown no less, and pull herself to safety, impressed him. He should have listened to her. Then he wouldn't have dropped the rifle.

"I suppose I owe you an apology."

The sound of the creek rushing around the bend roared in her silence. The tap of each raindrop smacking the surfaces around him increased in intensity. Her lack of sarcasm unnerved him. An uneasiness pricked the base of his neck.

"Miss?" He glanced over his shoulder and noticed her spectacles no longer rested on the bridge of her nose. He turned more toward her and took note of how her hair had come completely loose from its knot. His thoughts jumbled into a knotted ball of yarn. Before he could halt himself, he reached out to tap her shoulder and found his fingers brushing against her hair. Not one, but all of his fingers became captivated by the drenched ringlets. He could almost imagine spending his days like this, with her lounging on a crude, rickety raft in a muddy creek instead of spending his days being wooed by men with ideas bigger than their bank accounts, stiff collars and musky cigars.

A stone settled in the pit of his stomach and he jerked his hand back, his fingers snagging in her hair. He was surprised that she didn't cry out like he'd expect ladies to do when having their hair pulled.

He turned onto his knees and grabbed hold of her shoulders and began to shake her. Warm, sticky residue seeped through her gown, oozing against his hand. He eased his hand back, knowing what he'd find. That stone in his stomach began to mull around like boulders tumbling from a mountaintop. Blood spread from her shoulder and down the sleeve of her gown.

"Duncan Murray, you're as black-hearted as they come and you've done a lot of rotten things, but ye never shot a lassie afore," he told himself. He'd never shot anyone outside of the war.

He glanced around the small cove to see if Hamish had followed by land, but only drab gray trees waiting for their spring coats to sprout lined the river banks. The old man was nowhere to be seen. Rusa Valley lay east half an hour's ride by horseback. A well-worn path to the west would take him back toward Hamish and the hopes of shelter.

Duncan stood to his feet, the ferry rocking beneath them. Scooping her into his arms, he settled her against his chest, her head resting in the crook of his arm. The warmth of her breath filtered through the cotton strands of his soaked shirt, singeing his skin.

He stepped over the ledge, onto the bank and then readjusted her. Her arms snaked around his neck, causing his pulse to thunder. The clanging of bells, much like the ones alerting a town to a fire, roared in his ears, warning him he trod dangerous territory. He should just lay her right down on the muddy bank, forget about Hamish's offer and hightail it back to Topeka. Perhaps leave Kansas altogether, especially given the certainty the feel of her in his arms would never leave his memory.

This woman had managed to steal his wits. One touch of her left him rattled, ready to jump in his father's wastrel footsteps. In his father's case, married to one woman, his mind on another. Several others.

He ducked beneath the limb of a tree and came face-to-face with the end of a revolver and the barrel of a rifle. The revolver clicked as the mechanism slid back. He eyed the two women pulling a bead on him, and he nearly dropped the woman in his arms. The piercing dark eyes and matching scowls told him all he needed to know. These women were all sisters.

"How many more of you are there?" he asked.

The shorter one narrowed her eyes. "You railroad men have tried all sorts of things to get our land, mister."

"Kidnapping isn't one of them," the taller one added.

"Railroad man? Kidnapping?"

What did the railroad have to do with these women? Weston had briefed him on the latest plans to build the iron road through the county only days ago through the middle of Rusa Valley, and this bit of land was far from it. Before asking what they meant, the shorter one let out a high-pitched scream as she removed her finger from the trigger. "You shot Camy!" She whipped her head around and faced the taller sister. "He shot Camy."

He glanced down at the woman in his arms. Almond-shaped eyes rested in a sun-kissed, heart-shaped face. Her bow-shaped lips were slightly parted. Her dark curls formed a pillow for her head against his arm, and he couldn't help imagining gazing upon her beauty every day for the rest of his life and calling the name that suited her.

"Cam—Cameron Sims?" Dread curled in his stomach, pounding like wild horses in his head, and he nearly dropped her. So much for her not being Hamish's relation. So much for her not being the woman Hamish wanted him to marry. Everything in him told him to get away from her as fast as he could.

Her lashes fluttered and then opened. A pool of warm cocoa with flecks of gold blinked up at him, laced with pain. She blinked again. "You rescued me."

"Not exactly," he snapped, ashamed of his actions causing her need to be rescued.

Her eyes grew wide at his terse response, and at the moment he wasn't apologetic. He'd been a fool to follow Hamish out here with the promise of a home worthy of Scotland only to be swindled into marriage by a conniving old man. The woman in his arms was far from homely.

Her mouth opened and closed as if she wanted to say something. Instead she raised her head and looked from one sister to the other and back to him. She started to push against his shoulders and groaned in pain. Eyelids falling, her head fell and dangled over his arm. His protective instinct had him rolling her closer into him. The curve of her cheek resting against his chest.

The sisters lowered their weapons and rushed toward them.

The taller of the two sisters probed Camy's wound. "Is this her only injury?"

Duncan shrugged. "It's the only one I see. However, she was washed down the river."

"You shot her. And you tried to drown her just like

the last prospector promised to do," the younger sister accused as she jammed a fist on her hip.

Duncan's pulse skipped a beat. Someone had threatened her? A man claiming to work for the railroad? A man Duncan's money helped pay wages to? No wonder she'd been adamant about him leaving. Now wasn't the time to be interrogated by this younger sister, nor was it the time for him to ask questions. Camy needed medical attention, and quickly. "If I meant to drown her I wouldn't be carrying her, now, would I?"

The sister inspecting Camy for injuries glanced at the shorter one. "You best get Dr. Northrop."

"I don't like it, Ellie." The shorter one looked over Duncan from head to toe and back again, before resting on her injured sister. "If any further harm happens to either one of my sisters, you'll regret it, mister."

"Ye need not worry, Mara Jean." Hamish stepped from the shadows and over a log. "He'll not be causing harm to his future bride."

Obviously Hamish sought Duncan's protection for his family, but that didn't mean hot anger didn't boil in Duncan's blood at being manipulated. If Hamish had been truthful about his intention of Duncan marrying Camy from the start, Duncan never would have left Topeka, and she wouldn't now be suffering from a wound in her shoulder.

The sisters spun around, their faces white as snow.

"What have you done, Hamish?" Ellie held up her hand. "Never mind. We'll hear the tale soon enough. Come along, let's get Camy home."

"Northrop won't be too happy when he finds out about this." The younger sister giggled.

Camy flinched and curled tighter against him. Her

eyes once again opened, pooling with tears. Tears caused by the wound in her shoulder, when she hadn't cried before? Had she heard Hamish's revelation? Or was it the mention of the doctor that caused her to seek his protection, a stranger? Either way, he didn't like the lines of distress creasing her forehead and mouth. Somehow he couldn't help wanting to play the knight in shining armor to this damsel in distress. After all, he owed her that much after shooting her. No matter how loud the warning bells clanged in his head, he wouldn't leave her side until he was assured she was well, and then he'd be gone without a second glance. Before Hamish and his daughter convinced him a marriage of convenience held appeal.

"I won't leave you." She closed her eyes as the huskiness of Duncan Murray's voice, colored with his accent, vibrated through her and curled her toes. "Unless you ask mc to."

She gave her head a slight shake and then wrapped her arms around his neck as he followed Ellie up the path. Her behavior toward him had been monstrous to say the least, and yet he continued to offer her help. She'd almost be willing to slave over the fireplace and make him a month's worth of dinners.

The wall of his broad chest and his brawny arms reminded her of the days when her da had held her tight during a frightful storm, or when he'd taken her riding. Those days had been forever ago, before her mother had died, before he'd left her and her sisters with Hamish. She hadn't felt safe or protected since. She wanted to soak it in, and yet she did not. She opened her eyes.

"You may put me d-down now," she stuttered, releasing her arms from around his neck and pushing at his shoulders. He tightened his grip. She smacked his shoulder and grimaced at the fire burning in her arm. "Oaf!"

Ellie halted her steps. "Something wrong?"

"I'm not a child, Ellie. I can walk." She released a puff of air. She didn't want to trust that he had good intentions. There had been too many men of recent months travelling through Rusa Valley seeking land along the river, and some unsavory fellows vying for Sims Creek. However, she didn't wish to be overly rude, given that he seemed intent on helping her. "He's injured and has no business b-bearing my burden."

"Cameron is as stubborn as my Millie." Hamish's thick, gravelly accent warmed her heart, even if she took offense at being compared to his mule. He'd inform Mr. Murray that the Simses' land was not for sale, because Hamish promised it to her when she turned of age on her next birthday, and perhaps he'd help Ellie see reason as to why they shouldn't give up their home and allow bounders to take over their home.

"I've noticed," Duncan mumbled as he released Camy's legs. "Far from biddable."

His fingers anchored around her waist, leaving her light-headed and breathless. Her swim in the river had taken more of her strength than she'd like to admit. The pulsating, searing pain in her arm churned in her stomach.

Peeling his fingers from her sides, she shuddered at the loss of his warmth and wobbled. Duncan's palm, branding the curve of her back, offered support and propelled her away from him and the delight of his protectiveness. She wouldn't covet something she could never have. Not from him. He was too handsome by far, and she was too plain. Too unladylike.

She lifted her foot over an exposed root, and a wave of dizziness spun around in her head. Reaching her hand out to steady herself against the tree, she missed and lurched forward. Before she hit the ground, she found herself swept back into the arms of Duncan Murray.

The rumble of his laughter shook through her. "I'm afraid she'll find I'm just as stubborn."

Ellie and Hamish laughed too, and if Camy hadn't been so offended at their jests over her stubbornness, she would have released the tears of pain and frustration begging to spill from her eyes. Ellie rarely smiled anymore, and she hadn't laughed since she returned home.

Camy crossed her arms over her chest and scowled. "I'm glad to amuse you, but can we go home now?"

The sooner they were home, the sooner she'd be out of his arms, and the sooner they could correct him about purchasing their home. Then he could be on his way. But then one of the Northrops would soon arrive, and no doubt, Miller Northrop would hear of her mishap. She could handle Duncan Murray and the emotions he elicited, but she couldn't handle Miller's persistent pursuit. The last time almost cost her her freedom, in more ways than one. Camy shivered at the idea of being shackled to that boy. Only a year older than her twenty, Miller had gone from a polite young man to acting like a petulant child over the last year.

"Are you cold?" Duncan's slight accent rolled over her, somehow setting her nerves on edge, yet giving her a great deal of comfort as it reminded her of her parents.

"I'm fine."

He snorted, as if she'd tell an untruth, and then pulled her closer. If word caught on that a man carried Camy, no matter the reason, Mrs. Smith would call for a wedding. This man confused her, and she'd no more wish to marry the yellow-bellied oaf of a Scotsman than Miller.

A life with Miller would be worse than tea with Mrs. Smith and her daughters. The socialite had taken it upon herself to mother the Sims sisters, as they had no mother, and Camy always walked away from her teas with a stiff neck from sitting all prim and proper like. Not to mention her nose nearly took on a permanent wrinkled disposition. It was no small chore containing a sneeze, especially when Mrs. Smith insisted on waving her fan, stirring up every imaginable fragrance she'd doused her person with moments before the appointed time of tea. Third Tuesday, every month, weather permitting. A necessary evil, according to Ellie. After all, Mrs. Smith knew all the going-ons within three counties, which kept the Sims sisters ahead of the railroad. Most of the time. All they had to do was smile, nod and sip tea while they listened to drivel about the latest fashions and how a woman should glide and not amble in the presence of polite company. If Mrs. Smith had known about Duncan Murray, she certainly failed to mention it. The old goose needed to step up her game if she intended to continue tea parties in her parlor room. Unless, of course, she had intended to keep him a secret. But then, only men with fat wallets perked Mrs. Smith's ears.

"Do you always talk to yourself?"

Camy wrinkled her brow. Her gaze shifted to his. The sharp retort clinging to the tip of her tongue halted when she caught sight of his moss-colored eyes. She jerked her gaze from his and pushed her finger up the side of her nose. The wire rim that should be there was gone. No wonder everything but Duncan Murray seemed to blur before her.

"What's that, you say?"

"My spectacles."

Duncan flexed his arms around Camy as he stepped over another large limb that had fallen during the last winter storm a month back. He'd probably handle the oxen as if they were no more than small babes from their mother's womb.

"I didn't see them. You must have lost them when you fell in the river."

"Most likely." Even though Camy knew every inch of their land with her eyes closed, Ellie would insist on Camy staying in the house until they could be replaced. Mara wouldn't be too happy about trading chores with Camy and giving up the cooking, although their stomachs would be a mite grateful for the change. Mara's attempt at potatoes still soured Camy's gullet. Dr. Northrop would grumble about her being a simple-minded female who needed a husband, one like Miller.

"Can you see at all?" he asked.

"I'm not blind," Camy snapped, and then sighed. "I can see you. That's about it. My sisters treat me like I'm daft."

"We do not." Ellie's voice floated toward her. "The last time you lost your spectacles you stepped in a hole and twisted your foot. You hobbled around for weeks.

The time before that you nearly shot Hamish thinking he was a wildcat."

Duncan chuckled. "Hamish resembles a lot of things, but a wildcat?"

Camy shrugged. It was odd Duncan seemed to know her uncle well. "I knew it was him. I missed him on purpose."

"So the lass says," Hamish responded. "Too close for my liking."

"Too close? You have a hole in your hat," Ellie added. "We're almost to the path. Can you manage her up the hill?"

"Yes."

His accent curled her toes. "I can walk if it's too much for your head."

"We'll manage just as we are, Camy."

She liked the way he said her name. Not as a curse or as if she'd once again displeased her sisters. Her name almost sounded pleasant, even if it meant crooked nose. A name her da had given her because he felt all out of sorts at his wife producing another girl.

Camy's mind darted in all directions as Duncan maneuvered the path leading to her home. She didn't want to like him. She didn't want to like any man, given that they seemed to be as flighty as birds during the first fall of leaves. Her da always moving place to place looking for that one thing to fill the void her mother had left when she passed from this earth. Hamish leaving for months at a time.

Duncan Murray was handsome, and somewhat gruff, but somehow she'd found a bit of courage when he challenged her instead of constantly stuttering like a timid wallflower hiding behind a book during

Mrs. Smith's social gatherings. Beneath the layers he seemed to be caring and kind. He hadn't left her in the river, he'd come after her. She was tempted to giggle and become woolly-headed like Mara did whenever she talked about a gentleman, carriage rides and arm-in-arm walks beneath the light of the moon. Camy's younger sister didn't understand what it was like to have a man abandon them; she'd been too young to recall. Ellie knew, but she hadn't been the one to chase Da's coattails everywhere he'd gone. She hadn't been the one sitting beneath the stoop waiting for his return.

Camy promised herself she'd never do it again. She'd never allow her heart to be owned by anyone other than her sisters. She had the land Hamish promised to give her. That was all she needed.

"Mr. Murray, what is the truth as to why you're here?"

He halted his steps, his hold on her slackening. She could tell by the lighting that they'd reached the top of the path, and she could tell by his reaction that he hadn't expected what was before him.

"He's come to marry you, lass," Hamish said as he stepped past them.

Chapter Three

"No! I have no need for a husband," Camy said as she propelled out of Duncan's arms.

Although he felt a tad shaky on his own feet, Duncan grabbed hold of her arm and steadied her. He'd been both shocked and unsurprised at Hamish's revelation, and he didn't know which irritated him more, the fact that his friend hadn't been completely truthful about the acquisition of the land until last night, or that the Lady Hamish intended him to marry hadn't been told about the bargain. Either way, he wouldn't wed an unwilling bride. "It seems we are in agreement. I have no need for a wife."

"Excellent. Wh-why are you here?"

Duncan looked about him. Although the spring had yet to produce buds on the trees and the green of the grass had yet to sprout from the muddied land, the sight before him was more than he could have hoped for. In this Hamish had not exaggerated. A flat valley for planting gave way to gentle-rolling hills. Hens pecked around the yard. Several goats stood on top of a small wooden shed. A pair of oxen huddled beneath a lean-to. A hound as ugly as any he'd ever seen poked his head from around the door of a large barn before lying back down.

"This." Duncan motioned to the land stretched out before them.

"Is mine." Camy glared at Hamish. "You promised."

"You expected Hamish to keep his word?" Ellie crossed her arms.

"My shoulder's been shot, not my head, Ellie." She turned toward Hamish. "You gave your word. A Sims always keeps his word, right, Hamish?"

"Cameron, ye know I would if I could." The old man glanced at his feet. "The river is thawing."

A look passed between the sisters. Eyes narrowed, Camy turned toward the small cabin and wobbled. Duncan swept her into his arms. Her limbs turned to stone. "We can discuss the situation after the doctor tends to your shoulder."

"I agree." Ellie motioned for him to follow her into the small cabin.

Ellie went directly to the fire and poked at the logs in the fireplace, stoking the embers to life. She placed a pot on a hook over the flames. "Sit her on the bed, if you will."

Camy's cheeks took on a rosy hue. "I'll sit on the chair."

Ellie glanced over her shoulder. Her brow furrowed; she seemed unware of the awkwardness. After a moment, she gave a quick nod. "Do as you please. However, Northrop will have you moved to the bed before he examines you."

Camy shivered. "All the more reason I will insist on

sitting in the chair. I will not be perceived as a weak-kneed ninny. Besides, I could use dry clothes."

She had threatened him with a gun, demanded his obedience, received a bullet in her shoulder without so much as a bat of an eyelash *and* taken a dunk in the river. She was the furthest thing from a ninny, and his chest welled with pride at her courage. A shame he couldn't marry her. Unlike many of the ladies who'd vied for his attention in order to appease their vanity, she wouldn't demand his every waking hour, leaving him free to do as he wished. However, he feared her lack of dependence on him for her emotional well-being would only draw him nearer as she did now, intriguing him to get to know her even better. Realizing he was a little more reluctant than he should be about relinquishing her, he plopped her onto the nearest spindle-back chair.

"Ow." Camy teetered toward the table but caught herself with her good hand. She scooted toward the edge of the chair with her chin held high and her back straight as a plank. "If I was such a b-burden, you could have let me walk."

"My apologies." Duncan's cheeks flamed. "I should have been more careful."

Of course, he would do well not to touch her again. He wouldn't wish to be caught in her womanly charm. He scrubbed his palm over his face and winced as he brushed his hand over his eye. The cabin grew a few shades darker and the air closed in. Duncan needed to think about how he could seal the purchase without her as part of the negotiation. He turned for the door. Swinging it open, he stepped into the mud outside.

"Mr. Murray," Camy called.

His hand on the door. "Yes?"

"Where are you going?"

"To gather your belongings from the river." He needed air. He needed to get away from her to regain his wits about him. He'd found many ladies attractive over the years, but none as interesting as Camy Sims. The very lilt of her speech tempted him with a desire to sit and chat about nonessentials, a temptation he hadn't experienced in many years, since before his mother fell ill and lost the will to speak. He could imagine himself sitting across the table with her, sipping tea and eating biscuits, while she regaled him with some tale or another. All he had to do was agree to Hamish's terms. And gain Camy's acceptance to be his wife. Absolutely not.

"It is raining. You have no shoes."

"Rain has never stopped me from enjoying the outdoors." Glancing down, he held his arms out. "A little more won't hurt me." As much as he would enjoy a warm fire to dry his bones, he needed to walk, to think. Why had Hamish brought him out here to no more than a shack housing three sisters? To play on his charitable nature? The old man would find his charity didn't extend to marrying a brown-eyed lass with tumbling locks as wild as his beloved Highlands. He had to find Hamish and be done with his business so he could remove himself from Camy's presence.

"You'll catch your death if you're not careful."

If he was not careful he'd catch something much worse than death, like her for a wife. He'd much rather marry one of the simpering young ladies who cared more for proper social graces than was necessary, as it would be easier to maintain his distance. Besides, he felt at home with his bare toes in the cool grass—a little mud would not make a difference.

"I assure you I will be fine, Miss Sims. Besides, I wish to look for your father."

Deep lines creased her forehead. "My father? You'll have a time of that. He's not been seen 'round here in years. He left us with Uncle Hamish when Mara Jean was a tot."

"You cannot blame our father, Camy." Ellie dropped a pile of clean cloths into the boiling water and stirred it around. "He had no means to care for three little girls."

Camy scowled. "Either did Hamish."

"Hamish had Naomi," Ellie countered.

"Even so, Da dinnae even try." Camy's voice wobbled.

The soft lilt of her accent ignited the black heart confined behind the brick and mortar of his chest. Her words pummeled him like a battering ram. Her words were similar to those he'd said to his own mother after his father left them with a leaky roof, no wood for the winter and no food for their bellies. Even in her illness and after all his father's abuses, his mother had continued to defend him, but Duncan knew the truth: his father hadn't even tried. Duncan had done what he could, but there weren't many folks willing to help the son and wife of a scoundrel like Ewan Murray.

The pain of old wounds sliced through him like an ax splitting wood. To make matters worse, the sisters' raw emotions filled the room. Duncan understood the rejection and the loneliness all too well and he did not wish to recall the depth of pain he'd felt when his father abandoned him and his mother. However, he could not stop his heartstrings from pulling taut and drawing him closer into their midst, closer to Camy. The sheen of her brown eyes dulled, beckoning him to shield her from all the hurts of this life. If he stayed, as he'd promised, he wouldn't have the strength to resist his need to protect her. He reminded himself that he was no better than his father, no better than Camy's. No matter how much he wished it otherwise.

With escape the only thing on his mind, he pulled the door closed and stepped beneath the stoop and off the porch, his toes sinking into the mud. He lifted his face to the punishing sting of the rain. Would his father's past always chase him down and haunt his thoughts?

The land beckoned to him. However, the pounding in his head and the promise he'd made to Camy to remain by her side kept him from giving in to the need to run barefoot across the countryside as he'd done when he was a lad whenever his father had left, sometimes for months at a time, leaving his mother to suffer days of melancholy.

Camy slumped against the chair as the door closed behind him. The effort to act the lady almost forced her to embarrassment as she fought the roiling in her stomach. The sharp sting had long since turned into a deep burning, which seem to be spreading throughout her body. Although she was grateful he'd left, giving her a moment of reprieve from proper decorum, disappointment cut into her thoughts and she had a deep suspicion it had something to do with Duncan and his promise to stay by her side, and little to do with memories of her father's abandonment. She'd long since carved him from her mind.

There were few men of her acquaintance who kept their word, so she didn't understand why she believed Duncan would be different. Perhaps it had been the look in his eyes when he gave his word. As if he meant it. Hamish, with all his faults, had the same look when he meant to do as he said, which wasn't often. It was why she had been convinced Hamish would never sell the land. Her uncle might be a lot of things right down to a no-good yellow belly at times, but when he made a promise with a look of determination, he kept it. Until now, it seemed.

"Here." Ellie cupped her elbow and helped her stand to her feet. "Let's get you out of your wet things before Dr. Northrop arrives."

Camy groaned with each pull and tug as Ellie helped her change into a dry skirt and a loose-fitting bodice. She was near to suffering from the vapors by the time her sister fastened the last of the buttons after covering her wound with strips of linen. A quick tug of her hair had her knees wobbling and Camy didn't think she'd be able to stand much longer. Ellie released Camy's hair with an irritated sigh.

"We'll not worry about tidying you up any more than necessary, but we do need to get your hair dried." Ellie moved the chair closer to the fire and helped her sit. "Do you wish to speak about Mr. Murray before Northrop arrives?"

Turning sideways in the chair, she rested her head against the back of the chair, the spindles biting into her sensitive flesh as she sank against the hard wood. "There's not much to tell. I found him unconscious by the river, beaten and with no shoes. Once he woke up he asked after Hamish and claimed to be purchasing my, er, our land."

"I meant to discuss the wedding, Camy," Ellie responded.

"There is nothing to discuss."

"I tell you, Hamish is up to no good." The sound of Ellie scrubbing the table met Camy's ears. How many times could a person scrub an already well-scrubbed surface? A blur of purple squeezed between Camy and the warmth of the fire, chilling her limbs. The spoon clanked against the kettle. Camy didn't need her spectacles to see Ellie's frenzied state. Every brisk movement and every mumble beneath her sister's breath spoke clearly. Water cascaded as Ellie scooped another cloth out of the kettle. Everything in the cabin seemed to halt until the dripping of water subsided. Ellie's purple shadow swiveled away from the fire. The wet linen smacked against the table. "No doubt, he lost the land gambling."

Camy lurched off the chair with a yelp, her hand pressing against the wound. "He wouldn't. He promised. Besides, Mr. Murray doesn't seem to be the gambling type."

"And what do gamblers look like?" Ellie tossed.

"Miller," she said without thinking. The young man who'd once been a friend had since gained shadows beneath his eyes and hard lines of worry creasing his mouth.

"That just goes to show you that you shouldn't trust a man's words." Ellie scrubbed the table with a greater force than normal. "Not a Northrop's, not a stranger's and most definitely not Hamish's. Who knows what he does while he's gallivanting about leaving us here to fend for ourselves?"

"Our uncle may have left us at times, but he's never broken his word to us, Ellie. And he wouldn't gamble. He's too tight-fisted with his purse." Camy once again slumped onto the chair.

Ellie knew Hamish would never do such a thing. She had to. If she wavered and began believing the worst from their uncle, then Camy's faith in him would begin to waver too. Was it possible he thought marriage was the only way to keep her and her sisters safe? With Mara too young, Camy knew she was the obvious choice to sacrifice for her sisters, especially since Ellie's heart remained bruised from Benjamin Northrop's rejection. "You didn't have to send Mara for Northrop. You've tended all our scrapes and cuts thus far and we're still alive." With Dr. Northrop and his three sons practicing medicine, they had no way of knowing who would arrive. Camy didn't relish Miller treating her. Especially if Mara told him about Duncan, but for Ellie's sake she prayed Benjamin was nowhere close. And, no doubt, Hamish would shoot the elder Dr. Northrop once he crossed onto the Simses' property before asking questions ending years of disagreement between the two old men.

"A bullet is quite another thing, Camy. How did you get shot anyways?"

Even with the burning in her shoulder, Camy almost laughed. "Entirely by accident."

Ellie did laugh. "All of your mishaps are entirely by accident, dear sister."

Camy recalled the last incident when Hound took off after Uncle Tommy, her pet hen. The poor, one-legged gal nearly lost her other leg when she became tangled up in Camy's skirts. Somehow she was able to save the hen, but not without injury to her own shin. It wouldn't have been so terrible if she hadn't have been heading out to chop branches. Good thing Ellie excelled with a needle, leaving tight stitches and little scarring. Miller didn't need another reason why one of the Sims sisters needed a husband. Particularly him, to particularly her. If she were to wed Duncan, she would no longer have to concern herself over Miller's endless pursuit. She had no idea which would be the better of the two. Wedding a wastrel of a man who tried to dominate her with a heavy hand, or a man who would one day leave her broken just like her father had done?

"Sometimes I wonder if you enjoy having the Northrops over."

Camy's eyes grew wide. "Absolutely not! Besides, Mr. Murray carried the rifle and the bucket of water. I tried to warn him about the trap, but he didn't listen."

"He doesn't seem like the kind of man to take orders kindly." The table groaned under Ellie's scrubbing.

"Orders?" She *had* been quite rude to him, and she *had* demanded he stop when she could easily have told him about the trap. She wouldn't be sitting here wounded, and Duncan wouldn't be out coveting her land. Camy glanced at the weathered door and wondered if he'd decided to return to where he'd come from. Disappointment tickled her nose, as she'd like to interrogate the man Hamish had chosen for her. Was he a farmer or just a man hoping to tame the wild countryside? It was just as well, even if she worried over his shoeless feet and the bumps on his head. "I clearly thought to warn Mr. Murray, not give him orders."

"As I recall—" Duncan's voice rumbled into the cabin. A brisk wind blew in with him, proving the morning's warm spring rain had given way to the cold.

Camy eased to a proper sitting position, careful not to cause any more discomfort than she already experienced.

"—you demanded me to stop." Duncan Murray's shadow loomed over her as he moved closer, quickening her pulse. The smell of rain and freshly churned earth danced around her with each of his movements. She'd make a year's worth of pies to have her spectacles at this moment, to see the contours of his hardened jaw, to see how the rain fashioned his russet curls. Camy's cheeks warmed as she sensed his gaze on her.

"I could not find Hamish." He laid the rifle on Ellie's clean table and received an irritated huff from her sister. "Where would you like the bucket of water?"

"Right here is fine." Ellie snagged the rifle, her skirts swishing across the room. Camy heard it settle on the rack beside the door, and then Ellie once again began scrubbing the table.

"Don't mind her. Ellie doesn't like the Northrops and one of them is on his way."

"I don't dislike them, Camy. Well, not all of them." Ellie's voice softened to a near whisper and the scrubbing abruptly halted.

"Anytime we need a doctor, Ellie scours every nook and cranny."

"Which seems to only be when Camy has an accident. I've considered sending her to live with the Northrops to save us all the bother."

"I would never forgive you!"

"I know. And I would never wish it on anyone, not even Levina Smith."

Camy smiled at Ellie's teasing. Levina had done all she could to turn the eye of at least one Northrop, particularly Ellie's former beau. "No doubt, Levina would enjoy residing with the doctors."

"Does she have accidents often?" Although Duncan spoke to her sister, Camy sensed his gaze on her.

"Not Levina." Camy giggled. "Never once have I seen her falter. She glides across the floor with the grace of a queen and sips her tea without an unladylike slurp."

Certainly jealousy hadn't taken a foothold in her thoughts. Not of Levina. Just because Camy couldn't walk across the room with stacks of books on her head didn't mean anything. There were plenty of things Camy could do that Levina could not. Embroider without poking a finger, cook and plow a field. Those were practical things, things that would allow Camy independence to survive without a husband, not foolish things like useless chatter about the latest fashions and the weather that caused a man's eyes to cross and his mind to go numb in utter boredom. "Did I mention Levina bats her lashes in precise intervals?" Camy blinked and counted the required one, two count and blinked again for effect.

Duncan burst into laughter and then cleared his throat. "Exact intervals? Do ladies have a book for such things?"

"That, Mr. Murray, is a secret best kept." Ellie's mood lightened. "Besides, we've only heard tales of such a book."

"Tales spun by Mrs. Smith and her daughters," Camy mumbled beneath her breath.

"To answer your question," Ellie continued, "Camy does have a way of finding trouble when none should be had."

"Like today?" Duncan chuckled.

"Yes," Ellie answered. "Although I must say this is a first, as I've never recalled her having an accomplice."

"That is not so." Camy dipped her head to hide the embarrassment staining her cheeks as she recalled the time her sisters talked her into climbing a tree. "What about the time you told me Red had climbed the tree and couldn't get down?" She glanced at Duncan. "Red was an old tomcat, so old we made up stories about how he'd been on the boat with Noah. He couldn't climb over a pebble, let alone up a tree. In my worry, I never once thought my sisters were telling a tale."

"Oh, we weren't. I promise. Red had climbed the tree like a spry wildcat. Of course that was after Mara had dunked him in the water bucket to give him a bath. How were we supposed to know he'd gotten himself down while we fetched you?"

"It sounds as if you're quite the adventurer, Camy."

"Quite." Ellie laughed. "The exact reason the Northrops visit us often."

"At least, I'll be saved the sight of whoever attends me, even if I have to suffer their poking."

"Oh. I found these." Duncan lifted her chin with the pad of his thumb and then brushed the tips of her ears as he settled her wire rims into place.

Camy sucked in a breath as the lines of his face and the dusting of his dark beard came into focus. Or was it from the warmth of his fingers as they curved around her ears? The dark shadow gracing the curve of his jaw illuminated the gold flecks vibrating in the bed of his moss-colored eyes. Dark-colored curls clinging to his brow and curling near his collar dripped droplets of rain. She could have stared at him for hours, learning every detail, as if he hadn't already been branded into her thoughts. He'd make a fine husband. Too bad she would never be agreeable to the idea.

He glanced at her wound and then rubbed his palm over his prickly jaw. "My apologies for what happened at the creek. I should have listened to your warning."

A flutter swirled deep within her chest, a desire to have a husband as handsome as him, to be a wife. A mother. Her thoughts trailed into dangerous territory. She'd be a rabbit thoroughly caught in a trap if she didn't remove Duncan from her presence. A rabbit chasing a carrot never to be had. No doubt, Duncan had plenty of ladies vying for his attentions, ladies much more efficient at balancing books on their heads. "My th-thanks."

She tore her gaze from him and stared at the fire. Her heart cracked a little with each snap of an ember. Her faults would keep her from finding a decent husband, just as they had kept her and her sisters from having a father to love them and protect them. It had been one of her many accidents that had propelled her father to rid himself of his daughters. Did Hamish think to buy her a husband with her land because she couldn't find one any other way? Camy wasn't foolish enough to believe loyalty could be purchased. It had never worked with her father on the rare occasions he'd visited.

Duncan nodded. "Your spectacles must have flown

off before you started downriver. I'm just glad I found them."

"I cannot marry you."

"I know." He opened the faded blue curtains Ellie had made from one of their old dresses and propped his shoulder against the frame.

"Then why are you still here?"

Looking at her, he held her gaze for a moment. "I keep my word." He glanced out the window. "It looks as if you have company."

"Most likely Mara with the doctor," Ellie replied.

"By the looks of it, I'd say there is more than one man and they're armed."

Camy's heart climbed into her throat and then dropped to her toes. "Thugs."

She sprang out of the chair when she realized the possibility of the danger walking toward their front door. The room swam before her eyes and she pressed her palms against the table to gain her balance as Ellie grabbed hold of her arm to steady her.

"What, you think to take them on in your condition?" Ellie's voice teetered on bitterness and Camy knew that if these men weren't the Northrops, Ellie would have them moved from the farm before the sun set.

"I won't let them intimidate us, Ellie."

"Neither will I." Duncan yanked the rifle from the rack and swung open the door.

"You can't go out there!" Camy squeaked. Her heart pounded against her chest. Her ears began to roar. "You don't know what they're capable of doing. What they've done. What they said they'll do if we don't relent."

Fear tugged at her insides. Nightmares of masked men and torches had plagued her sleep for months. Cruel jests toward her sisters and the threats made against her came crashing into her thoughts.

"If they intend harm, I'll see them gone."

"This is not your business," Camy argued. She'd accused him of being one of them and he'd shown her kindness. He'd carried her from the river, up a steep incline. True, she didn't want a husband. True, she had wished *him* gone, but she did not wish him dead, which was a certainty if he came between the Simses and the men who coveted Sims land.

He looked over his shoulder and straight into her eyes. "Until we decide things between us, it is."

Chapter Four

Decide things between us? The words had rushed out of his mouth without thought, and he watched her mouth open and close like the wings of a butterfly. A response must have formed on the tip of her tongue, but not a single one released. And truly he knew how she felt, as he didn't have anything else to say either. Nothing could ever be between them, but for the time being he'd pretend otherwise and let her think so, as well. It wouldn't do anyone any good if she and her sister decided to stand against three armed men, and if these men were on a payroll financed by his bank account as the sisters seemed to think, it was his business.

"Camy, sit down before you fall over," he demanded, and prepared himself for a possibility that these were men hired by the railroad to torment innocent, helpless females.

As he stepped beneath the stoop, pulling the door closed behind him, a tall lanky man with a rifle propped against his shoulder jumped from the back of the buckboard before the driver even slowed his horse. Another man of smaller stature climbed from the passenger side and rushed to the other man's side. The driver slid the brake into place and dropped the reins. He pulled a black bag from the back of the buckboard, and Duncan eased the tightness from his lungs. These were no railroad thugs. "You must be the Northrops."

The tall one pushed his bowler above his brow and squinted through the pouring rain. "And you must be the one who shot my fiancée."

Duncan felt his brow rise beneath his hair at the news. If this man was Camy's fiancé, then why was Duncan's marriage to her part of the land acquisition? "Your fiancée?"

The man curled his nose. "Cameron Sims."

"Come, now, Miller. She hasn't agreed to be your wife." The more distinguished-looking gentleman with the black bag dried his palm down the front of his coat and held it for Duncan to shake. "Dr. Benjamin Northrop. This here is my brother Dr. Julius Northrop and of course this is my other brother, Miller, who has yet to gain the lady's agreement."

"That is a minor detail." Miller stepped onto the stoop and, hovering over Duncan, glared down at him. "She will be my wife."

Duncan did not appreciate the underlying threat, as it seemed more directed at Camy than himself even though she was on the other side of the door. Miller's hawklike nose, and ashy pallor reminded Duncan of a devious captain he'd encountered during the War Between the States who'd seized homes when he felt it necessary and stole food from the mouths of babes to feed his hounds. That reminder alone did not bode well for Miller, not if Duncan had anything to do about it.

Miller made to move around him, but Duncan

shifted, blocking his entrance, and glanced at Benjamin. "If, as you say, your brother is not Miss Sims's fiancé, I must insist only one of you attend her. Preferably you, Dr. Northrop," he said, nodding toward Benjamin. "As you seem to be a professional seeking to give medical help, not a jaded beau come to demean the lady."

Miller puffed out his chest like a rooster on the strut. "Listen here," he snapped as his brother Julius cocked back the hammer on his revolver.

Resting his hand on Julius's, Benjamin lowered the weapon. "Julius, he has the right of it. Miller, you are in no condition to speak to Cameron. Allow me to assess her, and then if she wishes to see you, you may enter. Until then you two may wait out here."

"What about him?" Miller's lip curled in disgust.

Benjamin shook his head. "I suggest he wait out here with the two of you."

The corner of Miller's mouth twitched in an arrogant smirk. Duncan didn't blink at the young man's bluster. He'd dealt with shiftier men in his days, men who'd threatened life and limb if he didn't bend to their will, men like his father.

"However," Benjamin continued, "I do not wish to treat another gunshot wound. After you," he said to Duncan, sweeping his hand in front of him.

Duncan opened the door and stepped into the dimly lit cabin. "It's all right, ladies. It's the Northrops." It took a moment for his eyes to adjust, but not long enough that he didn't notice Camy now sat on the edge of the bed, her hands properly folded in her lap, her cheeks pale. Despite the relief in her eyes at his words, lines of agony creased her brow. It also didn't go beyond his notice that the bed swayed as if she'd recently jumped on the mattress. Ellie's skirts had a similar motion while she hunched near the fire. He had no doubt the ladies had eavesdropped on the conversation between him and the Northrops.

As Benjamin Northrop closed the door behind him, Ellie straightened, ran her hands down her skirts and nodded. "Dr. Northrop."

"Ellie."

"Where's Mara?" Ellie asked, easing some of Camy's agitation at not seeing her youngest sister.

"I insisted she stay with my sister, Bella, until I knew what sort of trouble you ladies have gotten yourself into."

Ellie huffed. "You could have sent one of your brothers in to treat my sister if we're such a bother."

"Yet I am the one with experience with these sorts of injuries." He shrugged out of his coat and laid it across the end of the bed. "What have you done to yourself, Camy?"

Even in her discomfort she teased, feigning innocence. "I haven't done a thing. This t-time."

"So I've heard." Benjamin laughed as he pressed his fingers to her wrist. "Pulse is strong. That is good news."

Duncan knew he should turn away as the doctor pulled Camy's sleeve from her shoulder to inspect her wound, yet he could not tear his eyes from hers. He'd caused her this pain, and he intended to bear as much as he could with her. If only he could trade places with her.

"Mr. Murray." Ellie's voice pulled his attention from

Camy's crinkled eyelids. "Would you mind moving the table closer?"

Once he moved the table, Ellie placed a bowl of steaming water next to the doctor along with strips of clean linens and then scooted a chair beside Camy for Northrop to sit. It was as if the two had worked together before and the woman understood what he needed.

"Thank you, Ellie." He dipped one of the clothes into the water and cleaned the wound. Bright red rivulets streamed from her wound, soaking into her shirt. Camy groaned.

Camy's sister grumbled something unintelligible and then said, "I know you would save her the pain if you could…" Her words muffled beneath the hand covering her mouth. Dr. Northrop reached out toward her, but Ellie spun from him.

"I'll be fine, Ellie." Camy put on a brave face even as she grimaced.

Duncan sat next to her and took her cold hand in his. Although she wore dry clothes, she had yet to warm from her fall into the river. Dr. Northrop swabbed a clean cloth over the wound. Flinching, Camy gripped Duncan's fingers.

Dr. Northrop looked up from his work and frowned. "I'm sorry, Camy. I'm afraid your discomfort has just begun. Would you rather sleep until we're done?"

She shook her head, her damp hair dancing around her. Dr. Northrop pulled a silver implement from his bag. Duncan clenched his teeth and then positioned himself and turned her toward him so that they faced each other. He'd seen men die as they rushed into battle. And he'd seen men die in the surgeon's tent, not from the procedure itself, but from the chloroform. He didn't wish her to die, but he didn't wish her to be awake either.

She pulled her hand from his and brushed the tips of her fingers over the bruising of his eye. "Benjamin, you should tend to Mr. Murray's injury."

"After we see the damage done to your shoulder," Northrop responded.

Her attempts at distracting herself distracted him. The touch of her fingers against his skin near made him forget that she wasn't his wife. *Yet.* Where had that come from? She would never be. He pulled her hand down and rested their clasped hands between them.

"Are you ready?" Northrop asked.

Drawing in a breath, she closed her eyes and nodded. Northrop cleansed the wound once again and then inserted the probe into the wound. Tensing every muscle, Camy cried out and then pressed her lips into a hard line. She fell forward, her head resting on his shoulder. For a moment, Duncan thought she'd passed out, but the grip on his fingers and the tears warming his shoulder through his rain-soaked shirt told him otherwise.

Benjamin sat back. The probe dropped into the bowl with a clink. "It doesn't seem to have shattered the bone."

Camy pulled away from his shoulder as air rushed from Duncan's lungs in relief. He hadn't realized how much he feared she might lose her arm until this very moment. His closest friend during the war had lost his leg when bone fragments caused the limb to become gangrenous.

"However, the ball is tucked in there tight. Camy,

I know you don't wish it, but I'm going to have to use the chloroform to dig it out."

Pulling her lip between her teeth, she shook her head.

"I've seen grown men try, Camy. It's too much to bear." Ellie set another bowl of water on the table.

"Your sister's right." Dr. Northrop rested his elbows on his knees.

"I will not have my mind taken from me," Camy argued, and then her voice quieted. "I know people have died. Ellie told me so."

"That is true. I've seen it myself," Duncan said, worried either way, knowing Northrop had no choice. "Do you trust Dr. Northrop?"

After a bit of hesitation, Camy nodded.

"He seems competent. It is right as rain to be brave, lass." Duncan smoothed a wayward curl from her forehead. "I've been shot before." He pushed his sleeve above his elbow and showed her the scar. "I have another here," he said as he pointed to the middle of his chest. "And here on my leg. Chloroform was not always available on the battlefield. As much as I dislike telling you, the fact is, the pain is too much, even for a woman of courage such as yourself."

Her brown eyes pooled with tears. He'd give every coin he had to trade places with her, to go back and choose not to be swayed by Hamish's offer. "If it makes you more comfortable I will not leave your side and I'll be here when you wake."

She blinked. One lone tear crept from the corner of her eye and rolled down her cheek. She lowered her chin and drew in a slow breath. She glanced at him, the hint of a smile curving her mouth. "This is not your business."

He patted her hand and smiled back. "As I said before, your business is my business until things between us are settled."

"What things?" Miller ducked into the cabin, his bowler falling off as it skimmed against the frame. His straw-colored hair was plastered to his head, his hands were clenched at his sides and his face was ruddy. His bloodshot eyes, telling her he'd been drinking, narrowed when he caught sight of her hand held in Duncan's. His glare deepened when he lifted his eyes to hers. "There is nothing that needs to be settled other than *our* marriage. The sooner the better, since it's obvious you can't care for yourself. What sort of fool gets herself shot?"

Camy stared at Miller in disbelief. He'd called her many things over the last months, had insinuated even worse, but he had never outright called her a fool to her face. Her face must have reflected the sting of his words.

As he unclenched his fist, Miller's eyes softened. "I am sorry, Cameron. I don't like you being hurt. If you would quit resisting the inevitable...why can't you see that I am the only man willing to care for you?"

Willing. Camy had heard his argument before. There was never a confession of love, but what did she expect when her own father hadn't loved her? Did Miller always have to make her feel helpless? Worse, did he have to speak her fears aloud? No man wanted her. Her father had proved that when he left her with Hamish.

Even Miller's pursuit had everything to do with Sims Creek.

Suddenly she felt tired and weak. She wanted to curl up in a corner and cry until all her troubles disappeared. The only thing keeping her from doing so was the warm palm anchored to her. Duncan gave her fingers a gentle squeeze before releasing his hold on her hand. The mattress shifted beneath his weight and released as he rose and crossed his arms over his chest. The loss of his calloused palm had her lying back against the pillow. She closed her eyes in hopes of keeping the tears from spilling. For good measure she covered her eyes with her uninjured arm.

"First," Duncan said, "I will remind you that you are standing in Miss Cameron's home and that you would do well to respect all of the ladies of this house, even if they have an inclination toward accidents. Second, I have known Miss Cameron only a short time and I have concluded she is capable of caring for herself. She does not need a husband. Certainly not one who abuses her with his sharp tongue."

Despite the searing pain radiating throughout her upper body, and the ache in her heart, she felt giddy and had the urge to applaud Duncan's performance. It was a performance, right? After all, he'd met her only a few hours ago, not enough time to judge her capabilities.

"You have no right to tell me what she needs and does not need," Miller argued. "I have courted her for nigh unto two years."

Camy snorted and felt Miller's intense glare. His attempts at courting were akin to falling in a thornbush. His last attempt had landed him in the river near to drowning, and her under Mrs. Smith's condemning eye for breaking the unspoken rule about a lady pushing a man into the river after he stole a kiss. A rule saying she was compromised and must marry. Camy had yet to discover if it was the river washing or the stolen kiss that deemed a lady soiled. But given that Mrs. Smith felt the need to act like a mother to the poor Sims sisters, the woman was adamant that Camy save her reputation and marry Miller. Much to Camy's relief, Pastor Hammond came to her defense and spoke sound reasoning to Mrs. Smith, defusing the matter altogether.

Duncan stared Miller down. "At this moment, Mr. Northrop, I have every right."

The cabin fell silent. The pop and crackle of wood as it burned in the fireplace and the drips of water seeping through the roof plopping into strategically placed pots were the only sounds. Slightly lifting her arm, she peered at the occupants in the cabin. All of them seemed to be holding their breath waiting for Duncan's next words. Duncan leaned forward.

Lord, please don't let him say anything about Hamish's proposition. Please. I'm in no position to argue with Miller.

Although he was a head shorter than Miller, his fierce countenance caused Miller to shrink. "Miss Sims needs tending to without further delay."

Miller grunted. His cheeks looked as if he'd been attacked by rouge. "You've no business here. In fact, as I see it you should be in jail. Has the sheriff been fetched?"

"Miller." Ellie touched his arm. "Please, now is not the time."

"Outside, Murray." Miller circled his fists in front of him, ready to fight Duncan. Duncan looked as if he pitied the younger man.

Camy didn't think Miller meant much harm. Only a year older than she, he was foolish and young, determined to get his way in all things. Mostly with her. And Sims Creek, the property adjoining his father's. Miller's father had coveted Sims Creek for years, even before the railroad's interest, and it was obvious Miller carried on his father's determination, but why, as it was decent farming land, nothing more? And Miller despised the idea of plowing fields and milking goats. Worse, he didn't seem to like her much. He was always the first to tell her when her hair was unkempt. When the color of her dress was wrong. He even dared give her a tonic to do away with her freckles. Of course, she'd tried to scrub them away on occasion, but to no avail. She'd given up long ago on trying to obtain her sisters' perfect complexions.

"Miller, I think you should return home if you won't wait outside." Benjamin, always the calm one of the brothers, tried to defuse the situation.

Miller crossed his arms. "Not until I hear what rights he has to tell me anything about *my* fiancée."

Camy jerked her arm from her eyes. "I've never agreed to marry you, Miller Northrop." Nor would she ever!

"It seems we all have things we wish to discuss," Duncan added.

"Yes, we do," Miller added.

"I am not discussing marriage." Camy tried to sit, but Benjamin halted her progress by pressing a warm cloth to her shoulder. "To anyone."

"She is right. Everyone outside, now."

She could have kissed Benjamin Northrop's cheek for intervening.

"I'm not leaving." Ellie's soft voice cut through the tension. Camy knew it cost her sister more than she'd ever say to be in the same room with the man who'd broken her heart, but she was beyond thankful for the sacrifice.

"I'm not leaving either." Miller stomped his foot like a petulant child throwing a tantrum. "I am your apprentice and can help more than Ellie."

"Ellie is a better doctor than most," Camy argued, not wanting Miller and his unsteady hands to come anywhere near her.

"Any other patient and I would accept your assistance. However, brother, you've already done more harm than good by upsetting Camy. Her agitation has caused her wound to bleed more than it should. Besides, your hands are unsteady and your judgment is clouded by too much whiskey."

Relieved at Benjamin's soundness, Camy released the air she'd been holding.

"What about him?" Miller tossed.

"I'll be staying." Duncan's words were like a boulder, unyielding. He glanced at her, his voice softened. "I gave my word."

He had, and as much as she didn't want to admit it, Duncan soothed her fears and gave her a sense of peace. "All right," Camy said.

Miller huffed, swung the door wide and slammed it behind him.

"Shall we begin?" Benjamin asked.

Kneeling beside the bed, Duncan held her hand as

Benjamin took a brown bottle from Ellie. The white cloth hovered outside her vision and then over her head before covering her nose and mouth. Her head dizzied, and her eyelids became heavy. The deafening silence broke with the opening of the cabin door and Hamish's gruff voice.

"Ellie, lass, you best cook up a feast. The rev'nd will be here for dinner."

Chapter Five

Steam rose from his cup of coffee. The sky had long ago darkened with nightfall. What had begun as a warm spring morning had turned into a blistery winter night. White snow now fell, covering layers of ice left by the freezing rain. Thinking back over the last several days, Duncan wondered what had propelled him to follow Hamish out here in the country miles from the city. Of course, he knew. It had been the promise of a home with lush, rolling hills. It had been the promise of good farmland surrounded by untamed ruggedness. The promise of a home similar to what he'd left far behind. It had not been the promise of a wife with more courage than most men. An idea he was beginning to warm to but could never have.

He leaned against the window frame, his eyes resting on the woman who made him see that not all ladies were like many of his acquaintance, calculating behind their simpering. Her hair, long since dried, lay in stark contrast to the pale linen of her pillow in a wild array of dark curls. Thick, dark lashes rested against pale cheeks dusted with freckles. He didn't want a wife, did he? It didn't matter. He couldn't have a wife. Especially one who enticed him to take long walks with his head bent in rapt attention, to share more than a few meals, to steal a kiss. But if he could, he'd move Ben Nevis, Scotland's highest peak, to court her.

Why would Hamish make her part of the agreement? If he wanted her to keep the land, then why not let her have it? Because she had yet to turn twenty-one? Were their fears about the railroad genuine? Had unsavory agents threatened the sisters in hopes of gaining this parcel of land? Agents paid from his bank account? Did Hamish's generous offer have anything to do with the threats?

Duncan massaged his neck, wondering if his business associate, Calvin Weston, had anything to do with what was happening at Sims Creek. Calvin had, on the occasion, given red flags as to his character since the day he'd approached Duncan about helping finance a railroad to Santa Fe, New Mexico, but Duncan had brushed the flags aside as a doggedness to succeed. Now he wondered if his partner had had something to do with the attack on Hamish that nearly left him dead in a dark alleyway.

Fortunately Duncan had been unable to sleep that night and had been out for a stroll when he'd come across the miscreants beating the old man. It was the start of an odd, yet cherished friendship nearly a year ago. Duncan twisted his lips, digging through his memories of conversations he'd had with Hamish over warm cups of coffee. Not once had he mentioned his home in the country until a few weeks ago. And the old man had never said a word about relatives until they'd made camp on the banks of Sims Creek.

"Would you like more coffee?" Ellie pulled the black kettle from the fire.

"Thank you." He took a couple of steps toward her and held out his cup, which she filled with the dark liquid. "I am sorry for all this."

"It is not your fault," Ellie said, setting the kettle onto a trivet in the middle of the table. "I was just thanking the Lord that it was purely an accident and not a more purposeful deed."

The bandage on his forehead pulled as he raised his brow. More mystery? She had accused him of being a thug for the railroad, just as Camy had. Had other accidents occurred, accidents that were not purely accidents? What would they say if they knew he helped finance the road to be built through Rusa Valley, if they knew he was on the committee? "A more purposeful deed?"

She looked upon her sister with motherly affection. "It is not something I wish to discuss with or without my sisters, as it's been a source of contention between us. However, today's accident has made me realize that I can no longer put off making a decision."

"What decision is that, Ellie?" Camy uttered in a hoarse whisper.

Duncan set his cup on the table and then moved to her beside. He rested the back of his hand upon her brow. "No fever. How are you feeling?"

Camy tried to sit but fell back against the pillow. "Like I've been dragged by the oxen through a pile of rubble."

Ellie's skirts rustled as she neared the bed. "You should have listened to me then and not shot off the revolver while holding on the lines leading the oxen."

"Th-then I wouldn't have anything to compare my wound to," Camy gritted out with a slight smile.

Duncan chuckled, believing the banter between the sisters to be true.

"Here, this will ease your pain," Ellie said, holding a spoonful of laudanum in front of Camy.

"If I take that, will you tell me what decision you've made?"

"First, we need to know why Hamish felt the need to find you a husband." Ellie slipped the spoon between Camy's lips as she opened her mouth to argue. "And then I would prefer to wait for Mara to return, as it concerns her, as well."

Camy grimaced, swallowed the liquid and then tilted her head to look outside. The curtains had been drawn hours ago. "They haven't returned her yet? How long did I sleep?"

"As you know, the Northrops had her stay at their place with their sister until they could assess the situation here. The weather worsened and it wasn't safe to bring her back, but Dr. Northrop assured me they will as soon as they are able. Of course, your *fiancé* wasn't agreeable." Duncan winked to let her know he was teasing.

Camy's eyes grew wide. Ellie laughed as she handed her the spectacles. "You shouldn't tease her. Miller's obsession isn't exactly her fault, nor has it been pleasant for any of us."

"No, you shouldn't," Camy said. "And we should not discuss our personal matters with mere strangers."

Duncan winced. True, they'd met hours before, but he felt as if he'd known her his whole life. Perhaps, given the distress in her eyes, it was his teasing her about Miller that caused her to be surly. However, curiosity about the personal matters between Miller Northrop and Camy stirred in his mind. Any man with a lick of sense would be obsessed with gaining her hand, which obviously proved Duncan didn't have any sense. And he intended to keep it that way, at least until all was settled and he returned to the city far from the unsettling peace he experienced watching her rest.

He cleared his throat. "My apologies. You've slept the afternoon, and beyond dinner. As I said, Dr. Northrop will escort your sister home tomorrow when he comes to check on you."

Camy rolled her eyes. "Ellie is a fine enough doctor to treat me."

"We've discussed this. I know nothing about these sorts of wounds." Ellie laid the spoon in a pan of steaming water. "Are you hungry? Benjamin said you could have some broth as long as your stomach can handle it with the medicine."

"Where is Hamish?"

Duncan had hoped Camy held no memory of her uncle's announcement before entering the cabin. He didn't want her upset any more than what she was, and any mention of marriage would certainly do just that.

"I banished him to the barn." Ellie dipped broth into a bowl. "Mr. Murray, would you mind helping Camy to sit?"

Careful not to jar the arm held against her in a sling, he pulled back the heavy quilt and scooped one arm beneath her knees and the other behind her back, and settled her against the headboard. He stuffed pillows and a folded quilt behind her back for support.

"And Pastor Hammond?" Camy whispered near his ear as he settled the quilt around her.

So much for her not recalling Hamish's words. "Fortunately—" he smiled at her "—for both of us, winter decided to reappear. It gives us the evening to rest and enjoy one last snow."

"But—"

He touched his finger to her lips. Soft and warm. Dangerous. He jerked his finger away and began tucking the blanket beneath her legs. "No buts. We will worry about tomorrow when the sun rises. Today has had enough cares of its own. Sip your broth, renew your strength and enjoy the peace. I have no doubts Hamish will be rambling before your rooster cries."

Duncan stepped away from the bed and glanced around the small cabin for a place to escape. He'd kept his promise. She was awake, and seemed well, but he had far too much experience to believe she was truly well. Memories of men writhing around incoherently, only to slip beyond the here and now, pressed into his mind. He would never forgive himself if she died. He most certainly did not wish to watch her in the throes of agony. He could leave if he chose. However, he wouldn't be able to until he knew for certain she was well. Besides, Hamish had yet to return his horse and his shoes, Duncan's toes would freeze if he left. He'd been too concerned with Camy to interrogate Hamish. He believed what he told Camy, that tomorrow would be soon enough to demand the return of his shoes. For now, he needed to determine how to occupy the time without losing his wits, *er*, or regaining them. Massaging his neck, he contemplated making a run for the barn to seek shelter with Hamish. No doubt, he would be tempted to throttle his old friend for placing them all in a difficult situation.

"Would you like to join us for our nightly reading of scripture?"

He glanced over his shoulder to see Camy toying with an invisible string on the quilt. How long had it been since he'd opened a Bible? Since the war?

She lifted her chin and looked at him from beneath her thick lashes. "Afterward we pray, and then Ellie knits while Mara and I play chess. I suppose you could stand in for Mara."

He was still caught on the word *pray*. "Pray?" he repeated.

Camy released a nervous giggle.

The last time he prayed, he'd been holding Geoff Walters's hand as the young soldier took his last breath. He promised himself he'd never pray again. His earlier mishap of releasing a prayer as she washed down the river was an act of desperation and he wasn't yet convinced that it had been his prayers that had been answered, for surely she had cried out to God too.

Ellie laid a thick Bible on the table. "Do not feel obligated, Mr. Murray."

"Are you not a praying man?" Camy asked.

He jammed his hands into his pants pockets. "I, uh, haven't in a few years. Seems God doesn't hear much of what a Murray has to say." After all his father's sins, who could blame Him?

"What would ever make you think that?" Ellie sounded dismayed at the idea.

"I didn't realize God was selective when it came to surnames," Camy added. "Selective when it comes to the intention of a man's heart perhaps, but never with his name. Did we not read from the tenth chapter of the book of Acts last night, Ellie? I believe verse thirty-four said God is no respecter of persons. He does not show favoritism whether rich or poor, male or female, Murray or Sims. If He does not show favoritism, He certainly does not decide to ignore a man because of his name."

The tips of his ears burned at her chastisement. Their responses made him sound like a child seeking pity after not receiving bread pudding. They made it sound as if he pitied himself, because God chose to lend him a deaf ear whenever he prayed. Duncan despised some of his choices. Despised his past. He definitely despised his father. But he never pitied himself. Had he confused pity for self-loathing? He didn't wish to examine the question any further at the moment, nor did he wish to discuss his reasons as to why he believed God seemed to ignore his petitions.

"My experience tells me otherwise, but maybe you are correct. Maybe it has more to do with my heart than it does my name." He grabbed his coffee and sipped the hot brew. What would it hurt to read with them one night? "How about I listen while you ladies read, and then if you are up for a match I'll play chess?"

"Nonsense, Duncan. We read every night and as you are our *honored* guest, we must include you. We would not wish it to be rumored that the Simses are inhospitable, would we?" The corner of Camy's mouth twitched. The lass teased him. Very well.

Duncan gathered the heavy tome in his hands and settled in one of the spindle-back chairs. Ellie sat opposite him. "Where shall I read from?"

"The Good Samaritan," Ellie announced.

Camy's jaw slackened before she snapped it shut. Duncan dipped his head to hide his smile. He didn't know what Camy's sister was up to, but it seemed as if he might have an ally for the moment.

Camy glared at her sister. They should be reading the next chapter in the book of Acts, not some random story and one about a Good Samaritan. Everything Duncan had been and nothing Camy had displayed. And for what purpose? Was it to remind Camy of how she'd fallen short?

"Very well," Duncan said without seemingly being aware of the tension between her and Ellie. She supposed it served her right for trying to push Duncan into reading and praying when he'd rather not. However, as much as she did not want to marry, she absolutely refused to marry a man who did not honor God, which was one reason Miller and his propensity to drink too much was off her list, not to mention that he only wanted the land.

"I believe that is found in the book of Luke, chapter ten, beginning with verse thirty," Duncan said as he thumbed through the pages.

Camy stared in disbelief. If Ellie could read her thoughts she'd chastise her for judging a book by its cover. What sort of man didn't pray, yet knew where to find an exact scripture? She nearly laughed aloud. Of course, she was being a ninny. Everyone knew about the story, didn't they? Duncan didn't have to be a minister to know the reference.

"Here we are." Duncan laid the Bible on the table and leaned forward.

He brushed his hair from his brow, revealing more of the bandage.

"What happened to you?" Camy's thoughts tumbled out of her mouth.

Duncan glanced at her, his brow furrowed. "Pardon?"

"Your head?" she continued. "I never asked since finding you at the creek."

He touched the bandage, and then his fingers danced down to the bruising around his eye. He chuckled. "Hamish caught me unaware with the butt of his rifle. He hit me hard enough to knock me out. I landed on a large rock, causing the wound on the back of my head."

"Oh." She toyed with one of the ties on the quilt.

"Sometimes I don't understand that man," Ellie said as she scratched her nail over an invisible speck of dirt on the table.

"He was adamant I marry your sister," Duncan responded to Ellie. "And when I didn't agree…well, this was the consequence. I've known Hamish to act rashly, but I've always been able to reason with him."

Heaviness pressed against her chest as she tried to swallow past the knot in her throat. She didn't know what bothered her more, the fact that Duncan took a beating when it was obvious he could have won the fight, or that he was as determined as she was not to marry. She chewed on her lower lip. "Has he seen to reason?"

"I haven't found an appropriate time to speak with him yet, but he will. He'll either grant me the land without an agreement of marriage, or he'll find another man to purchase Sims Creek and offer you marriage."

The heaviness pressed harder until she thought she'd

split in two. She didn't want to marry anyone, especially since his only interest was the land. No different than Miller. No better. She had an idea as to Hamish's reasoning, but his plan wouldn't work. She wanted to be worth more than a piece of land.

Duncan lowered his gaze to the Bible. "'And Jesus answering said, A certain man went down from Jerusalem to Jericho, and fell among thieves, which stripped him of his raiment, and wounded him, and departed, leaving him half dead.'"

Camy recalled the moment she'd first seen Duncan. Unmoving, beaten, thinking he'd been left for dead. Of course, once he'd gained consciousness, he'd seemed well enough, even if he had been a little unsteady on his feet.

"'And by chance there came down a certain priest that way: and when he saw him, he passed by on the other side. And likewise a Levite, when he was at the place, came and looked on him, and passed by on the other side.'"

Camy had done much worse. Seeing his injuries and lack of shoes, she'd demanded he leave her property. With good reason, or so the fear pounding in her heart at the time had convinced her. She should have known, she should have asked questions before threatening to shoot him.

Perhaps she had a bit of Hamish in her blood. They'd done nothing but abuse Duncan, even after he had attempted to rescue her from the river without thought to his own life. She had teased earlier about hospitality, but he still wore the same clothes he had on earlier. His feet were bare. How long had it taken for his clothes to dry?

"'But a certain Samaritan, as he journeyed, came where he was: and when he saw him, he had compassion on him, And went to him, and bound up his wounds, pouring in oil and wine, and set him on his own beast, and brought him to an inn, and took care of him.'"

An apology clung to the tip of her tongue, but she feared if she opened her mouth the broth Ellie had made for her would reappear. She leaned her head against the headboard and closed her eyes. Duncan's voice, as he continued reading the story, curled around her heartstrings. His accent thickened until it was no longer hidden beneath shame. The scripture filled the room with such a lyrical grace that it lulled her into a peace unlike any she could recall. He held more power and authority in the softness of his tone, than Pastor Hammond when shouting from behind the pulpit, shaking the rafters.

She heard the Bible close and the spindle-back chair squeak. "She's asleep."

No. She wasn't sleeping, only resting her eyes a moment. Her lids refused to open. Her mouth refused to utter a word. She wanted to hear his voice. For him to keep reading.

"Dr. Northrop believes your injuries need watching as well, so you may have the bedroom." Ellie's chair scraped against the floorboards. "I will sleep out here with Camy and keep watch."

Camy tried to lift her hand to gain their attention. She didn't want to miss their nightly prayers.

"Will you adjust her again while I see to the other room?" Ellie asked.

"Of course."

Cold air infiltrated Camy as he pulled the quilt back. Strong arms tucked beneath her knees and behind her back and she no longer missed the blanket, until he gently laid her back down on the mattress. The heavy blanket fell over her. He tucked the quilt beneath her chin and then brushed his fingers over her brow, smoothing out her hair on the pillow. She felt like a child being cared for, cherished. It was a moment she would both hate and love until it faded from her memory, if ever. As she drifted further into sleep, she prayed she wouldn't recall the tender touch.

"Dear God," he whispered, "I'm reminded by this brave, beautiful woman that You are no respecter of persons. Will You forgive me for believing otherwise? I am laying my all here and now and asking You to keep her well."

Even though her limbs grew heavy with each breath she took, she knew she'd never forget. This moment would remain with her all her days.

Chapter Six

A loud noise startled Duncan out of a dream of a dark-haired lass sitting beside him at the creek while he read passages of scripture. There were times in the dream he'd been no more than a boy watching his parents enjoy lunch by the loch. Then he'd changed into the man he'd become, only his heart was filled with joy and his belly bursting with laughter as he gazed upon—*Cameron Sims*.

He threw back the covers and jumped from the bed. His head dizzied from the jolt, forcing him back on the bed. The squeak and pop of the springs confused him for a moment, until sounds of female laughter, filtering beneath the door, warmed a spot deep in his chest and he recalled he wasn't in the room he kept at Mrs. Williamson's boardinghouse in Topeka.

Two nights ago, just as he'd finished praying for Camy, a fever had begun to attack Camy's body. Although Ellie seemed competent, Duncan had refused to leave Camy's side until the heat radiating from Camy's skin diminished. He knew what happened when delirium came. It either broke the fever or broke the person.

Fortunately Camy did nothing more than mumble a few words, which Ellie informed him was quite normal for the lass. However, he remained vigilant for two days and two nights, helping Ellie bathe Camy's brow, taking turns napping in the chair beside her, praying for a quick recovery. It had been the wee hours of the morning when the fever finally broke and Duncan stumbled to the bedroom, falling onto the covers.

The freezing slatted floorboards stung his feet. Still cradling his pounding head, he glanced around the small room that had only been shadows when he finally crashed onto the mattress. Crude logs formed three of the walls; bits of colorful fabric peeked out from holes in the mortar. Limestone and what had once been a source of heat made up the fourth wall. Rocks and debris rested at the bottom of the aging fireplace.

Spots of colored fabric stuffed in holes in the ceiling caught his attention. He scrubbed his hand over his face. He'd noticed small things over the past day in the cabin, but his focus had been on reducing Camy's fever. How long had the sisters been fending for themselves? And why hadn't Hamish been caring for them? Duncan supposed he'd have to take a closer look at what other repairs were needed before he left.

Duncan eased to his feet, the bed creaking as it gave up his weight. He took several slow breaths until the pounding in his head subsided. He grabbed the shirt and trousers, borrowed from things left by Camy's father, and pulled them on over his flannel underclothes. His own needed a good scrubbing, stained from Camy's wound and their muddied trek in the rain.

A loud push of air sounded from under the door, followed by a high-pitched bark. Duncan swung open the door and was met by the same mangy-looking beast he'd seen lounging inside the barn when they arrived. A long tongue hung out the side of the mutt's mouth as he panted. Duncan held out his hand for a sniff and was met with a slobbery lick.

"He likes you." Camy laughed. "Hound doesn't like many people."

"Most dogs are a good judge of character." Duncan patted Hound on the head and then brushed past him to Camy. He pressed the back of his hand to her forehead. Although she was cool to the touch, her cheeks were overly bright. He slid his fingers to the soft curve beneath her doelike eyes. Her skin remained warm, but lacked fever. He pressed his fingers to her pulse and counted. Strong, steady. "How are you this morning?"

"M-much b-better," she stuttered.

Frowning, Duncan wondered at the cause of her discomfort. He'd noticed her slight stammer before she'd taken ill with the fever, but he'd attributed it to the shock of her injury. Was this the shy wallflower Hamish had spoken of?

"Ellie is out gathering wood for breakfast."

"Oh." He glanced around the room and noticed they were alone. He released his hold on her wrist and took a few steps from the bed. "I would have done it."

"We know. I haven't thanked you."

"For?"

"For not abandoning me, and for helping me when I was so terribly rude. My apologies."

"None needed. Although I do appreciate it. I gather you ladies are under some duress, and that it has something to do with the railroad." He intended to find out the facts before revealing his position.

"You must understand that it is difficult to know who to take into our confidences. We have had some trouble, and when the people of Rusa Valley found out they began to split loyalties, which caused further trouble." She glanced at her folded hands in her lap. "I do not wish to say more. Again, I feel as if I must apologize, but please understand."

Although he wanted her to trust him, he understood. He often kept things to himself until he was certain of who was his friend and who was not.

"Are you a d-doctor?"

He laughed. "No, why do you ask?"

"You checked for fever and took my pulse."

"Ah, that. While I was recovering from a wound in the war, I assisted the doctor in our unit." Far more than he liked, his assistance had been to hold the hand of a dying man, praying for his soul, reading his favorite scripture and writing letters to families. For many, it wasn't enough.

A blustery wind burst through the cabin door as Ellie stepped over the threshold. Hound danced around her legs, yipping.

"Here, let me take that." Duncan gathered the pile of wood from her arms and set it beside the fireplace. He stirred the dying embers and then added a few logs.

"Thank you." Ellie patted the dog's head and then she removed her hat, gloves and coat. "I will be surprised if Benjamin and Mara show up today. There are drifts higher than my knees, and the snow continues to fall. Who would believe it's almost March?"

"What of Hamish?" Camy asked. "I'm anxious to speak with him."

"I believe we all are," Ellie responded. "He was not in the barn, and there was no sign of him."

"I am not surprised." Duncan pulled back the blue curtain and looked outside. Snow piled up along the sill, nearly covering half the window. "Are there chores that need completing?"

Camy laughed. "You have no shoes."

"I took the liberty of searching through Father's things. I found a pair of boots. I hope they'll fit you better than his clothes. Now that Camy is alert, I'll tend to the washing."

The trousers were a good few inches too short, hiking above his ankles. "I've been a bachelor many years. If you don't mind I'll save you the trouble and wash them myself, but first tell me what it is I can do to help." He looked at Ellie and winked. "Since your sister seems to want to lounge about all day, perhaps it would help if I did her chores as well as Mara's."

"Oh no!" Camy argued.

"Thank you," Ellie said.

Duncan shifted his gaze between the two sisters. Was Camy so mistrustful of him that she didn't want him helping? "I promise I won't cause you harm."

Camy closed her eyes. "I didn't mean to imply mistrust. Ellie told me how you've helped these last two days. Certainly I would know you don't intend us harm."

He knelt beside the bed and took her hand in his, so soft and small. "Then what is it?"

Camy looked over his shoulder. "We haven't been very good Samaritans to you."

The corner of his mouth lifted. "I promise, I will not speak a negative word against the Sims sisters. As far as the outside world knows, you have been the best of hostesses. Now." He unfolded to his full height. "If you will tell me what needs to be done, I'll get started."

Duncan sat in one of the spindle-back chairs and wiggled his feet into the borrowed boots as Ellie and Camy gave him a list. Feed the animals, check for eggs, clean the stalls and fill the bucket of water at the creek. There was much more that needed tending to. He could see it with his own eyes. And surely the ladies would prefer a heartier meal than broth. Once he was done with their appointed list, maybe he'd check out the hunting grounds. Perhaps he could catch a rabbit or two, and if not, there was always one of the hens in the barn.

Camy's heart fluttered at the sight of snowflakes in Duncan's hair when he shouldered his way through the door with the egg basket and more firewood. "How many eggs today?"

"Only three."

She was surprised he hadn't left for Rusa as soon as he pulled the boots on. No doubt, he wanted to, but then he'd been insistent on speaking with Hamish. And too, a man wouldn't leave without his horse.

The flutter in her chest plummeted. Why couldn't a man covet her instead of what she possessed? At least she knew what Miller wanted. After all, Miller's father had claimed her father and Hamish had stolen this land. Hamish had documentation, and nobody had proved otherwise, but that still didn't explain Miller's anxiousness to marry her, not when the feud had lain dormant for years. Yes, it was beautiful here, and yes, the soil was good for planting, but it wasn't worth the years of imposed hatred between two families by the crotchety old doctor and Hamish.

Duncan set the basket on the table and the firewood in the crate. He rubbed his hands together and blew on them. In all the times Miller had been here, he never once helped. Instead he sat with his nose curled in disgust demanding to be waited on. Duncan's wind-blown hair and reddened cheeks from the wintery cold brought a cheery disposition into the dreary cabin as if he enjoyed farm life. Would that make a difference to her? Could she marry him if he loved working on the farm, even if he didn't love her?

He held his hands near the fire. "I think the snow is lightening up a little and I can see a break in the clouds. It sure is nice to see blue skies after all the rain and snow."

"What are your plans?" Her question came out sharper than she intended.

Duncan glanced over his shoulder.

She ducked her head. "I didn't mean…" She pulled in a deep breath and released it. Her shoulders slumped. "I d-don't know what I mean."

He moved from the fire and pulled a chair next to her bed. He sat and covered her hands with one of his. Warm from the fire, his palm over her hands settled peace in her thoughts. "We are all a little anxious to have things settled, but until Hamish decides to make an appearance, I'm in much the same position as you, stuck waiting."

Stuck. Like with a shoe sunk in the mud, no matter how hard you pulled, the mire suctioned tighter until you ended up on your backside covered from head to toe. Was that how he felt? Trapped, suffocating, pulling and pulling, knowing if he didn't take care he'd be in a worse position. "So you're not leaving now that you have shoes?"

He squeezed her hand. "Even if I had possession of my horse, I'd stay. I'm sticking around until I'm assured everything is settled."

A part of her was relieved. Another part of her was scared. Who knew how long he would stay? But with every moment they spent together she found herself dreaming about what she'd never had before. Marriage, especially after Ellie told her how he refused to leave her side until the fever abated, insisting on bathing her brow. A wastrel wouldn't do such a thing for a mere stranger, only a man with character above reproach. A man who laid his life down for another as he'd done when he jumped in the river after her.

"Your sister was heading for the barn when I came in. I need to take the bucket to the river and get water. Will you be all right by yourself until one of us returns?"

All right? She'd spent most of her life convincing herself and others she was all right. Through the abandonment, through the loneliness, through keeping her head for her sisters' sake, through each of Mrs. Smith's comments that made her feel like a pauper. "I'll be fine."

He shifted out of the chair and placed it back by the table. He picked up the bucket and opened the door. "I'll only be a few moments."

She nodded as he walked out the door, leaving her to the company of the crackling fire. She leaned her head against the headboard and closed her eyes. Her limbs ached from misuse, and her mind raced from one thought to the next. It always had. That was why she enjoyed doing chores, much more than inane talk at Mrs. Smith's social gatherings. And she found more pleasure eating Mara's burned biscuits than pretending to babble about nothing.

"Hmm, biscuits." Camy tossed the heavy quilt off and scooted to the edge of the bed until the tips of her toes touched the planks. She slipped off the bed and tumbled toward the table. She rested the palm of her good arm against the table surface and took a couple breaths before pulling out a chair. Clearly she hadn't thought out her plan, but determined, she climbed to her feet and took the few steps to the shelf where the flour sat. She tugged on the sack of flour and then pulled. It fell against her chest, jolting her injured arm and causing a cry of pain before falling to the floor. She collapsed next to the sack in a heap of flour and cried.

Cold air swished around her and she prayed Ellie had returned, not Duncan. She did not want him to see how much of a ninny she really was.

"Are you hurt?" His deep tones rumbled through her. She heard the bucket settle on the floor, and then he was by her side. "Camy, what has happened?"

Tears rolled down her flour-dotted cheeks. "Biscuits."

"Biscuits? Were they burning?"

"No." She shook her head and sniffled in the most unladylike manner, which caused her to cry more. "I couldn't lie about another moment."

"Ah, I see."

The uncertainty in his words had her glancing at him through a watery fog. "You think I'm a ninny."

Duncan laughed. "Not exactly."

He scooped her up and sat her in a chair. He ripped a linen cloth from a hook and then pulled a chair in front of her and sat. Removing her spectacles, he drew the cloth over each eye, across her brow, down her nose and then over her cheeks. He paused when it came to her lips. His gaze shifted to hers. She drew her lip between her teeth and tasted flour. He brushed the cloth against the corner of her mouth and then along the seam of her lips, releasing her bottom lip from her teeth all the while holding her gaze. Her stockinged toes curled against the cool floor. He leaned closer, much closer than he ought. His breath danced over her tearstained cheek, followed by a gentle touch of his lips.

This time, with this man, the stolen kiss wouldn't get Duncan Murray dumped in the creek. Yet she also knew at that moment that if Pastor Hammond entered the cabin she couldn't willingly say "I do." Duncan didn't love her.

He jumped from the chair, knocking it to the floor with a loud clatter.

Had she said the thought aloud? She dropped her chin to her chest as fresh tears spilled onto her lashes.

"Don't." He lifted her chin with his finger. "You have no need to hide. Not from me."

She pulled away from him and stared at the bright flames in the fireplace. Besides Miller's gruff smash of his mouth to hers before Camy had pushed him in the river, no man had kissed her, and now that one did, and with tenderness, he seemed to regret the action. Even if it was only a brotherly peck on the cheek. "I am sorry."

"Again, you have no need to apologize." He raked his hand over his face. "It was I who overstepped bounds. I should have called your sister in to help clean the flour from your face."

He turned in a circle, fingers thrust through his hair. He righted the chair, plopped the flour onto the table and then held her spectacles out to her. Sensing his displeasure, she hesitated. She wanted to right the situation but was at a loss as to how. She took her spectacles from him but did not place them on the bridge of her nose. Instead, not wanting to see him leave, she laid them in her lap and waited, ears tuned, listening for his departure. Somehow she sensed he'd leave.

The door popped open and slammed closed. A stone fell from the wall of her heart and settled in her throat as she choked back a sob. It was just as well he left before he made her feel a spark of something. Something like what she'd seen between Ellie and Benjamin when they thought nobody was looking, something that was best left alone for the preservation of her well-being. If he stayed, he'd truly turn her into a woolly-headed ninny.

Chapter Seven

Duncan lengthened his stride across the snow-covered yard, snatched up the ax leaning against the barn and headed for a stand of trees near the river. How could he have been such a fool? Sure, he'd given her a peck on the cheek. Brotherly affection, right? Bah!

The bubbling pool of tears spilling off her lashes and down her cheeks had been the furthest thing from his mind when he walked through the door. Contacting his partner Calvin Weston, finding Hamish, patching holes in the roof. Daydreaming of strolling along planted fields with Camy by his side, gathering eggs, holding her hand as they prayed before their meals. Things he shouldn't be thinking about lest he find himself following his father's footsteps.

He halted before a rather large tree and rested his palm against the rough bark. A piece beneath his hand loosened and fell to the ground. Its girth, nearly the circumference of a wagon wheel, suspended a good fifteen feet above the river with half the root system protruding from the bank. Duncan pushed his weight against the tree. It didn't budge. The other half of the roots anchored to the earth. Arching his neck, he glanced up to the highest branches. Smooth patches where the bark had disappeared told him the tree had suffered some sort of wounds, but one tiny green leaf budding with the new spring proclaimed some life continued to flow. Large and imposing on the surface, clinging to life.

Duncan took a step back, swung the ax and halted before the blade made contact. He knew that with enough blows it would eventually fall. He also knew if left unattended the tree would fall victim to the weather. However, that one little leaf called to something deep inside him. It stirred a smidgen of hope in the depths of his being, just as that peck on Camy's cheek had.

Resting the ax handle on his shoulder, he said, "I'll leave you for the moment." And then descended the path to the river and walked alongside it until he came upon the first fallen tree he'd stepped over only days before. Swinging the ax near the base, he severed the last threads remaining and dragged the small log up the path and settled it near the chopping stump.

"Ellie! Ellie, quick!"

Duncan angled his head to see Camy dashing out of the cabin and around the backside, a bucket of water bouncing against her leg. Hound sped past her with a series of high-pitched barks. Ellie flew out of the barn. Duncan glanced around. Nothing seemed out of place. Excepting the wisps of smoke rising from the back room where he'd been lodging, several feet from the fireplace in the front room.

"Fire!" Camy's panicked cries echoed in his ears as he darted to where the ladies had disappeared.

He came around the corner and spotted Camy smacking flames with a damp towel. Ellie tugged and Hound nipped at Camy's skirt.

"Move!" he yelled.

Ellie dropped the fabric, grabbed Hound by the neck and took off running. "I'm going to get more water."

Camy continued swatting at the flames licking the hewn logs. Flames singed the hem of her skirt, sparks catching the fabric. Duncan snaked his arm around her waist and swept her into his arms. He dumped her in a drift. Gathering her skirt, he plunged his hand into the snow. "Stay put."

He ripped the linen cloth from her hand and rushed back to where he'd set down the bucket of water by the cabin. He doused the cloth in the water and then slapped the sodden fabric against the flames. The fire was coming from a pile of sticks tucked into the corner where the main cabin met the extending bedroom. The structure itself had yet to catch fire. He dumped the bucket of water onto the debris and watched the flames disappear.

Running his hand through his hair, he knelt and inspected the damage. Fortunately only the bottom two logs were slightly charred. It didn't take a great deal of investigating to realize the fire was set on purpose. The two questions begging for answers, did the perpetrator intend to burn the ladies out of their home or only scare them? And who was responsible? An agent with the railroad? An imposter pretending to be with the railroad? Or perhaps someone with another agenda, like Miller Northrop?

A hand dropped onto his shoulder, startling him. He spun around and jumped to his feet. A cry tore from

Camy's lips as she stumbled backward. He grabbed hold of her elbow to steady her. "I'm sorry. Did I hurt you?"

He glanced into her coffee-colored eyes as she gave her head a gentle shake. Afraid of staring at her, he jerked his gaze to the soft curls gracing her forehead. Without thinking, he ran his fingers over one ringlet. Deep lines furrowed her brow. The elbow still held in his palm trembled. He shifted his gaze back to hers and saw a frightened doe.

He wanted to pull her into his arms and settle the fear right out of both them, but charred wood lingered between them. And the hair at the base of his neck, standing on end, told him someone was watching them. Releasing his hold on her elbow, he squatted and inspected the snow for footprints as well as took a few peeks into the surrounding woods, but it required greater attention than he could give at the moment. "Are you certain you are fine?"

"Yes." She nodded. "But Ellie should be back."

"I want to check the inside of the cabin to make sure the fire didn't catch through the logs, and then I'll search for your sister." He also wanted to inspect the cabin before he left her alone and ease the gnawing in his gut. For the first time since his arrival, he fully understood Camy's reaction to him when she first found him on her property. He was also beginning to understand Hamish's motives to negotiate a marriage for his niece, but why choose him? If Hamish knew of his involvement with the railroad, the old man would, no doubt, rescind his offer and rightly so. Duncan needed to have a discussion with his friend as soon as possible, but first he intended to discover who was behind the threats against the sisters.

He led her around to the front of the cabin. "Wait here."

She started to shake her head but then tucked her uninjured hand over the sling against her midsection. He hated the worried lines creasing her eyes, the tight line of her mouth. And he knew at the moment he would do all within his grasp to bear the burden of her fears.

Worrying about what he'd find inside the cabin, Duncan stepped onto the porch and swung open the aged, weathered door. A soft glow emanated from the fireplace. Dust danced in the beams of light protruding through the portal. He glanced under the bed. With his back facing the wall, he crept into the bedroom and released the air held hostage in his lungs as he neared the far wall. Kneeling, he ran his hand along the hewn logs and then stole a glance under the bed to see if anyone hid in the shadows. He drew in a breath, unfolded his length and made his way out of the cabin.

Camy remained as he'd left her, in the center of the yard surrounded by melting snow with her arms tucked around her waist. If he didn't know any better, he'd think a young girl stood before him. His jaw ticked as anger frothed inside him. He hated seeing anyone abused and bullied. Tormented.

He jammed his hands into his pants pockets and stepped off the porch. "All's well. No sign of the fire inside." He wouldn't cause her further fear by speaking his earlier suspicions that anyone had intruded into her home. Not until he had to.

"Ellie?"

Hound barked as he raced over to Camy. She held her hand out for a lick. Ellie climbed the last bit of hill and set the bucket down. "Is the fire out?"

Duncan followed Camy as she rushed to her sister's side. Duncan took the bucket as Camy threw herself at her sister. "I was worried. Truly frightened."

Ellie pulled back and brushed her hand over Camy's hair. "I tried to hurry, but in my haste I dropped the bucket into the water. Thankfully it caught up in the bend, but I had to find a branch long enough to pull it out. Are you all right?" Ellie bent over and inspected Camy's skirt.

"Yes, I'm fine. Just a little shaken." The hint of a smile curved her lips. "I'm beyond thankful Duncan was here. To think we could have lost everything."

Her words rang in his ear. He had no wish for her gratitude, not when he might be partially responsible. He might not have ordered the deed done, but if the railroad was involved as the ladies believed, then his coin was involved, which meant he was just as guilty.

Camy watched Duncan shove his hands into his pockets. Shoulders hunched and head hung low, he disappeared into the barn. "Hamish best return soon."

Ellie sighed. "We sure are in a mess."

"We?" Camy raised an eyebrow. "You aren't the one he's trying to marry off."

Ellie's cheeks paled. "He knows I won't marry and Mara is too young." She looped her arm with Camy's. "You, dear sister, are our only hope."

Camy dug her heels into the melting snow. "I'm sorry. I didn't consider you and Mara."

She'd never thought of her predicament as hope,

only as a curse. She'd been too caught up in her fear of being abandoned. Again. Perhaps being married to an absent husband wouldn't be such a bad thing if it saved their home. Duncan didn't want a wife. She didn't want a husband. Could they come to an acceptable agreement?

"I'm teasing, Camy. As much as we love it here, we would never ask you to marry for anything other than love."

Camy knew Ellie had experienced love. Often she caught her sister woolgathering over what had been lost with Benjamin. They had been inseparable, but Benjamin left to serve as a doctor in the War Between the States, and when he returned something had happened to keep them from reuniting as Camy had expected, and even prayed for. "Duncan isn't so bad on the eyes."

Ellie smiled. "That is something. And he seems to have a decent idea of how a lady should be treated, which is more than I can say for Miller. Poor boy, lost his mother much too soon."

"Ellie, I could never love Duncan." Oh, she could, easily, but she wouldn't allow herself to be caught in that foolish snare.

"Then you shouldn't marry him."

"I could never marry a man I did love."

"Dear sister, at some point you must forget our father's leaving and gather the courage to live outside the shadows."

They stepped onto the porch. A trail of flour dusted over the threshold. Ellie glanced at her with a question in her eyes.

"You know I despise idleness," Camy said. "With

Mara gone, I thought to make biscuits. Before I could finish cleaning the mess I smelled smoke."

She would not think about the warmth of Duncan's lips on her cheek, or the giddiness that had curled her toes. He had looked at her as if she were beautiful. As if she was more than beautiful. No man had ever looked at her in such a way before. She'd become lost in his gaze as he leaned closer. So close she'd thought she could hear the beat of his heart. Of course, she had only been woolgathering, and had given herself a thorough chastising after he ran out of the cabin in horror.

"I know this isn't easy for you, but until you're a little more mended I'd rather you remain still. Benjamin said there was a risk of your wound bleeding again, or even worse, becoming gangrenous. And with your fever the last two days, well, I'm demanding you stay in bed."

Camy sighed. "I'll perish from boredom."

Ellie rolled her eyes. "Unlikely. However, if it distresses you so much I'll see what I can find. I fear even a simple task such as gathering what few eggs we are getting would not be easy for you. You would need both hands to darn our stockings, not that you would volunteer for such a task."

Camy's heart still thundered in her chest after the fire. The exertion taxed what little strength she had, and all that hopefulness that had bubbled within her only an hour or so had dissolved. "For now I would like to rest."

Ellie halted her steps, and faced her. The back of her hand pressed to Camy's brow. "Are you well?"

"What's wrong?" Duncan's sharpness snapped Camy out of her melancholy.

She spun around, knocking her sister's hand from her brow as she wobbled. "Nothing."

"Her fever has returned."

"I am fine. What are you doing with Uncle Tommy?" The hen rested her head on Duncan's shoulder like she did whenever Camy carried her around.

"Uncle Tommy? This hen?" He glanced at the bird. "I thought you would like something other than broth to eat."

Camy hiked up her skirt and strode across the way. She wanted to snatch Uncle Tommy from Duncan's clutches, but she didn't want to drop the hen. "And you happened to think I would like to eat her?" She pointed her finger at the bird in his arms.

A deep V formed between Duncan's dark eyebrows. "She is a chicken with one leg. Most people I know eat chickens."

"She's *my* chicken. Mine. And you will not pluck a feather from her. Not a feather, you hear?"

Elllie burst into laughter. Camy spun around, hand on hip. "I see nothing to laugh at."

"Mr. Murray, you look as if you're choking on a fly." Ellie took Uncle Tommy from Duncan. The hen let out a raspy cluck as she settled into Ellie's arms.

Camy faced Duncan. He did have the look of a man in panic, a look that likely mirrored the brewing storm of emotions in her chest. Not because he thought to eat Uncle Tommy for lunch, but the realization that if she chose to negotiate a marriage agreement with him, she would quite possibly regret it later, or much sooner than she'd like to admit.

The fading bruise and the lack of swelling from his face unveiled hooded eyes and high cheekbones. She dropped her gaze to his mouth framed by a thickening beard a little darker than the color of his dark hair. He snapped his lips into a thin line. His pupils shrank, intensifying the gold flecks. It was as if she were seeing him for the first time. He no longer displayed a disfigured oaf, but more like the tales her mother had spun of the dark knights come to steal young maids' hearts, never to return them.

Camy's legs begged to run far from Duncan where all her hopes and dreams would remain safe tucked away in her imagination, but her body refused to move.

"If you intend to stick around the farm and marry my sister, you ought to learn the rules." Ellie's voice broke through the mire imprisoning Camy.

For no reason at all, tears pricked the backs of her eyes. Fortunately for her pride, Duncan pulled his gaze from hers and glared at her sister as if she'd shot his dog. "I've yet to speak with Hamish, and until I do so I can't say what I will do."

"You're still here." Ellie held up her hand. "Before you argue, I provided boots for your feet. You could have left."

"The fire."

"You could have left before that. You could have left with the Northrops, but you didn't."

"My horse."

"Is in the back pasture if you'd like to see her." Ellie half smiled. "She's a beauty."

"What?" Camy asked. "You knew this?"

"I walked out there this morning. I knew Hamish wouldn't have taken her far, and I was right."

"Why didn't you say anything?" She looked at Duncan. "You could've gone home or to Rusa, where you could find room and board."

"What is wrong with here?" he asked as if he hadn't been sleeping in a room with holes in the roof and eating vegetable broth and biscuits. It was as if he *liked* it here.

Why did he have to be stubborn? And likable? She didn't want him to be likable; she already liked him too much. A slight breeze blew through the yard, causing the beads of sweat on her brow to chill. She shivered. "We don't eat pet chickens," she snapped.

"If it makes you feel any better, I intended to ask permission before placing her head on the chopping block."

Camy narrowed her eyes and shook her head in disbelief. Was Duncan lying or was he that considerate? She thought back over the last few days. Of course he was considerate. He had jumped in the river to rescue her, carried her home in his beaten condition and stayed by her side while Benjamin extracted a bloody bullet from her arm. And he had even gone against his own convictions and read scriptures to her when she so rudely dared him to. Then according to Ellie he'd stayed up and watched over her while her fever raged.

Ellie's hand rested on her uninjured arm. "He won't leave you, Camy."

"Of course not," Duncan confirmed.

"Leave?" Camy's head spun. The fever had returned, burning on the inside, freezing on the outside, which, no doubt, stirred her irritation with Duncan. Why would her sister think it mattered? This was about Duncan taking over the farm chores, her chores. Chopping enough wood to get them through spring, assuming he could have her pet for dinner. It wasn't about him staying or abandoning her, was it? The way he shouldered the burden of the fire and checked the cabin before allowing her to return without even knowing she feared entering on her own had given her a sense of peace that she hadn't known since she had been a wee child. He acted like a man who knew how to care. Who could care. Who did. But she didn't want that, did she? "Why is that, Mr. Murray? Why won't you leave?"

She couldn't help wondering why she didn't want him to stay, to care. She didn't need to dig too far into her inner recesses for an answer. She knew exactly what it was, could see it even now fourteen years later. There had been no kisses to her cheek or waves good-bye, not even a glance back. She'd only seen six summers, but she'd never forgotten the moment her father had left. There had been letters, and this property many years later, and the occasional brief visit that had faded to nothing after a year or two. And she knew if she allowed Duncan a place in her life, he'd leave her just the same. Especially given that he didn't want a wife. And that terrified her.

Chapter Eight

Duncan didn't have a direct answer for her. At least not one he was ready to give. He certainly didn't want to tell her he needed to assuage his guilt, not when he wanted to be here for reasons he couldn't explain even to himself.

Shivering, she wrapped her arms around her waist. The air had warmed considerably and continued to melt the snow, but it was not warm enough to cause the beads of perspiration on her brow.

"As I have told you before, I'm staying until all is settled between us. I think we should continue this conversation after we have lunch," he said, hoping the return of her fever was nothing more than her body reacting to the stress of the fire. Perhaps if she rested, the fever would diminish.

"That is an excellent idea." Ellie looped her arm through Camy's and they stepped into the cabin. Duncan followed close behind them in case they needed his assistance. The high color in Camy's cheeks didn't set well in his gut. In fact, it scared him.

Ellie dusted off one of the spindle-back chairs before assisting Camy to sit, and then settled the one-legged chicken in a box at the end of the bed.

Duncan scrubbed his palm over his face. What had Hamish gotten him into? One thing was for certain. Camy was far from the simpering ladies with their batting eyelashes. However, she was also far from biddable, but Duncan found he didn't mind the way she challenged him. No doubt, an obedient wife would bore him, but then what did that matter if he didn't intend to stick around?

"I'll be right back." Ellie stepped outside.

Duncan knelt in front of the fire and stirred the logs with a long stick that had been resting against the stone. He swiveled on his heel and caught Camy starring right through him. "What can I do to help?"

She blinked. "Nothing."

Her tone remained surly. Had her renewed fever increased her discomfort and caused her to act like a stubborn mule with a sour disposition? His suggestion of eating something other than broth as well as her worries over the fire had no doubt taxed her gracious demeanor.

"I can either clean your flour mess or make you lunch."

She closed her eyes and slumped against the chair, resting her head against the back. "I'm not hungry."

His attempts at drawing her into an argument and out of her drudgery met with failure.

She swallowed. "I am thirsty."

"Are you in pain?"

She peered at him with one eye. "Truth?"

"If you trust me." He smiled as he handed her a cup of water. He knew the answer either way. He'd experienced more than one bullet piercing his flesh. One took nearly two weeks for the discomfort to subside.

"Worse than when Mara Jean accidentally dumped scalding water on my foot." She closed her eye. "Please don't tell Ellie. I don't think I can handle another spoonful of medicine."

He swiped a clean cloth across the table, knocking flour dust to the floor. "Your secret is safe with me for the moment."

He dusted the chairs and then began sweeping the floor. Curiosity burned in his gut. He wanted to know more about the threats against the Sims. "Was this the first fire?"

Her head rolled along the back of the chair. Her brow furrowed. "Someone set fire to the barn last spring. It was a month after a Mr. Henry had arrived with a *generous* offer from the railroad. I had no choice but to refuse, given that the land isn't mine, yet and Hamish was gallivanting somewhere as usual."

The tension that had been knotted in his neck and shoulders since the fire loosened. He didn't recognize the name. It most definitely wasn't his partner, which removed the burden of guilt he'd taken on.

"Of course, his idea of generous and ours were as wide as the Mississippi River. There had been incidents before the fire. Our crops trampled, animals missing. Every few weeks something happened. The night of the fire, it was dark. A storm brewed just west of us. We were trying to settle the animals."

As he listened to her story he had hoped there was the possibility that lightning had struck, causing the fire.

"The animals were restless, making noise." She

shivered as she closed her eyes. "Eerie screams, the oxen were restless. The Old Nag even reared up. The whole time we thought it was the storm, and before we knew it we were surrounded by torches."

Anger burned in his blood.

"I had never been so frightened. I still see them. The torches darting at us, threatening to set us on fire."

He clenched his teeth. It was by the grace of God his partner wasn't involved in tormenting Camy, because Duncan didn't know what he'd do if he had been. He'd served under a merciless captain, and although the man confiscated homes and stolen food, he hadn't treated women in such a manner.

"We never saw their faces. They're always faceless shadows."

She didn't need to tell him the shadows visited her dreams. He knew, he had experienced many fitful nights. Many nights he'd been the monster chasing soldiers too young to grow facial hair. Other nights he was no more than a young boy himself reaching for his mother to save her from his father. Duncan knelt beside her and took her hand in his. His mind raced to earlier in the morning when he'd kissed her cheek without a thought to the consequences.

Tired doelike eyes looked at him, and he longed to pull her into his arms and comfort her until sleep found her.

She sipped the water. "I said more than I should. It is our problem and ours alone."

"Camy, nobody should have to endure that sort of fear. Ever. I am sorry you and your sisters have been left to defend yourselves. I cannot pretend to know Hamish's reasons for leaving you, but I don't understand his cowardice." He rose and raked a hand through his hair. If he told her he was an investor for the railroad, he'd lose what little trust he'd gained. "I would like to find out more about this Mr. Henry. He could be an imposter."

"We have thought of that, as he was young and shabbily dressed, but Hamish seems to think the rotter is a hired hand."

The door pushed open, and Hound bounded into the cabin. He nudged his nose against Duncan's hand for a pat and then sat near Camy's feet. Ellie shouldered her way through the door with a water bucket and a large pot. Duncan took the bucket from her and set it down near the fireplace.

Ellie held the pot in the air. "Chicken for our guest."

Duncan's stomach rumbled at the prospect of a heartier meal.

"Unfortunately it will be a while before it's ready." Camy stood to her feet and wobbled. "I should rest."

Duncan didn't think Camy was the type to claim weakness. She was either avoiding further conversation or she really didn't feel well. The crimson color of her cheeks and the dark circles under her eyes told him the truth. Her steps looked laborious. Duncan thought to aid her, but Ellie was quick to grab her elbow and walk Camy to the bed.

"The road to town looks to be clearing. If Benjamin doesn't arrive with Mara today, he'll be here first thing." Ellie slid off Camy's shoes, scooted her legs under the covers and tucked the blanket around her.

"I'll be fine. I just need rest."

Duncan's heart clenched at the mere whisper of her words. He wondered how much of the morning's fire had to do with her downward turn. He silently prayed she had only overtaxed herself and needed to rest. He swept up the remaining flour and tossed the dust into the fire and then sat at the table. The heavy family tome lay in the center where he'd left it two nights before. He pulled it to him and traced the intricate gold letters spelling out the word *Bible*. He opened the cover. Heavy scripted ink detailed the sisters' lineage as well as their births. Ellie had been born in Scotland, Camy and Mara in Indiana along with another sibling, a boy by the name, who'd died at birth with Camy's mother. His heart ached at the loss of her mother, knowing how much he had loved his and how much it had devastated him when she fell ill.

He turned the book to a random page, Proverbs eighteen. He read over each verse, reciting it in his mind until he came to verse twenty-two. *Whoso findeth a wife findeth a good thing, and obtaineth favour of the Lord.*

He rested his chin on top of his intertwined fingers and gazed upon the woman beneath a mound of covers. Her soft snores intermingled with Hound's louder ones from the rug beside the bed and the hen's purring. He truly did not want the bother of a wife. At least he hadn't until he realized she was the one his friend had intended for him to marry. And even then he knew he wouldn't offer her a real marriage, and that was the battle raging inside his mind. Because now he wondered what sort of husband he would make her, and what sort of wife she would make him. He chuckled to himself; she was the sort of woman who kept a mangy mutt and a crippled hen inside her home.

His mother had done that. Not the chicken, but

goats, pigs and rabbits. Every lame animal that had crossed his mother's path had ended up in their home until it was nursed back to health. It drove his father to madness whenever he cared to come home. Duncan had a feeling Camy was the driving force behind the care of the animals rather than her sisters, and it actually warmed his heart instead of making him want to run back to the boardinghouse in a panic.

Camy was strolling arm in arm with a faceless man in the budding fields when the oddest noise broke through her dream, pulling her awake. She listened a moment, gathering her bearings, and heard the deep rumble. Peeling one eye open, she found Duncan slumped against the table, his head resting in the crook of his elbow, the palm of his hand on her family's open Bible.

She scooted to a sitting position with her back against the wooden headboard. She was pleased to feel the flush of her fever gone and couldn't wait for the pain in her shoulder to relent. Her hands begged to care for the animals, gather eggs and plow the fields for the early spring planting. How long would it be before she could work the oxen? The potatoes needed to be in the ground before too long. She would have to plead with Hamish for help, if he was even capable. The small glimpses she'd caught of him the other day made it look as if he'd finally succumbed to his old age.

She sighed. What purpose did she have in staying on the land if she couldn't care for it?

"You are awake?" Duncan lifted his head and smiled. The dimple in his cheek winked at her. "How do you feel?"

"Better." She tugged on the quilt. "The fever seems to be gone. Where is Ellie?"

"She went to milk the goats." He sat up, arched his back and stretched his arms over his head. "I forgot how much work there is on a farm."

"I prefer it to tea parties." She would much rather trudge through the field after a good rainstorm than host a social gathering.

"Being here brings back memories I had long forgotten."

"In Scotland?"

His lashes fell against his cheekbones as if to recall his home. A home in a land she had heard of and dreamed of, but had never seen. "Yes."

She wanted to ask him about his home, to know if it was the same as her mother had shared on those cold nights sitting before the fire. Camy hadn't been very old, but there were times when she could still hear the lilt in her mother's voice, hear the tales as they rolled off her tongue. "You must miss it."

"Some." He closed the Bible and slid it to the center of the table. "It's the reason Hamish's offer appealed to me."

She exhaled her frustration. Leave it to Hamish to stir up a grass fire and disappear without dousing the flames. "Until you heard I was part of the bargain?"

"It was unexpected, and yes, the thought of taking on a wife left a sour disposition in my gullet."

She dropped her eyes to her hand, twisting a loose thread on the quilt. "And now?"

He cleared his throat, drawing her gaze. "It's getting easier to swallow," he said with a wink.

Camy blew air from her lungs and relaxed against

the headboard. Although her thoughts were all twisted about how to feel toward the situation, it eased her mind to know he was beginning to consider their marriage as an option for her sisters' sake.

"Although, Camy," he said, his voice taking on a serious tone, "any marriage we have will be one in name only."

Before she could question him further Ellie, Mara and Benjamin entered the cabin. Hound barked, his tail wagging, and Uncle Tommy hopped over to Mara with her excited raspy squawk.

Mara picked up Uncle Tommy and plopped onto the end of the bed. Camy grimaced at the jarring of her shoulder. Her younger sister crossed her arms over her chest and glared at Duncan. "Ellie tells me you've been perfectly attentive, which is quite fortunate for you, Mr. Murray. After an hour in the Northrops' house, I was ready to spit nails. You can imagine my thirst for revenge up to the time good ol' Benny Northrop decided it was safe to travel through the snow to bring me home."

"Only upon my father's request after discovering you and my sister Bella dangling from the second story window," Benjamin countered.

Camy's jaw dropped.

"You didn't!" Ellie gasped.

"I never had a second-story window before." Mara ran her hand over Uncle Tommy's feathers.

"Ladies do not climb out windows." Camy quickly chided herself for sounding like Mrs. Smith.

Mara cocked her head. Her eyebrows rose. "As I recall, your skirts became caught on a nail when you snuck out of Mrs. Smith's parlor during her Christmas Social."

"It was not a second-story window." She would not recant the tale of how Miller had hounded her every move until she thought she'd go mad.

"How is our patient?" Benjamin untied the sling and pressed his fingers to her wrist to determine her condition.

"Ready to be done with this," she responded.

Benjamin laughed. "You never were one for holding still." He glanced over his shoulder. "Any fever?"

Ellie told him about her fever and how she and Duncan had cared for and brought the burning under control. "She woke this morning cheerful and seemingly well. And then the fever returned."

Light from the fire cast Duncan's shadow over her as he moved in closer. "An effect from exertion? There was a fire outside the cabin and she thought to douse it with a wet towel."

"Is that so?" Benjamin's jaw tensed as he pulled a stethoscope from his bag, placed the ends on his ears and leaned forward. "Exertion is a possibility."

"Thank you for leaving Miller at home," she whispered. "I don't think I could handle any more discord."

"Perhaps one day you'll return the favor when I attempt to fall back into the good graces of your sister," he whispered back. Benjamin then tugged the stethoscope from his ears and dumped it in his medical bag. "Has there been much pain?"

Duncan shifted into her line of sight and raised an eyebrow. Would he call her out if she didn't speak the full truth? She didn't intend to find out. As much as she disliked taking the bitter concoction her sister had spooned into her mouth, she despised telling even the littlest of lies. "Some, but not enough to warrant laudanum."

"I agree," Duncan added. "She has shown very little discomfort and mostly after taxing her strength with fighting the flames."

"Sounds like you have a champion, Camy." Mara Jean nudged her leg.

She looked up at him from beneath her lashes. Arms crossed over his chest like a sentry, he looked fierce, as if he'd willingly fight all her battles if she asked him to. Although she was irritated that he kept bringing up the fire and yet thankful that Benjamin hadn't probed into the incident further, her heart swelled with an emotion she didn't understand.

Instead of examining the feeling further, she pushed it aside and covered it behind the fear of rejection she'd been carrying on her shoulders since she could remember. It was better that way, safer, especially if they decided to enter into a marriage agreement that would allow her to safely keep her home, and him the land that gave him memories. Of course, she had never considered before now how she could live in such close proximity to him. "He's only speaking the truth."

"Ah, Camy, you're no fun," Mara Jean said. "Can't you once think about a man sweeping you across the dance floor until you're breathless?"

Benjamin chuckled. Ellie gasped. Camy's face burned. Her eyes darted toward Duncan and witnessed the darkening of his tanned cheeks before she stared at a red piece of fabric crammed into a hole in the chinking. What would her dear sister say if she told her she experienced breathlessness whenever Duncan walked into the room? What would she say if she told her how her toes had curled with happiness when he pecked her on the cheek? Camy would never know because she would never tell her.

"Mara Jean," Ellie said in a low motherly tone. "Your fanciful daydreams of capturing a beau will never happen if you continue with your outspoken tongue. Take Hound and Uncle Tommy to the barn and busy your idle hands."

Duncan stepped back when Mara Jean scooted off the bed with Uncle Tommy. The termagant she called sister stuck her tongue out at Camy as if she'd been the one to get her into trouble. "Come on, Hound. We know when we're not wanted."

Camy drew in a breath, and released it after her sister stomped out of the cabin. Her eyes found Duncan's. "Are you still finding Hamish's offer easier to swallow?"

He scrubbed his hand over his face and then burst into laughter. The sound echoed in the small cabin. "More so now than I ever was."

Chapter Nine

Duncan's coat hung on a nail by the door, the deed to the Simses' property nestled within a pocket. All that remained were the required signatures, which Hamish and Duncan had agreed to do upon their return to Topeka, to pay the measly sum Hamish asked for and for Duncan to agree to marry the woman tying his innards into a tangle of knots. Duncan meant what he said; he was closer to accepting the offer without reservation. If he was to be honest with himself, his life would never be the same whether he stayed here and married her or if he refused Hamish's offer and walked away. She'd be engraved in his mind like a cattleman's brand on his cattle.

"I didn't want to press the cause of the fire with Mara here," Benjamin said as he removed Camy's bandage. "But now I insist."

Duncan's eyebrows rose. His suspicions that there was something between the doctor and Camy's older sister renewed themselves, making him wonder why Hamish hadn't offered Benjamin the deed in exchange for Ellie's hand. Unless, of course, the old man was determined to keep Sims Creek from falling into the Northrops' hands. "It wasn't an accident, but I gather you already know that."

What would the good doctor say if he knew Duncan suspected his brother was the culprit?

Northrop peeled back Camy's bandage and inspected the wound. "This is the second or third time. I insist you ladies move to town." He looked pointedly at Camy's sister from the corner of his eye.

"I will remind you, Dr. Northrop, you've no right to insist we do anything. Not now, nor ever." Ellie swiveled on her feet, grabbed hold of the stick leaning by the fireplace and poked at the glowing logs.

"He may not, but I do," Duncan said with more calm than he felt.

Camy sat straight up and slapped the mattress with her palm. "How dare you?"

Northrop excused himself outside. Ellie followed behind the doctor. The door shut with a soft click. Their footfalls receded off the porch.

"I dare because it is a matter of your life." Duncan drew in a breath, deliberately puffing out his chest.

"We haven't come to terms." She attempted to kick her legs out from the quilt but quickly gave up and rested her head against the headboard.

"It doesn't matter, not the way I see it." He crossed his arms in front of him.

Her doe-colored eyes became mere slits. Her cheeks stained crimson, her mouth pressed into a thin line. He couldn't help the shift of his thoughts. Her anger did little to douse the hope stirring inside him. Instead it renewed with vigor. He wanted to kiss her. Not a fond brotherly peck. No, he wanted to ease the tension in her lips, to see her eyes give way like the dusk to a starry night.

"If I do not agree, you have nothing," she snapped.

Duncan took two long steps and yanked the document from his coat pocket. He skimmed over the lines. There wasn't a word about marriage in the document, but he had a feeling Hamish wouldn't sign the deed unless his niece was safely wedded, and for good reason. Duncan shook the deed between them. "Without word from your uncle, sweetheart, it seems all I have to do is sign this document, pay the sum required and the property is mine. I fear it is you who will have nothing."

Her lashes fell, draping the dusting of freckles. A tear leaked from the corner of one eye. Duncan wanted to kick himself for causing the tears, but more so for committing the very high-handed manipulation he'd witnessed his father commit. The ink blotted on the document hadn't even dried, and he was lording over her as if he owned her. His stomach churned in disgust. He tossed the deed on the table and thrust his fingers through his hair.

"I will not say I'm sorry." Even if regret spiraled to his toes. He'd heard his father say those empty words plenty of times. Never once had Duncan believed them, not even while his da cradled his mother as she gasped for her last breath after she'd fallen ill, because he'd left them with nothing more than a drafty shanty and little funds for food. He snagged his coat from the nail, yanked the door open and slammed it closed behind him. After donning his coat he jammed his hands into his pants pockets and rocked back on his heels. How would he fix this? Could he? No matter his threats he wouldn't force her to leave her home, but he could not allow her and her sisters to stay here with no more protection than a lazy hound and a garbling chicken.

"Is everything all right?" Dr. Northrop said.

Duncan jerked from the haze of his thoughts. Ellie and Benjamin appeared from around the cabin. "Ellie showed me where the fire had been. What are your thoughts?"

He shook off the disgust with himself and focused on the immediate conversation. The one outside his head. "The fire was intentional. Yet it doesn't seem to have been set to cause harm to the ladies. If it had been, there would have been more kindling, and there are several holes between the logs where the fire could have been more effective."

Northrop rubbed his chin. "I agree. It is not like before. You don't suppose this was a different person, do you?"

"Given that I've recently discovered what is going on here, I cannot rightly answer that question. What I do know is that someone intended to scare the ladies, and I intend to find out who." Duncan pinched the bridge of his nose. How could he protect Camy from whoever intended her and her sisters harm, when he knew he could possibly be the biggest threat to her?

"Have you had many pains since the bashing to your head?" Northrop asked.

Duncan lifted his head. "What?"

"Do you have a headache?" Ellie asked.

"No, but you ought to see to your sister. I fear that out of my desire to see her protected I caused her to cry."

Ellie nodded and slipped past him into the cabin. Northrop placed his foot on the bottom step, rested his arms across his knee, and glanced at him. "I do not envy you, my friend."

"Why is that?"

"Well." Northrop unfolded his length. "I know what you're going through, especially when you love the woman and you don't quite know how to get it through to her."

"Love?" Duncan had never said anything about love. The emotions tugging at his insides were far from love. "I don't love Camy. I've only met her a few days ago."

"And you think it takes years?" Northrop twisted his lips. "I suppose for some it could, but for men like us we see what we want and we take it. Or in this instance we speak flowery words, write poetry, bring flowers, take chaperoned walks and still, we're left scratching our heads."

Duncan hadn't done any of that stuff. He'd shot her, argued with a former beau and threatened to take all she had. "Up to several days ago I never wanted a wife."

"What man truly thinks he wants the bother of a wife?" Benjamin shifted his weight. "The endless chatter, the tightening of the purse strings with her whims, the insistence of having her way. The pouting." He smiled. "My sister could teach lessons on the aforementioned. But I've also come to realize not all women are like Bella."

Duncan couldn't picture Camy pouting to get her way. She might threaten to shoot him when he didn't follow the rules, but for the most part she seemed rational and straightforward. She didn't simper and bat her lashes. He looked forward to conversations with

Camy, even when they argued. And at the moment, he'd give over his entire bank account to make her problems go away. She'd never be a bother, not when he willingly wanted to make her smile.

"I'd rather do without the trouble," Northrup said, "but some women are worth it, I guess. And I'm thinking in a few weeks' time you'll understand a little more about what I'm saying. And perhaps you'll humble yourself and admit you might have feelings for Cameron Sims. After all, my friend, it's written all over your face."

Duncan shifted his stance and halted the urge to scrub away whatever it was Northrop saw. "You speak as a man who loves."

"I do." Northrop's gaze turned distant and full of heartache. "Perhaps too late, though. Now, what are your plans?"

"It's obvious the sisters can't stay here without protection, and until Hamish returns we can't settle the negotiations. Of course, I would see Camy's wound healed."

"There's no sign of gangrene if that is what bothers you."

"Yes," Duncan said. "I saw more severed limbs than I'd like to admit."

Northrop held his gaze. "The choices we doctors made were not easy. The war was distasteful, but as my father said, a necessary evil to halt a greater evil sweeping our beloved America. I counted my blessings every day, and thanked the Lord when I did not have to sever a limb or request another pine box."

Duncan recalled the surgeon he'd worked beside and how mechanical he had become as if he lost a piece of his soul with each victim. "I would say it is fortunate your patients had you to tend them."

Northrop took on a solemn look. "I don't know about that, but I did what I could." He was quiet for a moment.

"I should see to my patient." Northrop climbed the stairs. "I would ask you to try not to agitate her much over the next few days, until her shoulder heals more."

"I understand. I would not willingly cause her harm." Yet he had done so when he tried to manipulate her. He would do well to remember to keep his emotions under control whenever he spoke to her. He'd erect walls and become much like the surgeon he had worked beside during the war.

"Northrop?" The doctor halted before he entered the cabin. "Do you mind keeping watch over the ladies for a moment?"

"Of course not."

Duncan nodded and cantered off the porch. He intended to discover who set the fire and if it was the same men who had previously threatened the sisters.

Camy's eyes continued to sting from Duncan's sharpness. She hadn't expected him to apologize, not when it seemed obvious that he was thinking of her and her sisters. He could very well boot them out of their home without hesitation or regret, even if they married. Hamish had given him every right. What disturbed her was the shock, followed by the intense pain in his eyes, after he'd threatened to take all she had. He might not have said the words, but every line etched on his face said he regretted his actions, said he was sorry.

"Here, sip this." Ellie held a steaming cup toward her. "It'll ease some of your discomfort."

"I don't want any more laudanum," Camy said. She wanted all her faculties about her when Duncan returned.

"It's a tea made from black haw," Benjamin responded as he slathered an ointment onto her shoulder. "A Cherokee woman introduced it to me when my regiment was sent to Oklahoma. You may feel tired, but you need the rest. Other than that, it'll help your muscles to relax and I hope it'll quicken your healing process. I know how anxious you are to return to mucking stalls."

Camy smiled and took the tea from her sister. "Anything would be better than this." She sipped the hot brew and grimaced. "Where is Duncan?"

"The last I saw him he was heading around the cabin. I imagine he intends to trail whoever set the fire."

Images of shadows brandishing torches flashed through her mind, threats of dumping her and her sisters in the river roared in her ear. Camy knocked Benjamin's hands away from bandaging her shoulder. Spilling some of the hot tea, she swung her legs out of bed.

"Camy, what are you doing?" Ellie squealed as Camy thrust the tea at her sister.

"Those men are dangerous." She adjusted her sleeve over her shoulder and stood. "This is our battle, not his."

"You aren't going anywhere." Ellie crossed her arms in front of her, and then looked at Benjamin. "Do something."

"Cameron," Benjamin said, resorting to her given name. "If you do not allow me to finish dressing your wound, there will be nothing to stop the bleeding if it renews the flow. You wouldn't want to remain in bed any longer than necessary, would you? And with your recent fever, bed rest will be a doctor's order if you continue to sabotage what healing has already occurred."

Camy plopped onto the mattress. As much as she wanted to chase Duncan down, she knew the dizziness could return at any moment and render her incapable of helping.

"Besides," Ellie continued Benjamin's tirade, "Mr. Murray has shoulders wide enough to carry our burdens for the time."

In that, her sister spoke the truth.

"And," Benjamin added, "I have reason to believe Mr. Murray knows what he's doing."

Camy hoped so. She'd hate never to get the chance to discover what lay beneath Duncan's exterior, not just the man, but the child inside the man. She'd do just about anything to heal the wounds he kept hidden, hidden except for the small moment before he rushed out the door.

"Very well." Camy scooted back against the headboard and dropped her hands into her lap. "If I'm not allowed to go, Benjamin, then you'll have to do it for me."

Benjamin didn't respond. Instead he busied himself with tending her wound, which irritated her, as Duncan was out there by himself and he did not know the terrain. "You know, Ellie can treat patients as well as any doctor."

Ellie glared as she blushed. She turned toward the fireplace, her skirts swirling angrily about her ankles. Shame slapped Camy like a wet rag. She knew better than to add logs to the long-standing argument between her sister and her former suitor.

"I have no doubt about that." Benjamin smoothed another layer of salve over her wound, laid a brilliantly white, folded sheet of linen over the salve and then wrapped it before tying the sling back in place. "But I am not leaving you ladies unattended at the moment."

An ache formed in her temple from the argument. She removed her glasses, laying them beside her on the bed, and closed her eyes. "You needn't worry I'll chase after him. I know I'm weak at the moment and would only cause him further trouble."

"No." Benjamin's bag popped open. His tools clanked into his bag.

"Dr. Northrop," Ellie said, her use of his title telling Camy her sister would begin scrubbing every surface in the cabin. "I'll see to it she remains in bed."

"No. I gave my word to Mr. Murray. I'm to keep watch over you."

Camy sat up. She squinted. All thoughts of wanting to see the pain in Duncan's heart mended flew out of her mind like the fluff of a dandelion in a Kansas wind. How dare these men rush into their lives and act as if they've come to rescue them? They didn't need rescuing, from anyone. She might have been a tad frightened, but she and her sisters had gotten along fine without a man, and they could continue doing so. "As if we're incapable?"

"He didn't imply that. He's just—"

She flew off the bed. "He's just acting as if he's my

legally wedded husband, which I will remind you both, he is not." If he continued with his high-handedness, he never would be. The gall of these men.

"Camy, how can I convince him I'll see that you remain in bed when you keep getting out of it?"

She ignored Ellie, felt around for the broom resting near the door and held it between a blurred Benjamin and herself. "Count yourself fortunate, Dr. Northrop, that I cannot handle my rifle at the moment. I believe you've overstayed your welcome."

The door opened behind her and a large shadow loomed, chilling her. She spun around. The sunlight pouring in around the dark figure further blinding her. She pulled back the broom and swung. Wood connected against hard flesh with an "umph." The stick jerked forward, and she tumbled after it. She cried out as she jarred into a thick wall. An arm curled around her back, steadying her. She didn't need her spectacles to see Duncan. Several days' growth of his dark beard rested against her brow. Wet earth and woodsy trees clung to his person, cloaking her like a warm spring day.

She arched her neck. Her gaze collided with his sharp and searching green eyes. Butterflies swirled in her stomach at the memory of him holding her hand. Of him leaning in close and then kissing her cheek. What if he'd kissed her, truly kissed her? She blinked. And blinked again. He seemed to lean closer. The gold flecks in his eyes narrowed and then widened and she wondered if there was something to Mrs. Smith's counting method. Problem was, Camy couldn't recall which number came after one, not when it took all her concentration to remember to breathe.

Oh dear, she was becoming such a ninny. A swooning, wide-eyed ninny. Next she'd be twittering about nothing, dancing from room to room and gazing at the sky thinking about...*him*.

"What is going on?" His chest vibrated against her palm. He loosened his hold, but his gaze held her captive.

"Cameron was attempting to convince me I should leave," Benjamin said.

Duncan's brow lifted beneath a dark-colored lock. His eyes turned cold, his lips thinned. "Is that so?"

Turning out of his arms, she searched for her spectacles. "We are more than capable of caring for ourselves. Besides, I'm certain Dr. Northrop has other patients to tend."

Duncan reached over her and handed her spectacles to her. "And I'm certain Dr. Northrop would have greater concerns if we didn't seek out the men threatening you and your sisters."

She went and stood beside Ellie and propped her hand on her hip. "This property might be your concern, Mr. Murray. But I assure you we are neither of your concerns. Until our uncle returns and sees the deed signed, I'm requesting that you both leave."

Duncan drew in a breath, expanding his chest like a rooster, making the cabin seem much smaller. Ellie shifted, bumping her on purpose. Camy drew her lower lip between her teeth and prepared herself for Ellie's motherly, bossy side to expose itself.

"Considering this morning's fire, I think it best if Mr. Murray stays," Ellie said, siding with the men. Camy opened her mouth to argue, but Ellie held up her hand. "However, with Mara home, he'll have to bunk in the barn. Is that a feasible compromise?" Ellie looked from Camy, to Benjamin, to Duncan and back to her.

"I will rest easier knowing Mr. Murray is here," Benjamin said.

"Not that this is any of your concern, Dr. Northrop, but I will rest easier, as well." Ellie swiped her hands down her skirt. "Mr. Murray? Camy?"

She didn't want to admit it, but she didn't want Duncan to leave. Even though the fire had occurred while he was here, she felt much safer with him around. The barn wasn't too far. Less than a stone's throw.

As if he could read her thoughts, he said, "I can sleep on the porch if you'd be more comfortable."

All the irritation she had with him crumbled to her feet. He really was a Good Samaritan. "That is not necessary, Duncan. Besides, it's too cold for you to sleep outdoors."

"I've slept in far worse elements."

"Well, then, it is settled." Ellie snatched an apron from a nail. "Dr. Northrop, would you care to join us for lunch?"

Camy wasn't surprised Ellie invited Benjamin for lunch, as she was always hospitable, and always did the proper thing even when it caused her pain.

Duncan slipped outside and Camy's heart sank. Ellie and Benjamin's conversation became a hum as she moved to the window and pulled back the curtains. His head high and shoulders straight, he strode across the yard and disappeared toward the back of the barn where Ellie had moved his horse. Had she misjudged him as one of the most caring and kindest men she'd ever met? One moment he couldn't help himself and act the protector; the next he seemed angry over his decision. Was it her? Was there something wrong with her that made him war within himself? After all, hadn't her own father, who'd seemed to dote on his children abandoned them? And Camy had no doubt her father's leaving was her fault.

Chapter Ten

It had been a week since Duncan moved to the barn and Hamish had yet to return. Neither had the man who had set fire to the cabin, giving Duncan little to investigate. Fortunately the weather had warmed, providing him ample opportunity to plow the fields and mend the roof of the cabin. He patched what he could in the chinking on the outside but avoided stepping foot inside. He worked from before the sun came out until after it set, taking his meals in the barn only when Ellie or Mara brought him a basket. He thought if he didn't see Camy, he wouldn't think about her and all the advantages there were to marrying her.

More often than not, his work took longer than it should because he kept daydreaming about living here on the farm, with her. Working here, for her, to give her a real home, not a decaying cabin like what he and his mother had lived in. Not to mention that there seemed to always be a one-legged hen and an ugly hound at his feet demanding attention. A welcome distraction he could fully blame on the woman who spoiled them.

He scrubbed his hand over his bearded chin and

gazed across the plowed field. He never wanted a wife, and he should hang Hamish by his toes when he did arrive for making him want Camy. The longing to see her smile, to hold her soft hands in his calloused ones, to kiss her, to just be with her had begun to banish the horrific memories of his father and mother from his mind.

Uncle Tommy's hoarse cluck became even more excited than normal. Hound pounced on his feet with his front paws. Hoping to appease the mongrel, Duncan patted the dog on the head while he continued woolgathering about one tiny woman who had his innards all tied in knots.

"Hello."

Air caught in his throat. He rolled his shoulders and drew in a tight breath. "Hello," he returned. He didn't want to catch sight of her for fear that the last threads of his hatred toward his father would disappear altogether.

But he couldn't quite ignore her either, not when he had wondered over her condition since that day nearly a week ago when he'd left her standing in the cabin. It hadn't been an easy decision to walk away, to pretend he no longer cared for her well-being. Or to remain out of sight today when Dr. Northrop arrived to check on her, when all he wanted to do was sit at the small table inside the cabin and listen to Camy's quiet stammer, to read scripture with her.

He wondered if her color had turned back to normal, or if her hair sprung around her head in curls. A whole week he'd gone without catching even the slightest glimpse of her. It had been difficult, but he had survived. If he went a week, could he go a lifetime?

He turned. A jolt slammed against his chest. She was even more beautiful than he recalled. The sun captured the thick waves curling down her back, turning the dark strands to gilded copper, a stark contrast to the white sling holding her injured arm in place against the dark green dress. "Are you well?"

She dropped her head and looked at the ground, but not before he witnessed the staining of her cheeks. "Y-yes, Benjamin said I'm fine."

Although he was elated at the doctor's report, he was displeased to hear the stuttering more now than before when she spoke. Had his absence caused her confidence to wane? He hoped not. He moved to a safe topic. "The field is plowed. Mara told me about your planting. If the weather holds I should have potatoes in by week's end. Would you like to show me where you want them planted?"

She peeked at him from beneath her lashes. "Of c-course."

He recalled the niece Hamish had described to him, biddable, homely, a woman who preferred her nose in a book rather than sipping tea and gossiping. The woman he'd come to think about morning, noon and night was none of those things. Besides the stuttering when she seemed nervous, or the tendency to chew on her lip, she'd been anything but those things, spitting mad, courageous, determined and tenderhearted. But now he was seeing her shyness. Why?

He held out his arm, and although the sleeve of her gown, his shirt and his coat would form a barrier between them, he mentally prepared himself for his reaction to her arm resting against his. An image of her head tucked against his shoulder as they watched the sun disappear behind the trees had his toes curling in her father's boots. "Shall we walk?"

She hesitated, drew her bottom lip between her teeth and then looped her arm with his. They strolled along the fence to the gate. He released her and held it open for her and their two companions to pass through. Hound bounded through and ran into the field, and Uncle Tommy strutted after him. Camy glided through as if she were on a dance floor rather than strolling through the dirt.

He closed the gate and returned his arm through hers, this time taking delight in the warmth created between them. He guided her toward the edge of the barn, halted and reluctantly took three steps from her so he could breathe without inhaling freshly baked bread and spring. He needed to focus on the planting, not on the many ways to court her when he didn't know if he should, or even could. "Mara said you've planted the potatoes in the back field and the peas beside them."

She shielded her eyes and glanced toward the area. "Yes."

"Does the sun bother you? Do you not have a bonnet?"

She quickly gathered the thick strands together and pulled her hair over one shoulder. Although the movement was meant to hide the wildly untamed curls from him, it revealed the curve of her jaw and the porcelain length of her neck.

He shortened the distance between them. "Don't." He loosened her grip on her hair. He clamped his tongue on the next word bursting forth. He wanted to claim her as his bride. But he wasn't ready to commit to forever with her, especially since he now knew if he married her he'd never be able to leave her as he had first intended. Once she bore his name, once they became partners in cultivating the land, they'd become partners in all things. He knew that in the depths of his being, no matter how much he tried to deny it. "I only mentioned the bonnet for your comfort to shield your eyes."

Lifting her chin, she searched him with her gaze. He was supposed to be talking to her about peas and potatoes, not losing himself in pools of coffee. But he couldn't remove the thought of her from his mind. His gaze dropped to her mouth, that bottom lip pulled between her teeth. "You have no reason to be nervous, Camy."

The words tumbled from him. She dropped her chin, but he lifted it with the tip of his finger. "No hiding."

From the moment he discovered she was his intended wife, he'd fought the inevitable. He still did not know what choices he'd make, but he knew he couldn't go another moment without knowing one thing. His heart thundered in his chest. He held her gaze as he leaned in. Their breaths began to mingle, to dance between them, and her dark lashes fell against her cheeks. He leaned closer. Even with a whisper of air between them, the warmth of her mouth radiated to his.

"Camy!" Mara's voice came from around the barn.

Camy's eyes blinked open. Duncan jumped back.

"Here, Mara." Cheeks flamed, Camy ran her palm down the front of her skirt and strode toward the gate. She paused and tossed a glance over her shoulder. The corner of her mouth turned upward in a smile with a hint of solemnness. The rest of her was cloaked in timidity. Did she regret they almost kissed, or was she saddened that they were interrupted?

He ripped his hat from his head and slapped it against his thigh. He willed his racing pulse to settle. The energy pumping through his veins was much greater than when he had dodged bullets on the battlefield. One wrong move and his life would have been extinguished. He stared at the empty place near the gate and knew he'd dodged a bullet. Problem was, he didn't know if that was a good thing or a bad thing.

Uncle Tommy squawked and then pecked at his boot. "You think I should have tried harder?" he whispered to the animals.

Hound's wet nose nudged his hand in response. Duncan patted Hound's head. "We'll see, Hound. We'll see."

If he tried any harder he'd be caught, trapped in a noose tighter than the rope he'd swung from when he'd first met the doe-eyed beauty. Funny thing was, his feet had been firmly planted on the ground for over a week and his head continued to feel out of sorts.

White puffy clouds danced across the brilliant blue sky. "Lord, I do not know what to do. I need You to direct my paths. If there is any of my father in me, take me far from this place because I cannot subject Camy to such callousness."

Camy quickened her strides around the barn and came alongside her sister. "Why did you do that?"

"Do what?" Mara twirled the water bucket as if she were twelve, not almost eighteen.

"Call my name." Camy considered what had almost

occurred, what would have occurred had Mara not interrupted her and Duncan.

"You told me to, remember? You wanted to know when I was ready to go to Rusa." Mara cocked her head, a V creasing her brow. A smirk twisted her mouth. "What happened?"

Camy's face burned with embarrassment. She rushed into the barn. Dust danced on beams of light from the open shutters, illuminating the inside of the barn. She collapsed on a stool hiding in the shadows. Resting her elbow on her thigh, she cradled her head and worked to slow her breaths.

"Did he kiss you?"

"No."

"Did he almost kiss you?"

Camy lifted her head, her cheeks still warm. She pressed her palm to her stomach to calm the swirling. "No. Maybe. I don't know. Maybe."

"Maybe. Ohhhh," Mara said as she rubbed her hands together. "This is more exciting than Ellie and Ben. Of course I was much younger whenever he'd sneak a kiss or two and didn't quite understand this whole romance thing, but you and Duncan Murray." She clapped her hands together. "I can't wait to tell Ellie."

Camy stood up and touched Mara's arm. "Please don't. Not yet."

"Why ever not? She'll be happy and it'll take a burden off her shoulders. Maybe she'll even consider loving Benny again."

"She's never stopped, but thank you for adding a burden to my own shoulders." She plopped back onto the stool.

Hamish was old and frail, unable to stand against the men who'd plagued them over the last year, but then Hamish had rarely stayed too long at Sims Creek. As Ellie had said, Duncan's shoulders were wide enough to bear their burdens. He was much younger than Hamish and well capable of protecting their home. All her sisters' problems would be solved if she agreed to marry Duncan, but marriage to him would be the worst torment. Certainly he made her feel beautiful, where Miller had made her feel like a disgusting bug, but Duncan didn't want a wife, her or any other. And if a man didn't want a wife, then he couldn't offer his wife companionship, or love. She didn't even know if he intended to stick around if and when the vows were said. Did she want to be bound by the laws of marriage never to truly be married? After all, Duncan said their marriage would be in name only. Was that to be her lot in life, childless if she didn't marry, childless if she did? Childless when her heart longed to nestle a babe against her chest?

"Camy," Mara said as she knelt in front of her. "Would marrying Duncan be so bad? He is brawny, after all."

"There is more to marriage than having a brawny husband, Mara."

"Like what?"

Mara was young and full of dreams of handsome, chivalrous men and Camy didn't want to crush her disillusions, not yet. "Companionship, affection, loyalty. Not abandonment."

"Do you expect Duncan to fill Da's shoes?" Mara rose. "Your measuring stick is flawed, Cameron Sims. Any man you meet will come up short, and not because of our father's merit but his lack. I've admired your strength and the way you carry this farm because you love it so, but I pity you, dear sister. If you'll not give any man a chance because of Da's failures, you'll never get the chance to be loved by anyone but me and Ellie. You'll always live in fear of our father's rejection."

Camy stared at her sister, stunned at the wisdom in her youth. Wisdom Camy should consider, but could she? Fear had been her companion since the day their father abandoned them. Could she leave it behind and discover what life had to offer, even if Duncan decided to never be a husband in truth? Could she step outside herself and believe that she was worth affection, maybe even love?

"Did you tell Duncan we're going to town?" Mara Jean asked.

"No." By the time she'd found him she'd forgotten what she'd sought him out for. After a week of spying on him from behind the faded blue curtains as he moved about the farm, she thought she had memorized every detail of Duncan Murray, but having seen him up close, she knew there was more to learn. She barely remembered her name at the sight of him.

"Well, don't you think you ought to?"

"Ought to what?" Camy gave herself a mental shake to remove the image of Duncan from her mind.

"Tell him." Mara rolled her eyes. "He's not going to like it if you don't."

"I'm not going to like what?" Duncan asked, scaring Camy off the three-legged stool.

"Oh, my sister here was supposed to tell you that she, Ellie and I are going into town for supplies, but she kind of forgot." Mara smirked.

"Forgot, huh?" Duncan's eyes twinkled as if he knew why she forgot. "Well, you won't be going by yourselves."

An hour later they pulled in front of M&J's Mercantile. Duncan lifted Camy to the ground and assisted her up the stairs as her sisters bustled in ahead of them. "They both seem eager to shop," Duncan said.

Camy pulled her arm from his. "We don't come to town much during the winter months. Ellie looks forward to seeing the new bolts of fabric, and Mara peruses the ribbons."

"And what is it you like?" he asked as he held the door open.

"Definitely lemon d-drops and p-peppermint sticks," she said, brushing his arm as she entered the mercantile.

"Is that so?"

"Of course, I inspect the jars every time I come to see if there's anything new I might like to try." She maneuvered her way through the displays until she reached the counter. "Hello, Mr. Davis."

"Well, hello there, Cameron. It's nice to see you." He wiped his hands on his apron and held his hand out. "Who is this young strapping fellow you have here?"

"Mr. Murray."

"Call me Duncan," he said, shaking Mr. Davis's hand. "I'm Cameron's fiancé."

Camy gaped at him, wondering why he would declare such a thing if he hadn't settled it in his mind yet, when they hadn't even negotiated terms.

"Oh," Mrs. Davis chirped as she came into view from the back. "You must be that young man who shot our dear one."

The dimple in Duncan's cheek appeared as he smiled at Mrs. Davis. "I assure you it was unintentional."

"I sure do hope so, Mr. Murray." Mrs. Davis came over and hugged Camy, careful not to jar her injured arm and leaving Duncan talking with Mr. Davis. "I see Ellie has found the new bolts. I do hope she'll take me up on my offer and set up shop in the back room. She makes the most beautiful dresses, but I understand that she wants to see you and Mara settled first."

Camy glanced at her sister and could see the plans running around in her head for the piece sliding through her fingers. Was that why things hadn't worked between Ellie and Benjamin, because she wanted to see Camy and Mara settled? Duncan laughed at something Mr. Davis said, drawing her attention to him. If she were to marry him, would Ellie be free to marry Benjamin or to open her own business?

"It looks as if your sisters will be a while. Will you walk with me?" Duncan asked as he received a brown paper bag from Mr. Davis.

"Yes, of course."

They stepped out onto the boarded planks lining the main street of Rusa. "There's not much here, is there?"

Camy's hackles raised in defense of the small town she loved. "It's certainly not the c-city, but it has the necessities, depending on what you're looking for." She drew him toward the little church with the white steeple and white picket fence. "This is where we attend services when we're able. Pastor Hammond and his wife have been here almost a year and are expecting their first child in May."

"Will we come Sunday?" he asked, looking longingly at the white doors.

"As long as it doesn't rain." They strolled toward the north end of town while she pointed out various businesses and gave him details of the owners. "The Northrops' home is over that hill," she said, pointing to the west. She then pointed to the east. "That is Mrs. Smith's mansion. And right here is where I understand they're going to build the railroad."

"You don't sound happy about it," he responded, leading her to the banks of the river.

"After the last year, do you blame me?"

"No."

"I'd much rather they build here than go through Sims Creek. I just don't see how it is beneficial to build it straight through the center of town."

Duncan glanced around, taking in the landscape. "It's flat here, making production easier and quicker. The hills on either side would take more man power and more time."

"How do you know so much?"

He picked up a few stones and tossed one into the river. "I have some experience."

A question niggled in her thoughts, but she couldn't form the right words, so she brought up the other subject unsettled between them. "I won't allow Hamish to force you to marry me."

He tossed another stone. "I am not a man easily forced into anything. Mightier men have tried and failed."

She held her tongue, waiting. After several long seconds, he took her hands in his and looked into her eyes. "When I was barely seventeen a neighbor had invited me to his home. Upon my arrival I was met with a gun at my back and a preacher at my front."

Camy's eyes grew wide. Letting her hand go, he picked up several more rocks and thrust one across the river.

"I was falsely accused of compromising a young woman, the daughter of a neighbor who insisted I marry her. She was several years older than my sixteen summers, but that did not seem to matter. Fortunately my father arrived and sent me home."

"What happened to her?"

Duncan glanced at her. "I don't know. My father was killed, and I left Scotland shortly after his death." After he discovered a wealthy inheritance as well as several half siblings his father had produced throughout the Highlands. According to the village gossip, the neighbor had found himself with no funds and intended on using Duncan and his father's money as a remedy.

"I am sorry." She laid her hand on his arm, seeking to offer comfort to the young man hurting inside.

"Don't be. My father was the worst of scoundrels. He left my mother to care for her child while he gallivanted wherever his heart desired. I grew up in a shanty with more holes than your cabin and watched my mother die." All because his father had kept his fortunes to himself. "He didn't think highly of women. My mother was nothing more than property to him, although there had been a time when he seemed content with her, happy even." He tossed all the rocks in his hand into the river. "I promised myself I would never become like him." He turned to her. "That is why I cannot offer you anything more than my name if we marry."

"Is that why you seem hesitant to kiss me?" The words were out of her mouth before she could take them back.

Chapter Eleven

It had been two long days since Duncan had poured out his heart to her. Two days since she asked him the stupidest question any lady in her right mind could ask. He'd kept silent when he thrust the brown paper bag with the lemon drops and peppermint sticks into her hand. He'd kept silent as they walked back to the buckboard. He'd kept silent while they rode the hour home listening to Ellie and Mara chat. And he'd not only kept silent these last few days, but he'd kept his distance, leaving her to revisit their conversation, to chastise herself for being too forward.

"I'm going to the river. Would you like to go, Camy?" Mara asked.

"Of course. We agreed that none of us should go alone." She hated that they couldn't walk around freely on their own land as they used to. Hated that fear owned too much of her life, fear of the men who'd caused them torment, fear of rejection, fear of becoming a spinster, fear of not being loved. Of being loved. Being loved by Duncan, as if that were possible, the man was determined to punish himself for his father's sins, just as she'd been determined to allow her father's sins to cause her fear. "Shall we grab the fishing poles and see if we can't catch something other than broth for dinner?"

"You get the poles and I'll tell Ellie." Mara skipped across the yard.

It delighted Camy to see her sister maintain her joyful demeanor through all that had happened the last year. She wished she could do the same. A little over a year ago, she had been content. Ellie and Benjamin had been reunited when he returned from the war, and it seemed as if they were about to marry, and then came the incessant offers to purchase the land. And the frightening night of the fire. Had the men been hired by the railroad, or someone else as Duncan had suggested? Someone who had wanted Sims Creek since her uncle had settled here? The elder Dr. Northrop was too old to cause problems, but he had money to purchase ruthless men. Were his sons involved? Benjamin? Was that why Ellie broke off their courtship? What about Miller? The threats had started after her last rejection of his marriage proposal. Had he decided on another approach?

Camy sighed and entered the barn. Examining every possibility would only drive her mad, and she was already having a difficult time keeping her sanity with Duncan stalking around the yard as if she'd angered him. He might have done all to avoid her, but that didn't mean she hadn't snuck a peek or two out the window while he worked. Mara was right about one thing, Duncan Murray was brawny, especially when he shucked his coat and rolled up his sleeves. She knew why he had avoided her, why he hadn't joined them for the evening meals. But she wondered how long his patience would hold if Hamish didn't return soon. Looking around the barn, she thought she knew the answer to that question. Things were as they should be, tidy and organized, not strewn around as they had been.

The hens' nesting boxes had been moved to the south wall, the goats were penned on the north and the gates on the stalls no longer hung at odd angles. All the things she had hoped to fix were completed. Even the blackened stone from last year's fire had been scrubbed clean, the charred boards replaced. Tears formed on her lashes, blurring the changes Duncan had made to her home. It warmed her heart knowing that if they couldn't make suitable negotiations between them, at least her home was going to someone who would care for it. Camy knew Ellie would insist they leave the farm if they didn't have Duncan's protection. If negotiations couldn't be made, there was no reason for Duncan not to purchase Sims Creek and make it his home. It would be easier leaving her home knowing someone who would care for the land remained.

"Are you coming?"

Camy faced her sister. "Have you seen this?"

"What, the barn? Oh yes. Duncan has been busy," Mara responded. "The fishing poles are over here. I guess I should have told you they'd been moved."

Mara disappeared into a shed built into the barn and then returned, handing Camy three poles. "Ellie wants to come."

"She does?" Camy couldn't remember the last time all three of them had fished together.

"Yeah, it'll be nice. Just like when we first came here and would fish with Aunt Naomi. Even if we don't catch anything because the water is still too cold, it'll be fun. We can sit and listen to nothing."

Camy burst into laughter. "Nothing? If that were the case we'd have to leave you here to burn biscuits."

Mara thrust her hands on her hips. "What is that supposed to mean? It's not my fault I'm easily bored and distracted while they're cooking."

"Whose fault is it, then? Tommy Lakin's?" Camy teased.

An overdramatic shiver shook Mara's shoulders. "Do you know that he told Levina Smith I'm a tomboy? I think he's sore mad because I beat him at the Harvest Run."

They stepped out of the barn and into the warm sun. Ellie waved at them from the porch.

"No doubt, you hurt his pride. Maybe you can make it up to him and let him win the races at Rusa's spring picnic."

"And why would I do that?" Mara tossed over her shoulder.

"Because you like him?" Camy propped the poles against her uninjured shoulder.

"Not anymore. I'm done with boys. It's time I start thinking about my future."

Camy sighed. If she married Duncan, Ellie and Mara wouldn't need to worry over their futures. If she agreed to marry for convenience, they would always have a home here. She would require it in the negotiations before she agreed to stand before Pastor Hammond with Duncan, but would that be enough for her, could she marry him without love?

The sisters disappeared through the tree-lined path leading to the river. They each carried a fishing pole in one hand. A rifle rested against one of Ellie's shoulders, Mara swung a water bucket and Camy carried a picnic basket looped onto her pole. Duncan longed to join them, but their bubbling laughter told him they needed time to themselves without the burden of daily chores wearing them down, and he didn't need the answer to Camy's bold question burning in his chest. He had been hesitant to kiss her. It had taken everything in his power to keep from doing so, and he was thankful Mara had disrupted the pull between him and Camy before he'd given in to his curiosity. However, that didn't mean he wouldn't follow and keep watch. The weather had been nice for too many days not to expect another incident.

He grabbed the rifle from the barn and closed Hound and Uncle Tommy inside their pens so they wouldn't alert the sisters that he followed them. He waited a few minutes before he traced their steps. He halted near the large tree with half its roots reaching toward the river and sat on the worn path, the rifle on his lap. He watched as Ellie pulled a quilt from the basket, snapped it out and allowed it to settle on a large flat rock.

Camy sat on the quilt. Pulling the sling from her neck, she rolled her shoulder and he wondered how she was faring, if the wound remained raw or was healing nicely. Duncan's protective instinct itched to demand that she return her arm to the sling, but he stopped himself, knowing Ellie had cared for her sister's wound and would reprimand her if she needed. Camy slipped off her shoes, gathered her skirt to her shins and began rolling her stocking down her leg.

Duncan turned to give her privacy. He arched his

head against the tree and counted the new sprouts on the dying mammoth.

A twig snapped. Duncan jumped to his feet.

Hamish appeared from behind the tree. "Are ye spying on me nieces?"

"Keeping watch." Duncan relaxed the tension knotting his shoulders. Hamish had finally made an appearance.

"Do they know that?" Hamish spat.

"I don't think so."

Hamish pointed toward the sisters with his chin. "Ye best think again."

Camy had removed her other stocking, both feet dangling off the rock and into the water, but her gaze was focused directly at him. Warmth infused his cheeks, and he ground his teeth together. The woman would be the death of him if she didn't stop haunting him.

"Have ye considered if my Camy girl will make a decent wife?"

That had never been a question in his mind. "Will I make her a decent husband?"

"I wouldn't have chosen you if I thought otherwise. Considering her only other offer, I'd say you're a mite better than Miller Northrop."

Duncan wouldn't argue with him. A hermit would be an improvement over Camy's suitor. "Are you staying for dinner so we can discuss your offer?"

"I don't need any funds from you. Just marry the girl. She wants to remain here in her home, and I want her to. I'm an old man and incapable of protecting the girls. I promised Camy the land before all the trouble, but I can't, in good conscience, leave her out here on her own like easy prey for the wolves. Not when her sisters are bound to marry menfolk from town."

"I can't take the land for free, and I have yet to gain her agreement."

"What have you been doing, son? I've given ye plenty of time to court her proper. Gossip all over town says you're marrying. That old biddy Mrs. Smith is throwing you an engagement party come this Saturday, so ye best turn on your charm." Duncan didn't have to look very far to see who had spread the rumors. But then hadn't he spilled the gossip out of his own mouth when he told Mrs. Davis he was Camy's fiancé?

"I told you I wasn't looking for a wife."

"Maybe not, but you found one anyways."

That he did.

"Tell me you can walk away from her? She's done stole yer heart."

"Now wait a minute, she hasn't stolen anything," Duncan said, his nostrils flaring.

Hamish squinted and pursued Duncan from head to toe. "No? Sure looks like it from where I stand."

Duncan looked down his nose at Hamish. "I think you need to look again. I'm fully intact. Any marriage negotiation we make will be purely in name only."

"How do you intend to protect her from that railroad you work for?"

He winced. All the air whooshed from his lungs as if he'd been punched in the gut. "I don't work for the railroad. I'm just an investor."

"Right, so ye give 'em money."

"If the railroad is the cause of the threats, my name will be enough to protect her, or else they'll lose me as an investor," Duncan snapped, and then regretted the venom behind his words. Of course, Hamish wouldn't offer his niece to just anyone. "Does Camy know that I've invested money in the railroad?"

"I ain't told her."

Duncan gazed upon the woman who caused his head to spin. "She won't agree to a marriage if she thinks I'm here to swindle her."

"'Xactly why I haven't said a thing, but ye can't marry her with it betwixt you."

"What makes you think I won't swindle her, or you? Why do you trust me?"

"Near a year ago you saved an old man's life. Others had walked on by. Not you. I followed you for a time and I knew you had nothing to do with my beating. And I know you've had nothing to do with the threats to my nieces, and if you knew of them you would have pulled your money from the road they're determined to see cut through this land. Besides, son, you've got character, good character."

Duncan winced. He'd spent his life running from his father's shadow. He never thought to hear anyone but his mother call him good. Could it be true? Was he good? Had he somehow outrun his father's abusive hand? "I appreciate that, my friend."

"No thanks needed. I've seen the charity you've doled out to widows and orphans. I've seen what you've done for that soiled dove left for dead by the river in Topeka, and I've seen ye help her help others." Hamish scratched his head beneath his hat. "I'll be staying for dinner. I s'pect them girls to bring in a fine catch, and Camy girl sure does know how to cook."

Duncan scrubbed his palm over his chin and blew out a ragged breath. The old goat knew more about him than Duncan liked. He only did what he thought would make amends for his father's sins so that maybe one day he could step out of the dark shadows of his father's past.

A lot of good his good deeds had done. How was he to tell Camy he was helping finance the very thing that might be causing her fear on her own land? For now he wouldn't. He would wait until he investigated who was behind the fires, and he prayed, for his partner's sake, it wasn't him.

A squeal, followed by feminine laughter, drew his attention to the sisters. The trio gathered around a pole held by Mara with a fish dangling from a hook. Ellie pulled on the line holding it up, and Camy grabbed hold of the fish around its belly beneath the fins and removed the hook.

Camy said something and all the sisters turned and looked at him. Camy waved him down. Not wanting to intrude on their family time, he shrugged and maintained his position, but all three ladies waved for him to come.

"Hurry," Camy hollered.

Her anxious call had him rushing down the path, pebbles and clumps of dirt rolling from beneath his feet. His blood hammered in his veins. "What is it?"

They laughed.

"We've agreed that as our guest you should do the honors." Camy held the fish toward him.

"The honors?" He stepped back. "You caught him, you clean him. Fishing rules."

Camy stepped forward, the fish between them. "You were willing to pluck Uncle T-Tommy, but you won't clean a fish?"

What could he tell them, that he'd never even been fishing before? "I don't fish."

"Stop tormenting the man, Camy," Ellie said. "It's obvious he's scared."

Duncan glared at the one sister he believed to be his friend.

"We're only funning." Mara laid her pole on the rock.

"Besides." Camy winked as she smiled. "He's going back in the river."

"He is?"

"Sure. We always release our first catch. It's our way of giving our first fruits back to God. Here," she said, holding the fish toward him. "Hold him here and watch out for the thorns by his fins."

Duncan wrapped his fingers over Camy's. A jolt of awareness smacked him in the gut. She must have felt it too, because her lips parted as she inhaled a sharp breath. If they didn't have an audience, no doubt he'd kiss her. He cleared his throat. "Now what?"

She removed her warm fingers from beneath his, leaving nothing but a squirming fish. "Put him in the water."

Duncan pulled back his arm.

"No," all three sisters chorused.

Camy shook her head. A patient smile and understanding eyes comforted him as if she were encouraging a child and he couldn't help wondering what sort of mother she'd make.

"If you throw him, you risk injuring him." She knelt on the rock, her bare toes peeking from the hem of her skirt, and let her fingers skim over the surface of the water. He knelt beside her and she guided his hand into the cold water. "Now let go."

He relaxed his fingers and watched the fish dart away.

Camy bowed her head. "Thank You, Lord, for the blessing of Your creation and for providing us with sustenance. In Jesus' name, amen."

"Amen," Ellie and Mara said together.

"Amen," he repeated.

Camy rose and dried her hands on her skirt. Duncan stood, as well.

Mara clapped her hands together. "Ellie, didn't you say you were going to help me make biscuits?"

"I—uh," Ellie stammered, and then Mara elbowed her. "Yes. What was I thinking?"

"I can do it," Camy responded. "You two stay and fish. Duncan will keep watch."

"You're the better fisher, Camy." Mara grabbed the bucket and filled it halfway with water.

"That is true," Ellie agreed. "Duncan, will you carry the bucket for her when she's done?"

"Ellie," Camy growled.

He knew when he was being swindled. His keen awareness had kept him from making bad deals, and filled his bank account, but he didn't know how to get out of this one. More important, he didn't know if he wanted to. "Of course."

Camy hoped her sisters could feel the arrows she glared into their backs. Their laughter as they walked arm in arm toward home told her they didn't care.

"My apologies for their behavior. If you have things to do, I understand."

"I wouldn't leave you alone. It's too far from the cabin, and secluded." He glanced at her bare feet.

"Oh." She sat on the quilt and pulled on her stockings as discreetly as possible and then her shoes. "I could be here for hours trying to catch another catfish." She hoped that had not been her sisters' intentions.

"How many do you need to catch?"

Camy threaded a piece of meat on the hook and dropped the line into the water. "One if he's big enough."

He sat beside her and crisscrossed his legs. He stared at the water.

"H-here." She handed him her pole, trying not to think about the last time they'd been together and her direct question. "Just hold on to the s-stick and don't let go. Our lines are short enough you needn't worry about the fish taking off too far."

She reached behind her and baited the pole left by Mara and dropped the line in the river.

"You saw Hamish?" he asked.

"Yeah." She didn't know how to feel about her uncle's presence. Soon she'd know her future, to be married, or not to be married. To stay at the home she loved so dearly, or to move into town where she'd be at the mercies of Mrs. Smith's incessant mothering.

"How long have you and your sisters lived here?"

"My—my father s-settled here some time ago. He built the oldest part of the cabin and began on the barn. At least that is what Uncle Hamish says." She didn't want to tell any more about her father than what she had told already. Duncan didn't need to know she was the reason her father had left them. "Hamish brought us here about ten years ago, after other families had begun to settle in the area and after Mr. Davis built the mercantile. Before that we moved from town to town. Mostly Hamish would hire himself out to a farmer, or a mill. Naomi worked where she could, doing laundry and cooking, and we girls were kept out of sight."

Memories of living in hovels near the rivers where all sorts of people crept about in the night caused her to shiver. "They figured if the rich folk knew about us, they'd work us until our fingers bled, like they did Naomi. One day Ellie befriended a young woman. Even I knew she was not the sort to associate with young girls, but she rescued Ellie from something terrible and after that she watched out for us until we moved here."

She glanced at him. "More than you asked to know, huh?" She shrugged. "If we're to be married you should know the sort of woman you'll be getting."

He stared at the spot where his fishing line joined to the water. The corner of his mouth turned upward. "I think I know the kind of wife you'd make, and I find no shame in you."

She dipped her chin, thankful he didn't hold that part of her past against her. "We had our mama for a time, and then we had Naomi. Mama taught me and Ellie how to cook and sew. Naomi taught us how to care for the animals, work the land and fish. Hamish wasn't around enough to mend the roof and fix the pens. I tried. Ellie tried, even Mara. Thank you for what you've done."

"I'll get to the rest in the coming days."

She rested her palm against his forearm. He glanced at her. Gold flecks vibrated in the bed of green moss and she caught her breath. "Thank you."

He leaned closer, bracing his palm against the rock. She blinked, drew in a shallow breath and blinked again. She lifted her chin a little. Her upper lashes fell against her cheeks and rested as she waited. A field of wheat blown by the Kansas wind seemed to be caught in her belly.

"Hey," Duncan grunted.

She flung her eyes open. The tip of Duncan's pole bent toward the water. Climbing to his feet, he pulled the pole toward him. The pole tugged him forward. Back and forth, Duncan warred with the fish caught on his hook, and all she could do was watch. After a few moments, Duncan jerked the pole. The line and fish flew out of the water. The fish smacked him against the shoulder and then slid down the front of his shirt until the edge of the hook caught in the fabric.

A horrified look crossed his face as the fish dangled like a pocket watch from a chain, gasping for air. Camy burst into laughter. He turned a sharp glare on her. "What do you find so funny, Miss Sims?"

She swiped at the tears of laughter leaking from the corners of her eyes and stood. "This." She waved a hand between them. *Us,* she wanted to cry. Twice, he'd been about to kiss her, and twice they'd been interrupted.

An eyebrow rose beneath the rim of his hat. "And?"

"You caught a fish."

"I did."

"And it seems, Mr. Murray, it has thoroughly caught you." She laid her pole down and examined the hook. Pressing her fingers against his chest, she pulled the hook from his shirt. "There. You're fr-free," she stuttered as she guided the fish and line so it would hang from the pole. She didn't dare look at him, because she knew what he'd see in her eyes, knew he'd know what she wanted, what she longed for, so she watched the fish spin.

He crooked his finger beneath her chin and gazed into her eyes. "I doubt that."

Before she could close her eyes, his mouth brushed against hers. Once, twice. She rested her hand on his chest. The fish plopped into the bucket, and Duncan's fishing pole clattered on the rock. The river trickled, the birds chirped, the beat of his heart thumped against her palm. If this was what marriage would be like, she'd never get her chores done. She already spent too much time daydreaming about what he was doing, and now it would be even worse. And what if he found her flawed? What if he left her like her father had done because she had too many accidents? Could she forget the measuring stick, as Mara called it, and allow Duncan Murray to be measured by his own character? But what if—what if he was no different than her father?

Duncan pulled away. A cool breeze rushed between them, chilling her. He didn't look at her, but rather busied himself with pulling the hook from the fish's mouth, gathering the poles and the rifle, all the while she stared at the river until it blurred into nothing.

"We should be getting back," he said.

She touched her finger to her still-tingling lips, tears of rejection stinging her eyes. "Y-yes, of course." She shoved her sling into her pocket, folded the quilt and tucked it into the basket.

"Is this fish big enough?" He picked up the bucket.

She didn't trust herself to speak without giving in to the tears, so she nodded.

"Camy," he whispered. He grabbed her arm as she moved past him. "Look at me."

She raised her head and blinked. A tear rolled down her cheek.

"Did I upset you?"

She shook her head.

"Why the tears?"

She chewed on her bottom lip.

"I shouldn't have kissed you. It has nothing to do with you, but we're not married," he said.

She nodded but didn't believe him. She'd seen Benjamin kiss Ellie, and they hadn't been married. She knew why he didn't want a wife, but she was finding she wanted to be one. To be his. One he kissed, more than once. Without regrets.

He threaded his fingers through hers. "You did nothing wrong, but you must understand that what just happened can never happen again."

A large chunk of her heart tumbled into her stomach. She yanked her fingers from his and rushed up the hill.

"Camy, we need to talk," he called after her.

She didn't want to talk, she wanted to run, but she had never been a coward. She halted at the top of the hill and rested her hand against the giant tree. She'd watched this tree grow, watched the river eat away at the bank and expose its roots. It was barely anchored to the hill, but it continued to bring forth life. She and her sisters had suffered many trials and they'd survived, and she had no doubt she'd survive Duncan's rejection too.

Chapter Twelve

"Ye've done a mite bit of work here since I've been gone." Hamish leaned against one of the reinforced gates holding the oxen and glanced around the barn. "Don't look like a man who intends to leave any time soon."

"I've been keeping myself busy awaiting your return." Duncan settled a crate he'd found beneath several rusted wagon wheels on the ground and pulled out an iron skillet.

"Looks like I was wrong about you, Duncan."

"How so?"

"Here I thought ye weren't succeeding at wooing my niece."

"I wasn't exactly trying, Hamish. You know how I feel about marriage. Why would I court Camy when I don't intend to make a real marriage with her? I wouldn't want to get her hopes up and crush her."

Although, recalling her tears after that sweet and tender kiss, he thought he might be too late.

Hamish pushed away from the gate and toyed with

the various equipment pegged to the barn walls. "I say ye've had a change of heart."

Duncan pulled out another skillet and a ladle from the crate. "What makes you say that?"

"This." Hamish spread his arms out wide.

"I don't understand." Duncan focused his attention back to the contents in the crate. What seemed to be three books wrapped in oilcloth lay side by side on top of a case he would recognize with his eyes closed. He'd had a similar one as a child, one of the only luxuries he recalled given to him by his father. He removed the books and ran his fingers over the worn leather case before opening it. The once shiny lacquer covering the spruce wood had dulled where a chin had rested. Duncan gingerly took the violin from the velvet and set it against his shoulder. He plucked one string at a time and then picked up the frayed bow. His fingers danced over the strings as he brought to memory a time when all had been right as rain between his parents. He drew the bow over the catgut, a sharp note sang into the barn bouncing off the walls, electrifying his nerves as if he'd been struck by lightning. The violin nearly fell from his hands. He settled it back into the case and secured the lid.

Hamish's shadow crept over him. "Ye play verra well."

"It's been many years. Since I was a boy." Duncan's father had given him a violin as a gift and had taught him to play while his mother sang. Those were fond memories, memories that had been buried by his father's fits of rage.

"It was my brother's, Camy's da. He made it with his own two hands."

"The craftsmanship is beautiful." Even though he wanted to examine the instrument and hear it sing, he shoved everything back into the crate, right along with any good memories of his father. "Seeing the skillets, I thought the ladies could use some of the items in here."

"I've kept his belongings hidden. Ellie and Mara Jean adjusted well to their father leaving. Camy never did."

"I never did what?"

Duncan positioned himself in front of the crate.

Hamish sidled close to him. "Ye never liked to cook, a shame too." Hamish glanced at him. "She makes the best pies this side of the Atlantic."

Camy blushed and kicked the toe of her shoe into the dirt. "Ellie says dinner is ready."

"Whelp," Hamish said, stepping forward and turning Camy away from her father's crate. "We shouldn't keep her waiting."

Duncan waited until their shadows disappeared and returned the crate to the corner. He gathered the wagon wheels and laid them on top just as they had been. His fingers itched to play the violin; he longed to hear the strings sing beneath the gentle glide of the bow. Strange how one old box held memories for both of them, memories best left buried in the dust.

Duncan stepped from the covering of the barn. Crossing his arms, he closed his eyes and listened to his surroundings. No wagon wheels or clanking of ironwork. None of the obnoxious noises filtering from the saloons, the occasional ruckus of rowdy rail men. No twittering females vying for his attention. He didn't miss the city. He much preferred the river and the birds, Hound and even Uncle Tommy's hoarse clucking. And

Camy, from her fiery protectiveness to her shy uncertainty. He knew he couldn't just walk away and let her fend for herself.

He dipped his hands into a fresh bucket of water on the porch and splashed his face. He had to convince her to marry him on his terms, and without resorting to becoming his father. If only he could get their gentle kiss out of his mind. Perhaps that was asking the impossible even for him.

"Cameron Sims." Duncan's silhouette filled the doorway as the door banged against the wall. The ladle in her hand trembled, spilling broth and dumplings onto Ellie's freshly scrubbed table. His kiss and the fierce glint in his eye remained with her, kneading her insides, rising like yeasted flour. "Your uncle informs me there is to be a party in town Saturday in our honor."

Her brow wrinkled. "Our honor?"

"Yes." Duncan crossed his arms over his wide chest. Hamish hid his face, Ellie busied herself with stirring the embers and Mara looked between them with excited eye movements. "It seems we're to be married." He stepped into the cabin, shut the door and paced. "Of course, you already knew that was a possibility. However, it seems to be sooner than we imagined." He halted and eyed her. "What are your terms?"

She dropped the ladle into the pot and dried her hands on her apron. "My t-terms?" *Companionship. To be honored and cherished. Kissed. To have babes in my arms and children pulling at my skirts.* "For my s-sisters to have a home here."

He tilted his head. "Nothing else?"

FREE Merchandise is 'in the Cards' for you!

Dear Reader,

We're giving away FREE MERCHANDISE!

Seriously, we'd like to reward you for reading this novel by giving you **FREE MERCHANDISE** worth over **$20** retail. And no purchase is necessary!

You see the Jack of Hearts sticker above? Paste that sticker in the box on the Free Merchandise Voucher inside. Return the Voucher today... and we'll send you Free Merchandise!

Thanks again for reading one of our novels—and enjoy your Free Merchandise with our compliments!

Pam Powers

Pam Powers

P.S. Look inside to see what Free Merchandise is **"in the cards"** for you!

We'd like to send you two free books like the one you are enjoying now. Your two books have a combined price of over $10 retail, but they are yours to keep absolutely FREE! We'll even send you 2 wonderful surprise gifts. You can't lose!

REMEMBER: Your Free Merchandise, consisting of **2 Free Books** and **2 Free Gifts**, is worth over $20 retail! No purchase is necessary, so please send for your Free Merchandise today.

Get TWO FREE GIFTS!

We'll also send you 2 wonderful FREE GIFTS (worth about $10 retail), in addition to your 2 Free books!

Visit us at:
www.ReaderService.com

Books received may not be as shown.

BUSINESS REPLY MAIL
FIRST-CLASS MAIL   PERMIT NO. 717   BUFFALO, NY

POSTAGE WILL BE PAID BY ADDRESSEE

READER SERVICE
PO BOX 1867
BUFFALO NY 14240-9952

NO POSTAGE
NECESSARY
IF MAILED
IN THE
UNITED STATES

Hamish cleared his throat, catching Camy's attention. Did he know she wanted more, but feared to ask? Was her uncle urging her to find the courage? "I would ask that we continue on as we have been." Duncan squinted and opened his mouth as if he were about to argue, but she held up her hand and continued before he could say a word. "My sisters and I, we've lived here and worked here. Perhaps not to your standards, but we've done our best. I ask that we freely continue on if we choose. That you would not hinder us. H-hinder me." She felt Ellie's eyes boring into the back of her head. Hamish scratched his white beard, and Mara's eyes grew wide. What had she said to cause them to act in such a way?

"Let me see if I understand you, you agree to a marriage if I allow you and your sisters to remain living here, and I allow you free rein to continue doing as you wish?" She nodded slowly at his question. "What if I want to build a house in the far west field overlooking the river? Or to raise cattle instead of work the field?"

What had made her think he would leave after they had said their vows and after ruffians no longer tried stealing her land? Because he didn't want a wife. How could she live close to him, watch him make changes to her home as he wished and live, not as a married couple, but as neighbors?

Hello, Mr. Murray.

Hello, Mrs. Murray, the sun sure is hot today.

That it is, Mr. Murray.

Do you think it'll rain, today, Mrs. Murray?

We can hope. Good day, Mr. Murray.

Her face flamed. She clenched her fists. The muscles in her shoulder tensed, the wound still tender.

Mara's words echoed in her ears, but the measuring stick her father had left her with was useless. From all accounts, Duncan didn't act like a man ready to abandon her. But what did he intend, and how would she know if she didn't give him a chance? The memory of his kiss tingled her lips, but the ensuing displeasure he'd displayed afterward remained, frightening her. His rejection would crush her, leaving her hollow much like Ellie had been the last few months. She didn't want to live like that, getting up each day just to put one foot in front of the other until nightfall. She didn't want to just live, she wanted to be filled with life, to breathe with expectancy, to be joyful.

"Hamish, Mara, come let's give them a moment." Ellie untied her apron and tossed it onto the back of a chair.

Duncan stared at Camy until they left, and then he stepped forward. Camy's heart hammered, thankful the table remained between them. "What if I don't want you going to the river by yourself? As my wife, would you heed my wishes?" He moved around the table, the tips of his boots touching her shoes, and he gazed down at her. "What if I want to kiss you again?"

Her thundering heart climbed to her throat. She bit the inside of her lip. Did he want to kiss her? Would he?

"Camy," he whispered, pushing his fingers through her hair. Eyes closed, he leaned his forehead against hers and then straightened, dropping his hand to the side. He stalked away from her and stared out the window. "I cannot be the husband you deserve."

"Wh-what sort of husband is that, Duncan Murray?"

He glanced over his shoulder. "You don't know?"

"How could I? My father abandoned me, leaving me

with Hamish and Naomi, and you see what sort of man Hamish has been, leaving us here for months at a time. Husbandly examples don't exactly fall from trees."

Duncan strode back to her, taking her hands in his. "Camy, you deserve more than a wayward vagabond. Even before the war I moved from place to place, never wanting to set roots lest I become my father. I can't guarantee I'll stay here."

The better for her, given the disappointment striking her when he didn't kiss her. How could he not see he was far from the man he'd described?

"You deserve a husband willing to give you children," he added.

She pressed her quivering lips together and pulled her hands from his. "Mr. M-Murray, I'm fully aware of the k-kind of marriage we are negotiating and I'm prepared for the consequences. I don't expect you to stay. I don't expect you to fulfill your husbandly d-duties. Upon our agreement, we will become b-business partners and nothing more." Until death do they part. "You will acquire the land and allow us to stay in our home as long as we l-like."

He stared into her eyes, and she nearly caved. After the kiss they shared, and even now, how could they remain cold and heartless, mere strangers, toward each other? It might break her, but she would survive. She had to do it for her sisters' sake. For hers.

"I do ask, Mr. Murray, that you would give me leave to live my life as I choose. You need not worry that I will b-behave improperly. I give you my word and I take any vow made, especially before God, seriously."

The door swung open. "Have ye come to terms? This old man's stomach is stirring up a storm."

Her own stomach was feeling a mite unsettled, but it had nothing to do with hunger. She held out her hand. "Are we agreed, Mr. Murray?"

Taking her hand in his, he lifted the back of her hand to his mouth, his gaze holding hers, filled with determination. He kissed her hand, her eyes widening. "Agreed, sweetheart."

She sucked in a sharp breath at his endearment and jerked her hand away. How dare he tell her he wanted a platonic marriage and then woo her with his charm? Frustrated with the man, she plopped into her chair. Mara took a chair opposite her, and Hamish's limped gait suddenly disappeared as he dashed across the room, stealing the chair beside her younger sister, leaving empty spaces on either side of Camy, one for Ellie and one for Duncan.

All through dinner, his forearm bumped against hers, his wide shoulders brushing hers. He conversed with Hamish about the planting as if he intended to stay. They spoke about the terrain and the best place to build a house. Camy pushed the fish around her plate with her fork, intently thinking about what it would be like to see him, to know he was close, to know she carried his name, and nothing more.

Camy glanced from her plate as Duncan pushed in his chair and noticed everyone had finished eating and the table had been cleared of all dishes except hers.

"Don't leave," Mara said to Duncan. "Stay and play a game of chess with me. Camy hasn't been any fun lately. She sits there staring at the fire."

She read the concern and the question in his eye.

"I would say she's had things on her mind," Duncan responded in her defense.

"Oh, certainly." Mara giggled as Camy held her breath waiting for her sister to say more. Duncan didn't need to know about her woolgathering moments, especially since she could blame her inattentiveness on his shoulders.

"Mara Jean," Ellie chided. "Set up the board if you're going to play."

Grabbing her dishes, Camy left the table and allowed Mara and Duncan to set up their game. She pulled a chair near the fire, next to Hamish, who snored beneath his hat, and took up the darning basket. From the corner of her eye she watched as Duncan patiently gave Mara pointers with each move.

Half an hour later Mara squealed in a fit of giggles as Duncan took her king. "It's your turn, Camy," she said as she abandoned her seat next to Duncan.

Duncan leaned back in the chair, his shirtsleeves rolled to just below his elbows. The crisp hair on his forearms a stark contrast to the tan shirt they crossed over. His brow rose, challenging her. "Well?"

She felt conspired against as if Duncan and Mara were in league together trying to drive her to the brink of insanity. The less time she spent in Duncan's company, the less chance she'd be affected by his charm. As if she hadn't already.

She took the seat next to Duncan as he set the pieces on the board.

"Black or tan?"

"T-tan," she responded as she wiped her palm over her skirt.

An hour later she chewed on the tip of her nail as she stared at the remaining pieces. Mara breathed over her shoulder. Ellie leaned across the table and Hamish puffed on his unlit pipe. Camy toyed with her rook. Duncan's leg slid across the floor, brushing against hers under the table. He quickly pulled it away with a "sorry." She glanced at him, her cheeks heating. Distracted, she slid her rook across the board, taking the pawn guarding his queen, leaving her king vulnerable.

Smiling, he leaned forward. He gazed into her eyes, the firelight reflecting in the green, capturing the gold flecks, and she wondered if he recalled their kiss only hours before just as she did now. "Checkmate."

Chapter Thirteen

Duncan left the ladies sitting at the table reading their nightly scripture and joined Hamish on the porch. The bowl of Hamish's pipe glowed orange. Smoke rings rose toward the full light of the moon. Duncan leaned against the bolster supporting the porch and watched Camy through the window, wondering what she would have done if he'd leaned across the table and kissed her in front of her family. After he'd finally won the game of chess, they had written out their negotiated terms and signed them. Mara giggled with excitement while Ellie and Hamish seemed to be reluctant witnesses. Duncan was certain the two had hoped for more than a marriage in name only, and as much as he wanted to offer Camy his heart, Duncan just didn't think he could.

Camy had claimed exhaustion and had tried to retire to the bedroom, but he had mouthed the word *coward*, which had prickled her spine straight as a board and her eyes to mere slits. She pulled her hair into a severe knot, every curl tamed, and lowered her spectacles to the tip of her nose as if to keep her from seeing too much. Even now she stared over Mara's shoulder. Her hollowness crept into his chest.

"You two are the most stubborn mules I've ever come across," Hamish said.

"You would negotiate different terms?" He wished he had the courage to do so. To require her hair to hang down her back whenever they were together. To steal kisses by the river while fishing or playing chess. To invite her to live as a man and wife should.

Hamish shot off the three-legged stool. "I didnae give ye my land to leave her a spinster in deed."

Duncan tore his gaze from the woman capturing his attention through the window and glanced over his shoulder. "Be careful how you judge me, my friend. You sold your niece for a piece of land. I've only agreed to her terms."

His words were harsh, and he was sorry for it, but he wasn't feeling charitable toward his friend for placing him in the situation. Although, if Hamish hadn't manipulated him, he never would have had the chance of knowing her.

"I gave it to you in exchange for her protection."

"Which I cannot, in good conscience, take. I'll pay the original amount requested. Do what you will with the money. Give it to the orphanage you so often visit."

Hamish growled.

"You're not the only one who's been spying." Duncan sighed, shoved from the post and jammed his hands into his pockets. "I am sorry, Hamish. My thoughts are in turmoil. I wish I could be a husband to her, a real husband." One who could offer his heart. "Don't worry, your secret is safe with me. I won't tell anyone about your exploits at the orphanage. As for your niece, she doesn't want a husband in deed, and for good reason. You may have found some good in me, but, Hamish, I tell you, I'm no different than her father." No different than his own.

"Uncle." Camy stood framed by the cracked door, her hand on the handle. Her gaze darted between him and Hamish. She stepped onto the porch, closing the door behind her. "Mr. Murray and I have come to an agreement, we've signed our names and you've given your mark. It may not be desirable in your eyes, but it suits us."

The old man's shoulders sagged. "Lass, I want more for you and your sisters. I know I've not been the best uncle, leaving ye here for months on yer own, but I care fer ye and I want ye to have love." He twisted his lips and glanced at Duncan. "I want ye to love each other, and if not love, then at least a fondness."

There was fondness between them whether Camy realized it or not. Even now he knew she was remembering their kiss, just as he was.

"Can ye not try?"

That was the crux of Duncan's dilemma; he was trying not to love her. He couldn't. He wanted to, but the risk of him becoming his father was too great. Perhaps he should tear up their agreement. She might not be able to keep her home, but at least she'd have a chance at finding a husband who would love her as she deserved. The thought of any other man attempting to love her soured his gullet, made him want to fight anyone who dared try to take her from him. He was the worst sort of guttersnipe, selfishly keeping her for himself.

"Hamish, it is useless." He regretted his words at the

pain of rejection etched in the lines of her eyes. "It's not you, sweetheart. You're worth any man's heart. I'm afraid mine is as black as they come." He clambered down the stairs and lengthened his strides across the yard until he disappeared into the barn.

He didn't need to light the lantern to find his bed, but his fingers itched to play the violin, to lose himself in the notes and forget about all that plagued him for the moment. He set the lantern on a hook and dug out the violin from the crate that had belonged to Camy's father. He felt like an intruder into Camy's life, into her father's belongings, but he didn't care. Hamish had invited him into their family. Camy had given him permission with the negotiations.

He slipped out into the field from one of the side barn doors and sat, leaning against the stone structure. The stars glittered in the night sky, seemingly mocking him. How many times had he slept beneath the stars and found hope that there was something much bigger and greater, that there was a Creator of everything around him? Even his father's abuse of his mother hadn't taken that away. The war had hardened him, but whenever the stars twinkled he had hope. Now he didn't know what he felt beyond the sadness stirring in his soul. The mystery of the stars was nothing compared to what he saw in Camy's eyes when she was happy, and somehow this very night he had diminished the innocent glimmer. As if he'd broken her heart, but how? Did she want him to offer her love?

Unlatching the case, he grabbed the violin by the neck and hugged it. Memories of sitting in a heather-covered field flooded him. His father had been kind and patient then, teaching him to play. His mother had been happy dancing through the fields, twirling her shawl. His father would tease, singing a tune of fond kisses and broken hearts. That was before the whiskey overtook him, leading him down a path of vulgarity.

Duncan never should have kissed her. If he remained and did as he said and built a home in the field, he would long for the touch of her hand, the warmth of her lips, and if he left to cease the torment, he'd long for the same. Perhaps even more so.

He picked up the bow and drew it across the strings. Back and forth as his fingers recalled every note.

Having met Camy, he now understood the conflicted melody of joy and longing singing into the night. His thoughts mirrored the long-ago penned lyrics, his twisted emotions bubbling over like a cauldron. He paused, Shakespeare's words on his tongue. "To be or not to be. To love or not to love."

No answer came forth, not even from Hound, who sprawled beside him. His parents had loved, and then they had not. His father's abandonment to alcohol and women had destroyed his mother to the point of her death. The years of brutality had scarred Duncan, his belief in love gone, but Camy stirred something inside him to life. Hope in faithfulness? In love? He knew, even if he chose to leave, she would remain faithful. Even if he never offered her his heart.

He resumed playing, each word echoing in his head, until he heard the brush of Camy's skirts against the hay and her soft footfalls pass through the barn door. Of course, Uncle Tommy's excited squawking had alerted him to her presence.

Her soft lilt as she sang lyrics from a Robert Burns poem reached out across the field and into the night.

His heart lurched and then pounded with fierce pride. Listening to Camy speak over the last week, he wasn't surprised at the beautiful notes matching the violin.

The song of heart-wrenching tears with promises never to be spoken, sighs of love and groans of despair poured out of her like honey from a jar, echoing across the fields, quaking his very heart and soul.

Enthralled by what she'd just heard, Camy sat beside Duncan, curling her legs beneath her. "You play my father's violin as if it were made for you."

He dipped his chin in acknowledgment and tucked the violin into the case. "I haven't upset you, have I?"

"Of c-course not. I didn't know it was still around. If I had I probably would have burned it." Tilting her head back, she looked at the stars and smiled. "I'm glad I didn't."

He latched the case. "So am I."

She felt the warmth of his smile and glanced at him. Only parts of his face were illuminated by the light of the moon; the rest hid in the shadows. "My father used to play all the time. He sang that song to my mother, holding her hand while she took her last breaths."

"I am sorry."

She touched his forearm. "Please don't be. It reminded me how much he had loved her." She pulled her legs into her chest and rested her chin on her knees. "I've always thought he left us because of something I did. I had fallen soon after she died in childbirth and broken my arm. He yelled his frustration at how I was always getting hurt. But now I wonder if he just didn't miss mama. Ellie and Mara have the look of her. It must have been hard to see his beloved in his daughters, and even more difficult knowing she had sacrificed her life trying to give him a son."

"Nevertheless, he abandoned his children." She heard the disgust in his tone and knew he'd never abandon their children, not that there would be any, but the knowing eased her mind about their impending marriage a little more.

"He did, but thinking that the pain he must have endured was what propelled him to leave us eases my own hurts. I can let it go and forgive him," she said.

And maybe lengthen the measuring stick a little in order to give grace to Duncan. For too long she'd measured all men by her father's abandonment. Perhaps now, realizing he had suffered from a broken heart, she could see differently. Maybe even trust Duncan a little. She didn't know why she told him what was on her mind, except that the dark made it easier to talk to him, and his playing had somehow began to heal unintentional wounds left by her father.

"His pain almost makes me feel fortunate that I'll never experience love, or to know it."

Somehow she thought the words might be wrong when they tumbled out of her mouth. Was she experiencing love right now? Unwilling to examine the question further and to dwell on the thoughts of her heart, she stood and dusted the dirt and hay from her skirt.

Duncan rose too and grasped her fingers. She locked her knees and willed her breathing to settle.

"You have my word, if you still wish to marry me, I'll give you everything I can."

But not his heart. Disappointment struck a chord in her much like the sorrowful tune he'd just played on the violin, but it was what it was. She understood, he had his own wounds that needed healing. And she'd never expected to be loved for herself anyway. "I understand. I've learned to be content, and you've already given me more than I could ask for."

His brow furrowed. "What is that?"

"The first buds of healing." She smiled.

"I played a song, nothing more. Nevertheless, I'm thankful I helped."

"Well, then, I'll see you in the morning." She stepped into the barn, the flickering lamplight bathing the barn in a soft glow.

"Camy," he said, following close behind her.

She turned. Their shadows intermingled, becoming one. She drew in the scent of hay and livestock, and him. A scent she sank her head into every night when she lay down to sleep. She hadn't asked to take over Ellie's room, the room he had stayed in before moving to the barn, but because of her injury Ellie had insisted, and because her sister had insisted, Camy dreamed of the man standing before her every night. Dreamed of long walks, picnicking by the river, him reading scripture to her. And now she would, no doubt, dream of him kissing her and then playing a heartfelt song with lyrics sorrowful enough to make her weep.

"I have business to attend in Topeka before we marry."

He was leaving? He was leaving her. Before they were even to be married? She clenched her fist to keep from grabbing hold of him and begging him not to go, to keep the little girl inside her from acting out just as she'd done with her da all those years ago. That little girl didn't exist anymore, no matter how hard she pounded against the walls of Camy's heart. Besides, they had an agreement, a contract, and she knew Duncan was a man of his word.

"I'll ask Hamish to stay until my return."

They didn't need Hamish to protect them, but she wasn't going to mention it and start an argument, lest she give in to the childish tantrum boiling inside her. He'd kept every word he'd given to her, and even though he'd keep this one, she couldn't help the fear clawing at her insides. Tight-lipped, she said, "Good night, Mr. Murray. I'll pray for your safe travels."

He grabbed her arm, spinning her around. His gaze bored into hers. The violin case bumped against her leg. "Camy, I give my word, I'll come back, but if it would ease your mind, I'll stay. We can go together after we speak our vows."

"M-Mr. Murray, you've made it perfectly clear our lives will be separate. Why would you take me anywhere?"

"Because you'll be my wife." He drew his hand over her hair. "And I do care about your feelings, sweetheart."

If he cared he wouldn't capture her heart with his kindness. The corner of her mouth quivered. The pad of his thumb wiped a tear from the corner of her eye. He pulled her into his chest, the pounding of his heart playing against her ear, reminding her of the song. She arched her neck and looked into his eyes. He dipped his head. Their lips met with a gentle brush of a feather. She melted against him and prayed he wouldn't sever the tie binding them.

Chapter Fourteen

"What are you doing?" she asked as Hamish dumped her mother's trunk onto the floor.

"Ellie girl asked me to bring it in."

Camy tucked the needle into the shirt she'd been fixing and laid it on the table. It was the one chore she was allowed, and truthfully she was thankful, given that her shoulder continued to cause her discomfort. "Whatever for?"

Ellie swept in on a ray of sunshine and clapped her hands together. "Before he left, Duncan asked if we had a gown for you to wear at your engagement party. Besides, I thought I'd sew a little myself."

Ellie loved to sew. She loved the challenge of making new things from old, mostly curtains and dresses for Mara. Her stitches were tight and perfect, where Camy's were loose and sloppy. Camy would rather milk the goats, or plant seeds.

"Isn't this exciting?" Mara said, dancing into the cabin. "Camy will stunning in Mama's dress."

Camy shook her head. "What? Ellie, no. It's to be yours."

The morning light and Duncan's departure had brought an uncertainty that Duncan would even return as he'd promised, even with the contract written between them. He hadn't returned yet. Of course, he'd left only hours ago, shortly after the rooster crowed. And although their farewell had lingered several long, breathless minutes, last night she couldn't help fearing he'd turn yellow-bellied and run. Especially since he acted like a man who wanted more than a marriage in name only. Which he most definitely didn't.

"Don't be a goose." Ellie opened the trunk and sifted through the contents. "It'll be threadbare with age by the time I'm ready to wear it. Besides," she said, glancing up at her. "You favor Mama and you'll make the dress look stunning."

Camy's cheeks heated. Ellie had Mama's straight, lighter brown hair that glinted beneath the sun. Mara had her brown eyes. Ellie was tall and graceful, just as she'd remembered her mother to be, and although Mara was short, she had Mama's curves. Camy looked down the front of herself and grimaced. She was neither short, nor tall. She was plain and far from desirable. Her hair, always in wild disarray, couldn't be contained like Ellie's. And her eyes were drab, lifeless, the color of dirt.

"That she does." Hamish's voice cracked with emotion. "You do your parents proud, lass." He slapped his thigh, drawing attention away from his misted eyes. "If ye need me I'll be napping in the barn."

"I don't believe it," Mara said. "Uncle Hamish, a caring, sappy old cuss."

"Mara Jean! Of course he cares," Ellie responded as she pulled out several paper-wrapped packages. "He wouldn't have brought Duncan out here to marry Camy if he didn't.''

"You mean manipulated." Camy spun from her sisters and the excitement of digging through their mother's belongings. She plopped in the chair and resumed her darning. The words spewed out of her mouth without thought, and even though she'd known from the beginning Duncan's reasoning behind their marriage, it hurt.

What had changed? She knew the answer immediately. Their second kiss. Last night's kiss had been filled with promises she knew would never come. Duncan had said as much. Yet there had been that one moment where their heartbeats fell into unison; she'd felt it beneath her palm. The memory of it had played in her mind through the night as she tried to find sleep, and it continued even now.

"You are sorely mistaken if you believe Duncan is a man to be so easily manipulated."

Camy rolled her eyes. Of course he wasn't. There wasn't one imperfect thing about him. Excepting that he made her long for more in their marriage than a signed document. "He desires Sims Creek."

"Why?" Mara sat on the edge of the bed and pulled a brush she'd found among Mama's things through her hair. "He could have any piece of land he wanted. According to Old Dr. Northrop he could buy all of Rusa Valley and not bat a lash. He has several properties in Topeka."

"He's rich?" And handsome? Everything Mara fancied in a husband. Camy's head spun. She realized she didn't know much about Duncan. He knew almost all there was to know about her. Her tendency toward accidents, her stammering tongue and her freckles. Her fear of rejection, the pain caused by her father, and still he agreed to a marriage between them. Why, when he could purchase any property along the river? And why, if the gossip was true, would he want to live like a pauper in the country? "I don't believe it, Mara. He doesn't have the arrogant air of a rich man."

He behaved nothing like Miller Northrop and some of the other men Mrs. Smith had introduced to her and her sisters. Perhaps that was because he hadn't grown up with money, having lived in a home worse than the old cabin. Duncan was kind, played the violin, longed for a home like the one he'd left in Scotland and after seeing all the improvements he'd made to the farm in the last week, he worked hard.

"Money shouldn't bother you, Camy. It would make life easier," Ellie argued.

If easier meant Mrs. Smith's household, she didn't want it.

Mara folded her hands in her lap and looked dreamily at the ceiling. "To think, we could have a real stove."

Not that a real stove would improve Camy's sister's cooking any, but it would be nice.

"A roof, and walls without holes," Ellie chimed.

No more pots and buckets to trip over would make life easier. "A well. I love sitting by the river, but I dislike carrying the water bucket up that hill several times a day."

"See, Ellie?" Mara giggled. "She does dream a little."

"Even so, I'd rather marry a man who is kind, caring and works hard than a man who has none of the above and money." She pulled the needle through the fabric and poked her finger. "Ow."

"No bleeding fingers. You wouldn't want to soil Mama's gown before your party, would you?" Mara hopped off the bed and dropped the brush into the trunk. She stepped to the window and pulled back the curtain. "When do you think he'll return?"

"He only left this morning."

"I know, but the party is in a few days." Mara glanced over her shoulder. "Besides, it is fun watching him watching you and you watching him."

"Whatever do you mean, little sister?"

"Here it is!" Ellie jumped to her feet, hugging the brown-papered package to her chest, before laying it on the bed. All three of them stood, shoulder to shoulder, with Ellie in the middle, staring at the brown paper as if waiting for the package to unwrap itself. Ellie glanced at Mara and then at her. "Well, are you ready?"

Clapping her hands together, Mara squealed. Camy reluctantly nodded. Ellie pulled the string and gently pulled back the paper. They gasped at the rose-colored silk with brown velvet bows on the sleeves. Camy drew her finger along the edge of the scooped neckline.

Ellie nudged her with her elbow. "Are you ready to try it on?"

Feeling a bit like Cinderella, Camy swallowed the lump in her throat. If it didn't fit, would she miss the party, or go in one of her working dresses? She meant to keep the promise she'd made to Duncan and wouldn't shame him by behaving improperly, not with infidelity, and most certainly not looking the pauper. If the rumors were true and he was as rich as Mara believed… Camy prayed the gown would fit.

Without asking her, Ellie removed the sling and Mara helped remove Camy's work dress. They unhooked the pearl buttons running down the back of the bodice of their mother's gown and held the garment open for her to step in. She brushed her palms over the silk as they buttoned the back. It fit! And it was prettier than she recalled. Ellie and Mara moved in front of her. Ellie grabbed hold of Camy's right hand and held it out to the side.

Mara swiped a tear from her cheek and then removed the pins of Camy's hair. "You are stunning, Camy."

Camy tried to pull her hand from her sister's and shrink into the shadows, but Ellie tightened her grip.

Ellie's lashes battled against the tears filling her eyes. "Oh, I wish Mama was here. She'd be happier than even I am at this moment."

"Ellie." She drew in her bottom lip, not wanting to douse her sisters' joy with the truth, but Camy couldn't sing, dance and twitter around as if this was to be a happy occasion when it wouldn't. "My marriage to Duncan will be as real as the Fountain of Youth, and nothing to get all misty-eyed over."

The cabin door opened. Ellie dropped her hand. Mara stepped to the side. Duncan's eyes locked with hers. She sucked in a sharp breath at the sight of his freshly shaven face and the fierce ticking of his jaw. She felt like a rabbit trapped in the eyes of a predator. She trembled, not afraid that he'd devour her like a coyote might his prey, but she did fear the shambles he'd leave her heart in after their vows were said.

"I think you're sorely mistaken, sister." Ellie glanced at Duncan. "I'm glad to see you've returned. We'll give you a moment." She pulled Mara out of the cabin.

"I made it as far as Rusa," he said, his brow furrowing. Although he wore the same dark rough-hewn trousers and threadbare shirt, she could sense the money, could see him decked in fancy suits and rubbing elbows with the hobnobbers. "Here, I brought you some sweets from the mercantile." He handed her a paper bag.

"Th-thank you." She blinked and tucked her chin to her chest.

He closed the distance between them. Crooking his finger beneath her chin, he lifted her face to his and kissed her.

He kissed her. For the third time in less than twenty-four hours, he kissed her. He would blame all three on his determination to prove to her she was a treasure to be held and cherished, not a guttersnipe to be tossed away. The truth of the matter, though, was that he was insane, purely insane. Sure, he wanted her to know he wasn't rejecting her. That he wasn't her father. That she was everything he could hope for in a wife. His perfect helpmate created by God for him. Too bad he couldn't say the same about himself for her.

He was mad to think he could have her and yet not have her. Each kiss sweeter, and more binding. He should have known once he gave in to the temptation of kissing her by the river that he'd become his father. Except…he couldn't imagine kissing any other woman. Ever. Only her.

"Hello." He leaned his forehead against hers and blew out a ragged breath to calm his pulse. If he didn't stop seeking her out every chance he got, their marriage would become more than what they had negotiated for.

"H-hi," she whispered. "You're back."

"Yes." He laughed. Molding her to his chest, he rested his chin atop her head. *Lord, help me.* He couldn't even leave the area knowing she was here, knowing he'd be gone for days, unable to lay eyes on her. Unable to know she was safe from scoundrels who set homes on fire. Unable to reassure her that their marriage was a good partnership, even if he didn't fully believe it himself. He only wished he could offer her more than his name. "I sent someone in my place."

She pulled back and looked up at him, her brow creased. "Who?"

"Benjamin."

"Northrop?"

He released her and paced to the window. "Yes. He was going to Topeka for supplies."

"Do you tr-trust him?"

Leaning against the windowpane, he jammed his hands in his pockets and shrugged. "Why wouldn't I? Besides, I'd rather risk trusting him than having you worry as to whether or not I was coming back." He laughed. A half-truth wasn't exactly a mistruth, was it? He didn't want to tell her how much he'd worry over her or else she might get the wrong idea and think he cared a little more than he should given their situation.

"I set it far from my mind."

He glanced at her and smiled. Her hands folded in front of her as if she were a young girl being chastised. "I don't believe you."

She shoved her spectacles up her nose. "You don't have to, Mr. Murray."

Unable to help himself, he closed the distance between them. "If we're to be married, I prefer you called me by my Christian name. It's Duncan. You've said it many times, haven't you?"

Her lips set into a stubborn line and his competitive instinct roared. She could be stubborn, but he rarely backed down from a challenge, and he wasn't about to this time.

"Here." He touched his fingers to her temple.

"M-Mr. Murray," she said.

"Here." He laid his palm above her thundering heart. Her eyelids slid closed as she shook her head.

"And here." He kissed the corner of her mouth, knowing the game was dangerous to his sanity. He should have her uncle commit him to an asylum after their vows were spoken.

She drew in a sharp breath. "Murray."

He kissed the other side.

"Dun—"

He grasped her arms and yanked her to him, capturing his name and her lips with his. She tasted of hot cocoa, something he had failed to notice with their earlier kiss.

"Duncan!" Mara burst through the door. He gave himself a mental shake and jumped away from his bride-to-be. Camy's cheeks flamed as did her younger sister's.

"Hamish needs you. Now!" Mara said as she grabbed a rifle and flew out the door.

Duncan snagged another rifle.

"Duncan." Camy's hand rested on his arm, worry filling her eyes.

He smiled. Wisdom told him not to demand that she stay in the cabin, protected. "Yes?"

"Be careful."

He rushed out of the cabin and spied Hamish flat against the side of the barn peeking around the corner. Mara leaned around her uncle's shoulder. A loud commotion echoed in the distance. Duncan strode across the yard.

"What is going on?" He spoke just loud enough to be heard over Hound's deep barking growls from inside the barn and his paws scratching furiously at the door.

Hamish jerked his head toward the field. "Them no-gooders is tearing up the field with their horses."

Duncan peered around the corner. Three riders tore up and down the south part of the field. Not doing any real harm, since they hadn't planted yet, but the bullying was enough to make him mad as a disturbed rattlesnake. "Where's Ellie?"

"She's in the loft ready to draw a bead if they come any closer," Mara said.

"Go to the cabin and keep your sister company."

She propped a hand on her hip. "Camy can handle herself."

"I didn't imply otherwise, but I would prefer there to be no accidents to keep us from our wedding. Now go!"

She clenched her jaw, reminding him of Camy, and then she stomped toward the cabin.

"What's yer plan?" Hamish spat.

"I'm not sure yet." He rested the rifle against his shoulder and sighted the distance. "They probably aren't expecting us. Where's your mule?"

"Right next to yer prized mare."

"No insult intended, my friend. What do you think about riding up on them?"

"That's a right fine idea. Ellie girl will cover us."

Duncan explained to Ellie what they were doing

while Hamish coaxed Millie out of her stall, which was fruitless even with the offer of an apple and Duncan didn't have time for her stubbornness.

Duncan tossed his derby to the ground and jumped on Heather Glenn's bare back. Charging out of the barn, Duncan released a war cry like a banshee as he swung an ax over his head. The horses reared. The men fought to keep their seats. A shot, then two and three, rent the air from behind him. The riders, white as sheets, tapped their heels into their mounts and tore away from the farm. Duncan chased them off the property with a high-pitched scream he'd learned from a Cherokee man he'd met in Oklahoma during the war, and then he rode Heather Glenn over the torn-up fields, thankful they had yet to plant one seed.

An object glinted off the sun, catching his eye. Duncan dismounted and walked the length of field until he found it again. Kneeling, he stared at the gold pocket watch as familiar to him as his own name. Etched in the gold in Gaelic was *We are Murray* and the clan motto *Quite Ready*. Nestled in the center of the script was their crest, an image of a mermaid gazing into a mirror. His father had given it to him on his thirteenth birthday as a reminder never to forget whence he came. He was Murray, through and through. No matter the scandals, no matter the whispers of treason, and they were always ready to face the consequences of their deeds, right or wrong, good or bad.

How had it come to be here when he'd left it tucked in his tartan buried in the bottom of his trunk in the room he kept at the boardinghouse in Topeka? It couldn't have been Benjamin Northrop's doing, since he hadn't even the time to make it to Topeka, let alone there and back again. He cradled the watch in his palm and swiveled around on his heel, checking for anything else out of the ordinary. A wisp of smoke rose from the ground.

Duncan stood and strode toward the spiraling stream of smoke. A freshly lit cigarette lay next to an entire roll of smokes. The foil packaging had an intricate design of flowers and a lady dancing with a man-sized rabbit dressed in military garb, complete with a sword crinkled in his fist. He clenched his jaw. He knew of only one man who smoked this brand.

He tucked the watch into his pants pocket and mounted his horse. Tobacco leached from the foil wrapping as he clenched his fist, spilling down his leg and onto the ground as he rode back to the barn. Now that he had an idea as to who was behind the threats, he could deal with the culprits. Camy and her sisters would be safe, and he wouldn't need to marry her. Hamish could simply sign the farm over to Camy when she turned twenty-one and there'd be no more worry. But what about the next mongrel who decided to prey on the unmarried women? Besides, he wanted to marry her. Now more than ever. He'd already settled it in his mind and had even spoken with Pastor Hammond while he was in Rusa Valley.

Seeing these men threaten the woman he lo—cared for made him realize he wanted to marry her more than anything. Or maybe it had been the prospect of leaving her this morning and not seeing her for days. It was by the grace of God he'd heeded his instinct and come home, instead of traveling to Topeka. He'd hate to think about what would have happened had he not been here.

He clenched his jaw. Only the lowest of lowest of all bounders would terrorize women, and why? What was so special about this piece of land that a man would go to such lengths to steal from them? That was one conversation he intended to have with Hamish and the sisters. Before he confronted his partner. After all, the watch burning in his pocket was his, his to own. He was a Murray, a fact he'd despised since he was a boy, but now a sense of pride welled up in his chest. Even through all his father's scandals and the stigma of treason committed by his clan against England during the Jacobite uprising, there had been a sense of knowing that he was a better man than the legacy left to him, and he'd pull on the tales of victory and triumph. He was a Murray, and a Murray was always quite ready. In all circumstances, no matter the consequences, even if it meant tearing down the walls of his father's past and relinquishing his heart to Camy.

Chapter Fifteen

Camy wrung her hands while Ellie gathered material here and there. More than an hour had passed since Duncan tore out of the cabin. "Where is he?"

"He'll be fine. The way those scoundrels scurried like mice, no doubt Duncan scared the life out of them. I wish I could have seen their faces, but they were too far away," Mara said, even though she stared out the window. "You should have seen Duncan racing across the field circling the ax above his head, screaming like two tomcats in a fight. Uncle Hamish laughed so hard he doubled over. I had to fire his rifle after I fired mine."

She jammed her hand on her hip, the stool wobbling beneath her feet. "Ow!"

"Hold still, will you?" Ellie poked a pin through the silk. "It won't take long, *if* you quit wiggling around."

"I can't help it. How do I know he wasn't ambushed, or shot? I'm not even married yet."

Ellie rolled her eyes. "Weren't you just saying how there was no need for us to be excited, as your marriage was going to be as real as the Fountain of Youth?"

"Oh, it'll be a real marriage all right," Mara tossed over her shoulder.

Camy glared thorns at her sister's back.

"Of course it will. They just need some time to figure it out," Ellie responded.

"I think they've figured it out. I saw them kissing last night."

"Mara!" Camy jumped off the stool. Her cheeks burned. "How dare you?"

"Well." Ellie tugged on her arm, motioning for her to stand back on the stool. "I am relieved."

Camy didn't know why her sister was relieved. A kiss was nothing more than a kiss. It didn't mean he was going to change his mind about her, about them. Their marriage. She'd become Mrs. Cameron Murray. Husbandless and childless, but at least she'd have his name, and his protection. If he stayed.

"He's back, and he looks as mad as Ellie when Hound comes 'round smelling like a skunk." Mara ran out the door.

Camy jumped back off the stool.

"Not in Mama's gown, you don't." Ellie pulled her back.

"Come on, Ellie." She tugged at the sleeves. "Unbutton me."

Her sister laughed as she unhooked the buttons enough for the gown to slide down her hips. She helped her don her green work dress, and before the last button was fastened Camy flung open the door.

"Shoes, and your sling." Ellie laughed. "I pray one day my heart will find someone to love too."

Her entire body skidded to a halt, even the pulse that had been fiercely pounding through her veins. "Love?"

Her breath caught in her lungs. She leaned against the door frame. "Is it possible?"

"Is what possible?" His deep timbre cut straight through her, like a nail through wood when struck hard enough.

He stood so close his warmth radiated, encompassing her. Churned earth, horse and him swirled around her, pulling her deeper into what she knew before their first kiss, maybe even from the moment he'd appeased Ellie and had read the Good Samaritan, she loved him. Her breaths shortened and quickened, tightening her chest. Spots danced before her eyes.

"Are you all right?"

She looked at him, his clean-shaven jaw, his soft green eyes like a bed of moss, the mouth that had so lovingly touched hers. *Oh, Lord, how am I to marry him when I love him? He doesn't want to be loved, not by me.* Like she was stuck deep in mire, she dragged one foot backward, away from him. She wobbled.

"Ellie, water please." He scooped her up in his arms and placed her on one of the chairs. He crouched in front of her and wrapped his hands around hers.

A warm stream of tears slid down her cheek. She swiped it away. "You must th-think I'm a n-ninny."

"Not at all." Eyes filled with concern, his gaze bored into hers, searching for answers she hoped he wouldn't find. "You're the first woman I've met who didn't swoon at the hint of rain."

No, just at the prospect of loving you.

Ellie pressed the cup into her hand. "We've had a lot of excitement the last week. I know I'm exhausted and I'm not the one who got shot and is getting married."

"I almost forgot," Duncan said. "I spoke with Pastor Hammond while I was in town. He'd be happy to marry us during Mrs. Smith's planned engagement party."

She shuddered.

His brow creased. "Is that all right with you, Camy?"

She stared at their hands. His surrounding hers, much larger. Stronger. Two days was a short time, and she was beginning to feel as though her head was underwater. She'd already agreed to the terms, had signed her name, but she'd never thought about all the benefits of having him as a husband would provide to the farm. If he stayed. She wouldn't have to search around the riverbank for broken limbs and branches small enough to carry and chop with her weaker strength when they couldn't afford to barter with the neighbors. And he had done more alone than what she and her sisters struggled to do each day as far as the chores were concerned.

The sooner they were married, the sooner she'd settle into how they'd move forward as Mr. and Mrs. Murray.

He gave her hand a gentle squeeze. "We can wait if you'd like."

She shook her head. "N-no, Saturday is fine."

"Just think, Camy," Ellie chimed. "You'll only have to be at one of Mrs. Smith's gatherings instead of two."

Duncan released her hand and rose. He smiled down at her. "That's one way of killing two birds with one stone."

She gulped down her water and tried to come to terms with her heart.

"Did you get a close look at the rotters?" Ellie asked as she handed Duncan a cup of coffee.

"No, but I'll know them if I see them again." He sipped his coffee. "By the way, thank you for your assistance."

"I'm thankful you decided to return instead of go to Topeka," Ellie responded.

"I am too." He gazed out the window. "I hate to think what might have happened if I hadn't. It seemed they were only about mischief, which makes me uncertain they are the same ones who have been bothering you. It's by the grace of God we had that late snow, keeping us from planting."

"Wh-why?" Camy asked. "Why did you c-come back?"

He blew across his coffee and she wondered if he stalled thinking of what to say. Would he speak the truth, or lie?

"I had an intense gnawing in my gut, and the further I traveled the worse it became." A corner of his mouth turned upward. "I did wonder if it might have been the extra amount of salt in the biscuits last night, but once I discovered Northrop was heading to Topeka the gnawing disappeared."

Ellie's laugh filled the cabin. Camy could only stare as the knot in her stomach tightened. She loved him. He'd eaten every bite on his plate, even had a second biscuit along with the rest of the fish, and not one grimace crossed his face, not one, and she would know because she'd watched him. Not only last night, but every time they'd shared a meal, especially when Mara helped prepare food. Camy had begun to pity the man, thinking he didn't have the luxury of good food, but of course, if he was as rich as Mara hinted, he knew what good food tasted like. No wonder the man had tried to eat Uncle Tommy, his poor stomach wasn't used to broth and root vegetables.

She had to know. After all, they were to be married. "Mara says you're rich. Is that true?"

His smile fell, and Ellie's laughter quieted. "Is that why you're so somber?"

She kept silent. If she told him no, he'd press, and she was far from ready to tell him the truth. If he knew what was in her heart, he'd leave, and the thought of him doing so caused her insides to tremble.

He pulled up a chair and sat. "Yes. Does that bother you?"

She chewed on the inside of her lip. "Why didn't you tell me?"

Ellie took Mama's gown, along with the sewing box, to the other room.

"I didn't think it mattered."

"It d-doesn't, not to me." She drew in a breath. "How will you be content to live here, when you're used to finer things?"

He set his cup on the floor and grabbed her hand. "Camy, you're sorely mistaken. I inherited money from my father. Money I didn't want. In my youthful foolishness I took financial risks investing in various inventions and companies trying to get rid of it. Many of my investments were blessed." He stood and paced to the window. "But everything I own fits in my trunk. I've gone from boardinghouse to boardinghouse."

"You never wanted a home?"

"Yes." He nodded and then looked her in the eye. "This one."

* * *

"Camy, there is something I need to tell you."

She looked up at him, her brown eyes curious and filled with innocent trust. He didn't want anything standing between them, not his money, not his investments, not the fact that his partner was a no-good rotter. It would be much easier to tell her what was budding in his heart, but he couldn't do that, not yet.

A clap of thunder shook the rafters and Camy tilted her head as if listening for something more.

"Is everything all right?"

She nodded. "Y-yes, but we need to make sure the animals are secured."

Ellie swished out of the room. "Hound will be pounding on the door soon."

Another clap of thunder, this one louder caused Camy to jump. "I'll see to the animals."

"I'll go with you," he added.

They raced outside and to the barn. Mara stood on the bottom rung of the gate to one of the empty stalls, tears sliding down her cheeks.

"What's wrong?" Camy strode through the barn.

"It's Miller."

"Miller? What is he doing here?"

"We went to bring the goats in and Hamish found him beaten." Mara jumped down, her face white as a sheet. She swiped at her tears. "He's not making much sense. I don't like him much, but his sister is my friend, and I've never seen anything so awful."

"It's all right, Mara," Camy consoled her sister.

Duncan peeked over the gate and bit back the words bursting forth from his belly. Hamish held a rag to the young man's face. Lanky legs and arms, one twisted at an odd angle, told him Miller was even younger than he first thought. The red bandanna Duncan had seen tucked in the vest pocket of one of the riders was now tied around his head, telling Duncan the kid had been one of the riders tearing up the field. Had Miller gotten himself mixed up with the others? Duncan slipped inside the gate and knelt in the hay beside Hamish. "Whew, the boy's been drinking."

"Like he's been swimmin' in the bottle," Hamish added. "I'm thinkin' it's not such a bad thing, considerin' his injuries."

Duncan pulled back one of Miller's eyelids and then the other.

"What can I do?" Camy sucked in a sharp breath. "Oh my."

"Get Ellie. Have her bring the sewing box. He may not need the laudanum, but have her bring it anyway." Camy hiked up her skirts and left for the cabin. "Mara, are all the animals in?"

"Hound disappeared when we found Miller, but he's probably at the cabin by now. He hates storms."

"Can you gather the lanterns? We're going to need them." Duncan pressed his fingers to Miller's pulse. Someone had done more than just beat him, they'd sliced an X in his right cheek from beneath his eye to the corner of his lip, from the side of a swollen broken nose to his jaw. A crimson-soaked handkerchief wrapped around his fingers. Duncan didn't need to pull back the makeshift bandage to know the damage done. "Where's his horse?"

"I dinnae see no horse," Hamish replied.

"If it isn't here, then it must have been taken." Duncan didn't tell them Miller was one of the men who'd been tearing up the field. If they knew, then they'd know he'd most likely been part of setting the barn on fire last fall, and the cabin a few days ago. Even though the hothead had tried to start a fight with him last week, Duncan didn't think Miller was the type to terrorize women. He didn't know what was going on, or how involved Miller was, and until he did, he'd keep his mouth shut. No need to stir up any more trouble for the young man.

Miller moaned, and Duncan wished he could do something more than sit here.

Ellie opened the gate. "How long before you think Ben will be back?"

"He thought tonight, but with the storm coming in…" Duncan didn't have a clear answer. "I can take Heather Glenn—"

"No!" Camy cried. "If these are the same men, look what they did."

Duncan went to her and pulled her into his arms. Her presence settled him, gave him a sense of calm. If these were the same men, and they were out there, they could do the same if not worse to Camy. "You're right."

Rain beat the roof, along with pieces of hail. A crack of thunder rent the air. Bright white light burst through the shudders of the barn as lightning struck something close by. "Where's Mara?"

Loosening his hold, Duncan glanced around the barn. "I asked her to gather the lanterns. She should be here. Mara!"

"Mara!" Camy hollered.

"She probably went looking for that mangy pet of yers," Hamish growled. "You two gather them lanterns. Ellie girl needs all the light she can get to stitch the boy up properlike. I'll look around for Mara Jean."

Hamish took up the rifle leaning near one of the doors and slipped outside. Duncan twined his fingers with Camy's. "You don't think she's gone searching for whoever did this, do you?"

He hoped Camy's sister wouldn't be so foolish, but the two youngest Sims sisters had a streak of spitfire in them. Camy dug her heels into the ground, her eyes wide with concern. "I—I don't know."

Knowing the answer to his question before he asked, he felt his heart hammering in his chest. "Would you?"

Her eyes searched his. "A few weeks ago, yes."

"And now?"

"If it was you who'd gotten hurt like Miller, nothing would stop me."

"I was afraid you'd say something like that."

"But Mara likes Miller even less than I do."

"That may be so, but you've seen him. Even I'm angered by the brutality of what was done. And his sister is her friend."

"Oh, Duncan," Camy cried.

"Is there any place she'd hide, a place to get away from everyone, to think?"

Camy chewed on the tip of her fingernail and thought for a moment. "When we first moved here, we'd find her in the root cellar playing with her doll, but that was years ago."

"You get the lanterns. I'll check there." He gave her a quick peck on the cheek. "Don't worry, I'll find her."

He went to leave, and as he passed the stall holding Heather Glenn he heard muffled sobs. He opened the latch and found Mara Jean with her face pressed against his mare's neck. "What are you about? Your sister and uncle are worried about you."

She lifted her head. Tearstained cheeks and red swollen eyes glared at him in anger as if he were responsible for what had occurred, and in a way he very likely could be, given that he now knew his partner was involved. Guilt pressed against him like a boulder, but he shook it off. This was no time to pity himself. Even if he had never met Calvin Weston, his partner would have found another purse, and for whatever reason, the situation would still be the same, except Duncan wouldn't be here to flesh it out. Of that, he would be forever thankful.

"I don't know how to ride," she snapped. "If I did I'd go after them and I'd give them a piece of my mind, and shoot them in the knees so they'd never walk again."

"A little bloodthirsty, eh?" He scrubbed his palm over his jaw. "I promise all will be well. First, we need to care for your friend. We'll find the men who did this, trust me."

"How are you so confident?" Camy asked. He'd heard her skirts swishing before she leaned against the stall, before he had smelled the hint of rosewater. She scratched Heather Glenn's nose. "We don't even know who did this or if they're the same ones who have been after Sims Creek."

They're the same, he wanted to say, but he didn't want to tell them that their friend was involved. Not yet, if ever. He didn't know why, but he had a gut feeling that Miller had been swindled somehow, blackmailed into participating. "When Miller wakes up, he'll be able to give us information." He looked Camy's younger sister in the eye. "Until then, it'll do us no good to race across the county in the middle of this storm."

"Duncan," Ellie hollered. "Would you come here?"

Closing the latch, he followed the sisters to the stall where Miller lay injured.

Fear flickered in Ellie's eyes, but then it was gone. "I need him moved to the cabin away from the animals. I've secured his arm the best I could."

Duncan scooped up the young man, careful not to jar his arm, and followed the sisters. The storm continued to rage. Rain and wind whipped around him, stinging his bare flesh. He hunched over Northrop when thunder clapped overhead, and lightning struck something in the distance. He quickened his steps and climbed the stairs of the porch. Fingers dug into his arm. Miller's eyes were mere slits in the swollen sockets. His mouth opened and closed, bare mumbles. All Duncan could make out were the words *forgive me.*

"You're forgiven," he said as he shouldered Miller through the door held by Camy.

Camy glanced at Miller, then at Duncan. "He's forgiven for what?"

Duncan laid the man on the bed, the springs creaking beneath his weight. "I don't know, but it seemed important."

And somehow giving the young man forgiveness changed something in Duncan; it gave him peace and a sense of resolution. If he could forgive this young man for whatever part he had in bringing trouble to Camy's door, he could begin to forgive his father, and then maybe he could forgive himself, freeing him to become the husband Camy deserved, the husband he desired to be. The kind of husband who gave his heart to his wife without hesitation. The kind of husband who loved his wife as much as Jesus loved the church.

Chapter Sixteen

Morning came too soon or maybe not soon enough. The storm that had started yesterday afternoon had continued through the night. At times the violent winds forced through the nooks and crannies of the cabin, vibrating the barred door on its hinges and causing Hound to whimper from beneath the bed. Duncan had hoped Benjamin would arrive and ease the minds of everyone hovering over Miller, but the rooster had crowed hours ago, and still no sign of the doctor. And according to her sister, Camy had disappeared nearly an hour ago. Enough time for her to find trouble. Anguish unlike anything he'd known, even throughout the war, churned in his gut, each second propelling his feet to move faster as his boots ate up the ground.

He'd checked the barn, the loft and the root cellar. Checked every animal stall, and the field, and now he paced along the porch worrying over her whereabouts and wondering if he'd misplaced his trust in Benjamin. The missive he sent with Northrop to his friend Deputy Nate Cooper had been of a delicate nature concerning Weston and the railroad. If it had fallen into the wrong hands, things could go horribly wrong. As if they hadn't already. Was Benjamin in league with Duncan's investment partner? Considering the condition of his brother, Duncan didn't think so. But what if he was wrong, and where was Camy? Could she have gone out to feed the animals and fallen into the hands of Weston's hired hands?

He was about to saddle Heather Glenn when Camy and Hamish appeared from the tree line. The jolt in his chest interrupted his sigh of relief, and all thoughts of shaking sense into her for scaring him vanished. He'd seen her looking like a river rat, soaked to the bone, in her work dress dusted with flour, and in a gown fit for a queen, but right now she was the prettiest picture he'd ever had the pleasure of seeing. A floppy hat shielded her eyes, covering the upper half of her heart-shaped face. Her hair, tied with a blue ribbon, hung over her shoulder. The fingers of her right hand peeked out from the sleeve of his buff-colored coat. She wore a pair of oversize britches tucked into mud-covered boots, two revolvers belted at her side. This was a side of her he hadn't seen, although he sensed it was there beneath the anxiety of being shot and the inability to protect her sisters.

Her animated conversation with Hamish came to a halt when she saw him. "G-good morning, Duncan."

More like good afternoon, but he wouldn't mince words with her. "Where have you been? And why are you prancing around in trousers?"

She flinched, and he immediately regretted his tone.

Hamish shook his head. "Son, if ye're marryin' her, ye best learn how to communicate."

Duncan narrowed his eyes. What was that supposed

to mean? He wouldn't mind his wife wearing such attire, but at least after they said their vows he would have the right to haul her behind a tree and kiss her senseless. "I've been worried."

"And rightly so, Mr. Murray. Hamish had a beastly time protecting me from the nasty little squirrels tossing sticks upon my head as I looked for you." She shook, her cheeks flushed with anger.

Duncan growled. Funny how when she became irritated with him her stutter disappeared.

"Camy girl, that's not a way to respect yer husband. He has every right to be concerned after what happened yesterday."

"He isn't my husband. Yet."

Duncan held his tongue before he dug a bigger hole for her to bury him in.

Foot tapping, she glared at Duncan until Hamish disappeared into the barn. "What was that about?"

"What?" He shrugged. "You weren't here when I came to check on you, and nobody knew where you'd gone."

"And just where have you been, Mr. Murray?"

"Duncan."

"For your information, *Mr. Murray*, I went looking for you to see if you would escort me to the river, but *you*—" she poked him in the chest with her finger, her freckles hidden behind the rosy hue filling her cheeks "—were nowhere to be found. Did you know there is a man lying in my home who'd not only been beaten but carved like a piece of soft wood? Of course you know, you carried him in there."

Which was exactly why he'd been concerned over her disappearance. Needing space to think without her overtaking his every good sense, he stepped back, before he grabbed hold of her and molded her to him until they were inseparable with no ending and no beginning. "If you must know, I was checking for signs of intruders."

She gave him a look that said she didn't believe him. "After the rain we had?"

Oh, he wanted to pull her into his arms and kiss her. A sweet gentle caress wouldn't do, not this time. He clenched his jaw and breathed through his nostrils, willing self-control into his mind. "Yes, Cameron. If they are here, I would know as their boots and their horses' shoes would leave impressions in the rain soaked ground."

Her mouth formed an O. She held out her hand. "Truce?"

He wasn't giving in that easy. "Where were you?"

She glared at him. "If you must know, I was worried about you, so I donned this ridiculous hat and went searching. And after all the rain last night I needed to check the river."

"And?" He crossed his arms in front of him to keep from grabbing her.

"It's high." She chewed on her lip. Her confidence wavering as the heat of her words cooled, why? "Maybe t-too high for Benjamin to cross when he gets to Rusa Valley. I never thought I'd say this, but we sure could use a doctor right now." She kicked the toe of her boot into the mud. "Ellie's doing the best she can."

"And? You were gone over an hour, Camy. It only takes a few minutes to walk to the river and back. Your sisters are worried." As had he been; now he just wanted to lock her up in a room and keep her safe until the men were captured.

"I checked the road to see if it was washed out. I wouldn't want to miss the party tomorrow."

All the tension in his shoulders drained. He pulled her toward him. "You don't seem the type to enjoy parties, even if you are an honored guest."

"Ha, most likely Mrs. Smith wishes to make a fool of me. But you're right, I don't like parties. I despise them."

"I know, then why the urgency? Why, after all that happened yesterday, would you go off on your own?"

"I was with Hamish."

Duncan had crossed up with Hamish less than an hour ago. The old man had been alone.

"Camy, he wasn't with you when you left, as he'd been with me."

Her mouth pressed into a thin line. He glanced past her shoulder, toward the roaring of the river. After meeting Mrs. Smith, he knew she wouldn't pass the chance to have a social occasion and would reschedule as soon as the road was passable. So what was so important about tomorr— Oh!

Smoothing his palm over her cheek, he dislodged the floppy hat from her head to her back so he could gaze into her beautiful brown eyes. "It will take more than a thunderstorm and a rain shower to stop us from saying our vows and sealing our business deal. You don't have to worry about losing your home."

"Business deal? Losing my home?" She pulled from him and rested her hand on the butt of her revolver. She'd been looking for him, but she'd been ready to shoot any man she couldn't identify who crossed her path. She was tired of standing and tired of fighting. And she'd do just about anything to keep Duncan from Miller's fate. Even hunt down the scoundrels herself. "How can you even think about our *deal* at a time like this? In case you've forgotten, I'll remind you once again that Miller is recuperating from very grievous wounds. It very well could have been you after you chased the bounders off my land."

His eyebrows hiked at the mention of her land, and she waved his silly argument off with her hand. "Whose ever land it is, yours, mine, ours it could have been much worse. You—" she poked him in his chest "—could have died!"

He could have died, and it would have been her fault. All because of her foolish, prideful heart. Didn't the good Lord's word say *Pride goeth before destruction, and a haughty spirit before a fall*? Pride had told her to fight for what belonged to her and she hadn't counted the cost to her sisters, to Miller. In her arrogance she thought she could keep the farm, to care for it on her own. She'd even tried to convince Hamish of such. Obviously, after seeing all the improvements Duncan had made, she couldn't. She should have pushed Hamish to agree to Mr. Weston's offer months ago and saved them all a great deal of turmoil. At least his offer was a mite higher than Mr. Henry's had been for the railroad.

"How will attending Mrs. Smith's party tomorrow change anything? How will we being married change that fact?" Duncan asked.

Her jaw fell slack. Was the man daft? Wasn't it plain? Every hobnobber in the county flocked to

Mrs. Smith's social calls. If Mr. Weston wasn't in attendance, Hamish could auction it off to the highest bidder. Or give it away to old Dr. Northrop, although that would have Hamish falling into an early grave. She wouldn't expect Hamish to keep his promise to her. She loved her home, but she didn't want it anymore, not when it was obvious someone else wanted it enough to cause serious harm.

"Camy, why were you so worried about attending Mrs. Smith's party if you weren't worried over sealing our business with marriage vows?"

"The business deal is off. I'm not marrying you." She stomped by him, angry that she had to remain Miss Cameron Sims instead of becoming Mrs. Murray, wife of the man she loved.

He grabbed her arm, spinning her around. "Why not?"

Stupid man. "Don't you see? Just because we marry doesn't mean this will stop. Before they were only tormenting us with silly games. Now they've nearly killed Miller. I will not allow that to happen to you, nor to anyone."

The muscle in his jaw furiously ticked. "The party. Why do you want to go if not for the wedding? I want an answer."

She huffed. "Shortly after the first fire, an acquaintance of Mrs. Smith offered to help us out by buying Sims Creek. He'll buy the land, and the railroad will no longer be my problem and you can go back to where you came from, and perhaps find a more suitable wife, one who doesn't walk around in trousers unattended on her own property."

Duncan winced as if she'd slapped him. His face darkened in anger. "We signed an agreement. It's legal. It's binding. This land is as good as mine, and you are as good as my wife. The only thing lacking is standing before Pastor Hammond and speaking our vows."

"You would force me to keep our agreement?"

"Yes."

She could love him from afar. She could love him close by without saying a word, but she couldn't love him dead. The very thought shattered her heart into tiny remnants like the twinkling stars surrounded by black nothingness.

"Cameron." The anger in his voice relented, but it still rang hard, unyielding. He ran his hand down her arm until he met her fingers. "I just joined this fight and I'm not backing down. I never back down. I'll fight for this land. I'll fight for your family. I'll fight for you."

Warmth filled her chest, filling every crevice threatening to render her apart. The unspoken promises in his eyes begged for her patience and understanding. No one had fought for her and her sisters. They'd been left, pushed around and passed around and left again. Why would Duncan be any different?

"I'll fight for us."

He left her standing in the middle of the yard, staring at his broad back as he disappeared into the barn. He believed every word he said. Why couldn't she believe them? Because she didn't want to believe them. Because he wouldn't fight if he didn't think it was worth the cost, which meant she needed to diminish the value by ridding them both of the problem.

She squeezed her eyes against the tears threatening to spill. The fight wasn't worth his life. It wasn't worth anyone's life. She only prayed Mr. Weston was still interested.

Chapter Seventeen

Benjamin Northrop jumped from his spotted horse and tossed the reins around the hitching post near the barn. "I left your friend at the boardinghouse in Rusa as you requested. Your trunk is in the back," he said, pointing to the brown leather trunk.

"My thanks for retrieving my belongings and delivering my message." Duncan hefted his trunk and set it inside the barn. Benjamin followed him. Duncan unlatched the buckles and popped open the lid. After discovering the theft of his father's pocket watch, he held his breath as he dug into the bottom and felt for the small lump tucked into the lining.

"I'm sorry it took me so long."

"I understand. There was a lot of rain." Duncan's fingers brushed against the velvet bag and he breathed a sigh of relief. Tucking it into his pocket, he closed the lid and returned outside.

"By the time I was able to cross the river, it was late, and it seems my father has had some sort of fit, maybe even an apoplexy, after he heard the news about

Miller." Dark circles underneath Benjamin's eyes were proof of the sleepless night.

Duncan paused. How would the elder Northrop have heard about Miller? Duncan had been planning on riding out to see Dr. Northrop to let him know his son was recuperating at the farm. "I'm sorry to hear that. We've been watching for you. Ellie fixed him up nicely, but—"

A V creased Benjamin's brow as he interrupted Duncan. "Who?"

Duncan raised an eyebrow. "Miller."

"He's here? He's not dead? How? One of his friends showed up at the house and told Father he'd fallen in the river and drowned. When I came home Julius had been out looking for him. He's here?" Benjamin grabbed his medical bag from his horse.

Duncan wasn't sure what to think about Miller's "friend." Was Miller part of the threats against the Sims sisters? Or had he been used or coerced and then beaten to a pulp when things had gone too far? Duncan had no idea. He also had no idea if he could trust any of the Northrops. Including the man standing before him.

"He didn't drown," Duncan said. "Hamish found him out by the goats' pen. Before you see him, I must warn you about his condition. He'll live, but he's damaged."

Benjamin paled. "How bad?"

"A broken arm, perhaps a few broken ribs. It remains to be seen if his fingers can be saved."

Benjamin stalked toward the house.

"Benjamin, there's more." Duncan gritted his teeth, knowing what he was about to say wouldn't be easy to hear.

Benjamin halted. His long black coat billowed around his legs.

"On the afternoon of the attack, three riders tore up the fields. No real harm was done, as I was able to chase them off, but you must know, Miller was one of those men."

Benjamin squinted. "Did you harm my brother?"

Duncan shook his head. "I didn't know he was one of them until Hamish found him and brought him into the barn. Even if I had known I wouldn't have done anything more than secure him and let the law have him. You should know, there was an X carved into his face. Like a mark left on a signature note."

A puzzled look creased Benjamin's brow. "What are you saying?"

"I'm not certain. Somebody wants this land. I know Sims Creek has been a source of contention between your father and Hamish for years, and Camy believes the railroad has been behind the attacks here. What was done to your brother was more than a beating, it was personal. Is there anyone Miller owed money to, or your father?"

"I wish I knew. I've only recently returned to Kansas. Miller was a boy when I left. Did you ask him about it?"

"No. He's been groggy much of the time." He massaged his neck. "Besides, the girls don't know he was one of the riders. Until I had proof of the extent of his involvement, I thought it best to keep quiet."

"I appreciate that. No need to have further discord between our families at the moment."

"By the way, does your father smoke?" At Benjamin's nod, Duncan pulled the foil wrapper from his pocket and unfolded it. "Do you recognize this?"

"No. Should I?"

"This was left out in the field around a package of smokes." Duncan didn't want to tell him he knew of only one man who smoked this brand. It was best to keep as much as possible to himself until he unraveled the mystery. "Ellie's been keeping a close watch on Miller. She stitched him up real good, but I know she's been anxious for you to arrive."

They entered the cabin. Camy glanced up from the book she held in her hand. "Ben, I've never been so happy to see a doctor before. Ellie's resting a moment. She'll be relieved to know you're here." Camy stood and laid the book on the table.

"Please, let her rest." Benjamin removed his coat.

"Of course. Would you men like some coffee?"

"Yes, please." Benjamin hung his coat on a peg and pulled a chair next to his brother.

She poured them each a cup and then stirred herself a cup of chocolate.

"Are you two ready for tonight?" Benjamin asked, the small talk, no doubt, a distraction as he prepared himself to tend to his brother. "Mrs. Smith is over-the-moon that one of her protégés is finally getting married."

Camy choked, hot chocolate sputtering from her mouth. Duncan patted her on the back.

"Don't let it distress you," Benjamin said. "I believe she means well enough, but I don't relish the day she sets her sights on Bella."

"At least Bella will have Mara Jean by her side.

Let's hope Jamie Muster finds a wife before the girls become of age."

Duncan had met the young man a few days ago at the mercantile when he bought sweets for Camy. The banker's son had nearly knocked over the displays tripping over his feet as he tried to get out of the way of a pretty maid. Duncan couldn't imagine him holding court with bold and mischievous Mara, but perhaps Duncan needed to make it a point to start chaperoning his future sister.

"Let's hope. Perhaps Levina will grow fond of the young man." Benjamin's hands shook as he sifted through his bag.

The lighthearted chatter seemed to be an attempt to keep Benjamin from looking at his brother. Duncan could only imagine how he felt, having not grown up with siblings. It was torment when Camy lay in the exact same spot with only one minor wound.

"He isn't rich enough for her tastes," Camy said.

"I don't know that King Solomon would have been rich enough for Levina's tastes," Benjamin replied, his voice quivering as his eyes watered.

"Camy, may I speak with you a moment?" Duncan asked.

She pulled a shawl around her shoulders and followed him onto the porch. He closed the door behind them and tucked a stray curl behind her ear. "I believe Benjamin needed a moment alone with his brother. He seemed nervous to even look upon him."

She gazed at him through her spectacles, her lashes brushing against her cheeks. The steam from her hot chocolate swirled between them. She shivered in the morning air, so he wrapped his arm around her and pulled her close. Her head rested against his shoulder.

He could become used to this, the two of them in the quiet morning with nothing but the cluck of hens, bleating goats resonating in the air, Hound brushing between their legs and Uncle Tommy pecking at his boots. The feel of her softness snuggled against him, the smell of warm chocolate and rosewater.

"Is that all you wanted to speak to me about?" She blew on her chocolate.

He moistened his lips and then faced her, his hands on her arms. "We've negotiated and signed the agreement, but I have yet to ask you proper."

He dug the velvet bag out of his pocket. Untying the ribbon, he poured the ring into his palm and dropped to one knee. He took her hand in his and gazed up at her. "Camy, will you do me the honor of becoming my wife?"

Camy stared at the gold knotted band. The purple stone glinting in his hand. She had fancied this moment since she was a girl, but as she had become older she'd lost hope and here it was, better than she could ever have hoped for even if it was a farce. Why did it have to feel so real?

His tenderness and kindhearted caring pulled her close like the river on a hot summer's day. It was so natural between them, and right. At least for her. She'd forgotten her resolve to distance herself from him and gave in to the moment. The bond they had, the friendship. The sweetest of kisses. She couldn't bear the thought of Duncan fighting for his life, potentially losing it because she wanted to keep her home. His life was worth more than a piece of land. And without the land, there was no bargain. No business. No deal. No marriage.

The ring winked at her, mocking her heart. If she said no, he'd know she intended to break their agreement, and she didn't want that to happen until after the land was sold. She prayed Hamish would see to reason and help her. If she said yes, it'd be a lie. "I—it's beautiful, Duncan."

"It was my mother's, passed down from mother to daughter-in-law for five generations." He slipped it on her left ring finger as if Pastor Hammond was here requesting the action, and without her consent as if confident of her yes. Duncan drew up alongside her. She leaned in, clinging to his shirt, wanting to hold on to the love burning in her soul for him, but it was that very love which propelled her to let him go. Her heart crumbled.

She pulled away and held her hand out as far in front of her as she could without slipping it from the sling, branding the image in her mind to hold her for a lifetime. The aged gold shone in the morning light; the purple gem sparkled. The weight of it on her finger was foreign. It made her feel like she was a part of something, of someone. Of him.

"We can have it adjusted to your size after we're married if it's too big."

The woman who'd birthed this wonderful man had worn this ring. Five generations of women had worn this ring and she wondered how many of them were marriages in name only. How many had loved their husbands before they said their vows? And how many of them had intended to leave their future husband waiting at the altar because of that love? "Thank you, Duncan, for honoring me with such a gift. I only pray I'm worthy of it."

The words came out before she could take them back. Odd how she'd spent most of her life fearing rejection and yet here she was, about to reject this man's proposal. His protection.

"I could have captured the moon and the stars for you, Camy, and you would be worthy of such a gift."

"Ohhh," she sighed. Her knees wobbled. Her toes curled. Her insides churned and swirled, ebbed and flowed, like the frothy river rushing out of its banks. It was quickly doused by heavy guilt pricking her conscience. She slipped the ring off, handed it to Duncan and grasped hold of the post holding the porch for support. How many times had she listened to her sisters giggling, trying to outdo each other with their romantic tales of chivalrous men? And here she was, experiencing a real romance that would bury theirs far from their memories. If only she could share it, keeping it with her forever. "Will you hold on to this until this evening? I would hate to lose it."

Especially since she never intended to marry him. He needed to save it for a real wife, one who would have more than just his name. A wife who wouldn't ask him to risk his life to save her home.

"Of course," he said, tucking it back into the velvet bag. "I would like to leave a little sooner than we'd discussed. I have business to tend to before the party."

Early suited her. Perhaps Mr. Weston would arrive at Mrs. Smith's early. "That is fine. I'm certain Mrs. Smith will wish to fuss over my hair before her guests arrive."

"They should be *your* guests." Duncan laughed. "I've asked Hamish to stand beside me and be a witness. I hope you don't mind."

"No. This is all his doing. It's only right he be in attendance."

"Shall we check on Benjamin and Miller? He was elated to hear Miller was even alive after thinking he'd drowned in the river, but he was obviously unprepared for Miller's injuries even though I tried to explain them to him." Camy listened to him as he told her all that had transpired, including the elder Northrop's apoplexy.

"I'm sorry for it, I am, but he has been a thorn in our side since I can remember."

"Camy," he said, his eyebrows dipping. "Do you know why Northrop wants this land?"

"I never asked. Hamish would know, though. Why?"

"I was just thinking, wondering if he might have had something to do with the attacks."

"Don't be silly. He can barely get around. His sons often carry him from place to place."

"He could have hired someone."

"No, although Hamish might agree with you, and even though the doctor has been a prickly thorn, he wouldn't cause or threaten harm to anyone, especially his own son."

"I didn't get the impression he was that kind of man. Besides Miller, Benjamin and Julius seem to be of good character. Even now Julius is caring for their father. I guess that leaves your railroad theory."

"It's not a theory when the man who came calling claimed to be with the railroad," Camy said. "I know you think he might be an imposter, but why do you think it's not any of them?"

"I've told you, I know some of the financiers and some of the men on the committee."

"You know them well enough?" She knew Miller, had known him for years, but after last night and Duncan's questions, she did wonder if he might be involved in trying to take her land.

"Some."

"So it's possible?"

He shifted his weight. "Yes."

"I should have listened to my sisters and convinced Hamish to sell the land before it came this far. Poor Miller will be scarred for life, bearing the mark that should have been meant for me."

"Don't say that, Camy. You don't know that for certain. Miller's attack may not even be related to what's been going on here."

"Then why was he here?"

"I've wondered that myself, but I think Miller is the only one who can answer that question."

She had wondered why Miller had been here. And maybe Duncan was right, maybe Miller's attack had nothing to do with Sims Creek, but something told her otherwise. At first, she'd thought the rotters hurt him to gain her cooperation. Perhaps, thinking they were to be married instead of her and Duncan. But now she wondered, Miller had coveted this land and had tried all sorts of tactics to gain her hand in marriage to get it. Surely he wouldn't have hired ruffians to leave him for dead, would he? There were too many questions to ask Miller when he woke up.

"Why do you think Miller asked you to forgive him?" she said.

Duncan massaged the back of his neck. He shifted his eyes to the fields. "His words were nothing more than mumbles. It's possible he didn't know he was talking to me."

"What aren't you t-telling me, Mr. Murray?"

He grumbled. "When will you stop calling me that?"

"When you s-start acting like a husband." She held her hand to stop him from moving closer. "My sisters and I have been on our own for quite some time. We've been dealing with men who think we are incapable of gathering eggs long before you came along, so please do not insult me by treating me like an imbecile, and do not, I beg you, try to distract me from the matter at hand. I am a grown woman. I can handle hard truths. What aren't you telling me?"

He adjusted his hat lower on his brow. "I don't have all the facts, Camy. I don't want to accuse an innocent man of something he's not guilty of. I've experienced such things and it wasn't pleasant having a man accuse me of compromising his daughter when I had never seen her before."

She sighed inwardly, frustrated that she wanted to know everything, but also knowing Duncan's honor would keep him from accusing an innocent man of wrongdoing. "What facts do you have?"

"That's it, I don't, only a suspicion that Miller was one of the men tearing up the field yesterday."

After spending the last two nights pondering Miller's actions, she had expected this truth, but it still fired her veins. She flew across the porch. Duncan grabbed hold of her before she could open the door.

"Camy, this is exactly why I didn't want to tell you. There are too many possibilities. He's young. He and his friends may not have been involved with the fires. He could have been reacting with a scorned heart, nothing more."

She searched his eyes. "Do you believe that?"

"I honestly don't know, sweetheart. I honestly don't know."

She wanted to know. Needed to know. If Miller had been the one behind the attacks, there was no need to visit with Mr. Weston. "I choose to believe he wasn't involved. What about his face, his arm? His fingers? Duncan, what sorts of friends do that to a man?"

"The kind who aren't friends. Maybe the kind who believe he owed them something." Removing his hat, he thrust his fingers through his hair. "I don't know, Camy. I could be wrong."

She hoped he was wrong, but couldn't help wondering if Duncan was right. Miller had become obsessed with gaining her hand in marriage over the last year. She hoped they found out the truth before the engagement party, as there was a possibility Mr. Weston wouldn't be in attendance. And if she couldn't convince Hamish to tear up the contract between him and Duncan and sell to another, she'd end up standing in front of Pastor Hammond, next to Duncan. She didn't want Duncan to marry her needlessly. And she didn't want to marry a man only to bury him. "What are we going to do?"

"We're going to pray."

He held her hand and bowed his head. She listened

to the prayer, but all she could think about was the prayer dominating her heart, a prayer of hope, one with a happy ending. One without her standing over fresh dirt and a grave marker.

Chapter Eighteen

After dinner, Camy and her sisters packed up the buckboard with the gowns they'd chosen to wear for the wedding, along with several pies for the reception afterward. Other than carrying one of the trunks, Duncan's attempts at helping were waved off. He stood in amazement watching the three of them in constant motion, even stopping on the occasion to check on Benjamin and his brother. Although Miller's condition seemed to be improving, he had yet to wake, causing Benjamin and Ellie to wonder if there were unseen injuries to his head.

Leaning his elbows against the side rail of the buckboard, Duncan waited for the trio to return, which gave him time to think about their future. He must learn to control the impulse to seek her out without warrant. Seemed his mind continually came up with excuses to be in her presence. Like now, did she need help donning her coat? Was that why she hadn't appeared as quickly as she should?

He heard Hamish's uneven gait come from behind him. "I thought ye might be needin' this," he said, tucking the violin case beside the trunk holding Camy's gown.

"I appreciate the concern, my friend." Duncan pushed his derby up with the tip of his finger, no longer shielding his eyes. "But I think I'll be occupied keeping watch over your niece."

"Ach, ye best be doin' more than that." Hamish squinted. "Something's not right. She's got her mind set on something, and it ain't marrying."

The hard kick in Duncan's gut confirmed the niggling that had prickled at the base of his neck ever since she handed him back the ring. A hollow determination had overtaken the glimmering gaze, and indifference had cloaked her like quills on a porcupine. She'd tried to act like an excited bride, and he'd even thought for a moment she might be reacting to nerves, but he'd seen the far-off stares as if she were in deep thought, calculating her next move. "What do you think she plans?"

"Considering she asked me how much I'd sell the land fer," Hamish said around a piece of hay stuck between his teeth, "she's lookin' fer a way outta yer bargain, and here I thought you courted her proper. Fer the record, Sims Creek is yers."

The land didn't matter. There were other tracts he could purchase, houses in town he could buy, but none of them had her. Only Sims Creek. He meant what he'd said, he'd fight for her, fight for them.

"And fer another record, Camy girl will cut off her own foot if she thought it'd save a man. She might not like Miller none too much, but what happened to him shook all them girls up."

Before Duncan could ponder Hamish's words,

Benjamin shouldered his way through the door of the cabin, bearing yet another trunk. The ladies piled out behind him and onto the porch in a cacophony of animated chatter. Their dresses, varying shades of spring, looked like a bouquet of flowers in front of the ash-colored log cabin. Camy's, the shade of a heather field in full bloom, caused her sisters' to pale in comparison.

"Ain't they pretty?" Hamish shuffled away from the buckboard. "Mind my words, keep her by yer side. No tellin' what she's got cookin' in that brain of hers."

Duncan's meeting with Deputy Cooper posed a problem. He wanted to hear what Nate had discovered before he told Camy anything more about Miller's involvement. Jumping into the driver's seat, Duncan pulled the buckboard alongside the bottom step. Benjamin deposited the trunk into the back, then helped Ellie and Mara settle on the trunks. Duncan assisted Camy onto the bench seat, then climbed up beside her.

"Thank you for riding out to the house and telling Julius about Miller," Benjamin said, handing him a rifle.

"I wish I could have done more. We can only hope Julius can get through to your father," Duncan said as he rested the rifle next to his leg.

Tilting her head, Camy peered at him from beneath the rim of her white-lace cap. "Are we expecting trouble?"

Duncan flipped the reins, propelling the old sway-back mare into motion. "Were we expecting trouble the other day?"

Her mouth firmed into a straight line as she stared straight ahead. Her pert button nose lifted a notch.

"You don't act like a lady about to become a bride."

Her eyes darted toward him, then back to the worn tracks ahead of them. "M-most brides have grander notions of love."

"And you don't?"

Her fingers knotted into the folds of her skirt, the only hint besides the occasional stutter she wasn't confident in their current predicament. "We have an agreement, a business deal. As I recall, love is not a requirement, nor was it mentioned."

His fingers itched to take her hand, to reassure her all would be well between them. If her sling hadn't been in the way, keeping her shielded from him, he wouldn't have just held her hand. No, he would have wrapped his arm around her shoulders and glued her to his side. The prospect of her trying to weasel out of their deal soured his stomach, made him want to ensure that there was no way around it. Made him want to take her straightway to Pastor Hammond's home and demand they marry immediately. He leaned close enough to whisper near her ear. "As I recall, neither were kisses."

Her cheeks turned a pretty rosy hue, causing his breath to catch. Conspiring giggles drifted from the back, the sisters' heads bent together. Duncan wondered if they were conspiring against him or for him. As long as Miss Sims became Mrs. Murray before the evening was out, he didn't care.

Hamish rode up beside them on Millie. "Gonna check things out up ahead. Keep outta the ruts. Don't need ye stuck in the mud before ye're hitched." Whistling a jaunty tune, Hamish bounced ahead of them. The old man's earlier warning remained with him like a festering splinter.

"What are your plans?"

She paled. "T-tonight?"

"Yes, Miss Sims, tonight." Would she outright lie to him, skirt the truth or avoid the topic altogether?

"You're to drop us at Mrs. Smith's so we can get ready for the party."

Skirting the truth as he suspected she would. Camy wasn't one to lie, he knew that, but he was discovering that when she got her mind set on something, she was as stubborn as Hamish's mule and would find a way to carry out her plans, unless he did something drastic. She turned from him and stared out across the greening hillside while he contemplated their course of action when they entered town. It seemed Pastor Hammond's would be their first stop, whether she and her sisters agreed or not. The sooner she became his bride, the sooner he could set her aside and focus on the other pressing issue. Calvin Weston and Miller Northrop.

Camy hadn't heard her sisters chatter with such excitement since before the attacks began, since before Benjamin broke off his engagement with Ellie. Perhaps Mara would one day find love and a romance to rival the fairy tales dancing in her head. Their whispers carried to Camy's ears like a chick's call to its mother, stirring guilt deep in the pit of her stomach. They couldn't wait to dress Camy in their mother's gown and watch her become Mrs. Duncan Murray. Her poor sisters would be sorely disappointed if there wasn't a wedding.

As Duncan pulled up on the reins, halting the nag, she realized they weren't at Mrs. Smith's house but rather parked in front of Pastor Hammond's home. Her sisters' hushed conversation about Camy's upcoming nuptials came to an immediate quiet. Cheery tweets and whistles from birds perched in a nearby bush mocked her inner turmoil. The sucking and plopping of Millie's hooves as Hamish ambled beside them.

Setting the brake, Duncan dropped the reins to the floorboard and jumped to the ground. With her jaw slack, she watched him lift her sisters out of the wagon, keeping their feet from touching the mud, then strode to her side of the buckboard. "Are you ready, sweetheart?" He held his hand out to her.

"For?" She purred like the barn cats begging for goat's milk and batted her lashes. Once. Twice. Exact intervals as Mrs. Smith had suggested, as it was a sure way to distract a man if he was about mischief, and it was clear Mr. Duncan Murray was about mischief. Without waiting for her response, he scooped her from her seat, cradling her against his broad chest. Her palm rested against the thundering of his heartbeat. The air in her lungs conveniently chose that moment to catch, leaving her breathless and thoroughly distracted from all thoughts.

"To become my bride."

She squirmed. If she had a rifle she'd shoot him good. It'd be better for him to suffer from a lead ball than wind up like Miller. The dratted man didn't know what was good for him. How was she supposed to contact Mr. Weston about the land, if she was here? Marrying Duncan. "We were to marry at the party. What about my friends?"

"As I recall, you despise parties, and I'm guessing

it's because you don't like many of the people who attend Mrs. Smith's social gatherings."

"Ye got that right, son." Hamish snickered.

She glared at Duncan, despising how well he knew her. She looked at Ellie for help, but her sister quickly pretended to pick at a speck of dirt from Mara's dress. And it was obvious Mara would be of no help with her eyes all dreamylike as if her head were in the clouds. Duncan climbed the three steps to Hammond's front door and rapped his knuckles against the thick wood. He didn't even have the gentlemanly decency to set her on her feet.

Pastor Hammond swept open his door with a toothy grin.

"My gown?"

"Will be fine." Adjusting her in his arms, he held out a hand to the Pastor Hammond, whose shock of blond hair hung over his eyes. "Hello, something's come up and I'm anxious to marry my bride." Duncan set her on her feet, his palm spread over the small of her back like a yoke.

"What about your meeting with your friend?" She squirmed.

"That can wait."

"I'm not ready."

Determination set in his eyes as his gaze roamed over her face. His fingers swept a lock of hair behind her ear and down her back. He leaned in, his mouth capturing hers. The gentle, lingering kiss demanded that she yield, accepting his proposition, demanded that her mind give way to her heart and risk all he had to offer, even if he promised no words of love, even if it meant he'd end up like Miller or worse.

"Oh my!" Mrs. Hammond's shocked voice pulled Duncan's lips away, but his gaze remained locked with hers.

"I'd say ye're more'n ready, Camy girl." Hamish chuckled.

Her face burning, the misty haze filling her vision cleared. Her focus dead center on Duncan. She narrowed her gaze as she could almost hear the word tumbling in Mr. Murray's head, *checkmate.*

She might not have fancied herself becoming the wife of such a handsome man with an obstinate streak as wide as Rusa River, but here she stood with Duncan's arm anchoring her to his side. Her mother's beautiful gown, which Ellie had spent numerous hours altering while keeping watch over Miller, lay tucked in her mother's trunk in the back of the buckboard, all the while she wore a mud-speckled lavender gown, much too big for her frame. At least it would match the ring he intended to brand her with as he put it on her finger.

Even though she'd discarded her sisters' romantic tales as foolish wastes of time, she mourned the inability to feel like a princess on her wedding day. And all because Duncan Murray had somehow seen right through her plans, had known she sought a way out of their deal. He didn't need to say a word; she knew he knew, she felt it in the anger vibrating in his muscles, saw it in his eyes. They were here, in Mrs. Hammond's living room instead of Mrs. Smith's parlor, two hours before the set time, all because he wanted to secure their bargain. To secure the land reminding him of his childhood, a home he'd tried to forget. "I—I need to freshen up."

"Of course you do, dear," Mrs. Hammond said with her hand resting on top of her belly swollen with child, her soft motherly voice and support easing Camy's nerves. As the pastor's wife pulled Camy down a narrow hallway, she gave in to the urge to glance over her shoulder at the man, then quickened her steps as if running from a rabid dog. "My apologies it's not more private, but there's a mirror and a washbasin in the corner. Would you like me to help, or send one of your sisters in?"

Chewing on her bottom lip, she shook her head.

"All right, then, I'll leave you." Her soft honeyed ringlets bounced around her shoulders. "By the way, dear, you look ravishing. It's no wonder Mr. Murray is anxious to marry you."

Dipping her head to hide her embarrassment, Camy waited for Mrs. Hammond to pull the door closed behind her, then stole a glance at her reflection in the floor-length mirror, a luxury they'd never had. The woman staring back at her with familiar dark eyes seemed foreign, unknown to her. Gone was the thin-faced little girl with prominent brown spots speckling her cheeks like a raccoon's. Her freckles remained visible, but they weren't the dominant feature of her face. She tugged the bonnet from her head and gasped as her hair tumbled in wild disarray around her shoulders and down her back, no longer the drab color of dirt, strands glinted like copper and gold. She was almost…*pretty*.

She rested her hand against her queasy stomach and drew in several deep breaths. Could it be Duncan actually found her attractive? That it wasn't just the land he desired? It would take more than seeing her reflection and a few stolen kisses to convince her his intentions were more than sealing their agreement. Besides, it didn't matter if he had feelings for her or not, her love for him wouldn't place him at the mercy of low-life scoundrels seeking to bring her harm through people she cared about.

Falling into an upholstered armchair, Camy looked at the ceiling. An image of Miller pressed into her thoughts. His swollen eyes had left him unrecognizable. The cut on his cheek would leave a scar, reminding him every day of his connection with her and Sims Creek, not to mention the possible loss of his fingers if infection took over. If Miller hadn't been involved, and her heart told her he hadn't, then someone meant to send her a personal message. Sitting up, she buried her face into her hand. How could she speak vows to Duncan, till death do us part, knowing full well he could die tomorrow, or even tonight?

There had to be a way out of this mess. As if an answer to her dilemma, Mrs. Hammond's sheer yellow curtains rippled with the breeze coming through the open window. Springing out of the chair, she skirted around the bed and shoved the window open farther. She sat on the edge, preparing to swing her legs outside, when a light knock tapped on the door. Camy slipped out of the window and directly into a pair of strong arms.

"Hello, sweetheart."

Heart pounding, she waited for him to say something more, to do something. "You left Pastor Hammond waiting."

"I know."

"You left your family waiting."

"I know."

Leaning back, he gazed into her eyes. The look lassoed around her heart and squeezed. "You left me waiting."

"I'm sorry," she whispered, her body trembling.

"Don't," he said, touching a finger to her bottom lip. "If I thought we didn't suit each other, I'd let you go, but we both know better. You know better."

She did, and she wanted to be his wife. A wife with more than his name. A wife who would own his heart, not a gravestone.

"Do you trust me?"

"I do." She did trust him. She trusted him more than she trusted anyone, including her own sisters.

"I suggest you freshen yourself as you implied to Mrs. Hammond and you meet me in the parlor. Promptly."

He helped her back into Mrs. Hammond's bedroom. As her feet touched the hardwood floor, she wiped her palm along the front of her skirt.

"Camy," he said, his deep timbre causing her to jump.

She glanced at him over her shoulder wondering if he was going to watch her until she left the room. "I trust you won't test me. I don't want to chase you down, but I will."

He disappeared, leaving nothing but an open field framed by the white window frame, draped with the yellow curtains. Shoulders sagging, she blew out a ragged breath. "Lord, why does the man have to be so stubborn?"

"Isn't it obvious?" Ellie's soft voice filtered from the doorway, frightening Camy. "You didn't answer. I was worried and came in. Why are you all of a sudden resistant to the marriage you agreed upon? It's not like you to go against your word."

Camy straightened her spine, her skirts swishing as she strode toward the washbasin. Pouring water into her hands, she splashed her face to cool her heated cheeks. "I don't know what you're talking about. We were to be married at Mrs. Smith's in two hours."

Ellie's reflection appeared beside hers. "Here. There. Now. Later. What difference does it make? The sooner, the less likely anything will occur to keep you from saying your vows. But I have a feeling that is what you were hoping for. Why, Camy, when it's obvious you love him?"

Tears brimming on her lashes, for both Ellie's loss and her own, she turned toward her sister. "Enough to want him safe."

"Oh, sister," Ellie said, pulling her into a hug. "You cannot control the actions of others. What happened to Miller was not your fault." She leaned back and swiped the tears from Camy's cheeks. "If you haven't noticed, your groom is quite brawny and more than capable of taking care of himself, and he's done a right fine job caring for you and the farm."

Sighing, she said, "He has."

"For better or worse, that man is committing himself to you and expecting you to hold to the promise you made when you signed the agreement to do the same. And I'm guessing, by the sound of Pastor and Mrs. Hammond's squeaking floorboards and the forlorn glances he kept darting toward the hallway, he would give Sims Creek away if it meant making you happy." Ellie ran her hand over Camy's hair. "He's been running from shadows so long he's ready to stand and fight, not because he's tired, but because he's found something worth fighting for, dear sister. You've just got to give him time for his mind to catch up with his heart."

He said he'd fight for her, for them. Because he kept his word? Because he had a misguided sense of loyalty? Because he had strong affections for her? Did it matter as long as she bore his name, became his wife? Was his determination enough?

"Now, let's get your cheeks scrubbed rosy before your groom tears down the door and drags you to the altar."

Chapter Nineteen

Duncan rolled his neck, releasing the built-up tension, when he heard the door open and close, but he didn't release the breath he'd been holding until the hem of her lavender gown appeared from the hallway.

"Thought I was gonna have to fetch one of the docs, son." Hamish's gravelly whisper forced a laugh from Pastor Hammond.

"One of the prettiest brides ever." Mrs. Hammond blotted her eyes with a handkerchief.

Even with her red-rimmed eyes she was the prettiest bride. None of the ladies who'd vied for his attention back in Topeka, hoping for access to his bank account, came close to the one walking toward him. She had no flowers in her hand, no veil covering her face, and he silently prayed she didn't mind. Perhaps he should have waited, to give her time to change into the rose-colored gown, but something in his gut, along with Hamish's warning in his head, cautioned him.

Coming up beside him, she took her sling off her neck and handed it to Ellie. Trembling fingers reached for his, intertwining them. The gesture set his mind at ease, gave him peace. Even though she was scared, she trusted him, and that was all he'd asked of her. "Are you all right?"

The corners of her mouth turned upward, her dark eyes shone with trust and something more he didn't want to examine, melting layers of steel long ago forged with bitterness. Pastor Hammond hadn't spoken a word, and yet he already felt united to her, as one flesh.

"Mr. Duncan Graham Murray and Cameron Andrena Sims," Pastor Hammond said, wasting not another moment. "Marriage is an important bond of two souls becoming one, producing children, going forth and multiplying God's earth as He commanded Noah in His Word."

Duncan shifted, surprised he didn't feel the need to drop her hand like a hot poker. Images of rosy-cheeked little girls with freckles and chubby-legged little boys with brown eyes pressed into his mind. And he didn't mind one bit. In fact, he quite looked forward to bouncing them on his shoulders.

"Do you, Hamish Sims, stand as a true and honest witness to this union?"

"Aye."

"Do you, Ellie Sims, stand as a true and honest witness to this union?"

"I do."

"Duncan Murray, do you take this woman to be your wife, to comfort her, honor her, to keep her in health and sickness?"

"I do."

"Do you promise to love her, forsaking all others for as long as you both shall live?"

His heart leaped, kicking against the wall of his chest, and he knew it was a promise he could keep. "I do."

"Cameron Sims, will you serve this man as a true helpmate, to honor him and keep him in health and sickness?"

"I do."

"Do you promise to love him, forsaking all others as long as you both shall live?"

"I do," she said, tears spilling down her cheeks.

"Now repeat after me."

"We promise to have and to hold, from this day forward for better or worse, rich or poor, until death do part us."

Turning toward her, Duncan crooked his finger beneath her chin and gazed into her eyes. He wanted to look into her eyes as they spoke their vows in unison.

"We promise," they said, their voices in perfect accord. "To have and to hold, from this day forward, for better or worse, rich or poor."

Duncan squeezed her fingers. Pausing, she blinked at him. "To love, honor and cherish," he said.

"To love, honor and cherish," she whispered as she swiped at a lone tear.

"Until death do part us," he said, wondering if she believed his words. Praying she meant hers.

Squeezing her eyes closed, her fingers tightened around his as if she were trying to keep him from leaving. "Until death do part us."

The emptiness in her eyes drew him closer, but Pastor Hammond clucked his tongue. "First, the ring, Mr. Murray."

"Oh." Duncan pulled the velvet bag from his pocket,

and as he'd done earlier in the morning he untied the ribbon and slid the ring into the palm of his hand. Earlier it had meant something, now it meant even more. The ring warmed against his palm. He took her left hand in his. As he slipped it on her finger, he said, "Cameron Sims, with this ring I wed thee."

His heart jumped into his throat at the sight of the shy, yet bold, courageous woman standing before him. His wife. *His wife.*

"Ellie, do you have something?" Pastor Hammond asked.

Stepping in front of them, Ellie drew three pieces of ribbon from her skirt pocket. A brown one matching the bows on their mother's wedding dress, a color matching the gem on the ring, and a pure white one. "We have a traditional blessing passed down through our family." With Camy's fingers still held in his, Ellie took the ribbon and twined it around their hands. "Like the wedding band forms an exact circle, so shall peace reign in your marriage. May there be nothing missing and nothing broken. May your home be filled with love and laughter, and may you always remember to keep God the Father as a cord binding you together. As Ecclesiasties four and twelve says, a threefold cord is not quickly broken."

After what seemed like a long testing of his patience, Pastor Hammond declared an amen. "Mr. Murray, you may now kiss your bride."

Now that it was over, Camy was glad the ceremony had been small and private. One of the reasons she disliked Mrs. Smith's social gatherings had to do with the woman putting Camy and her sisters on display for every eligible bachelor and then flaunting their faults as she spoke highly of her own daughters. She couldn't imagine the debacle had they waited to marry in front of all Rusa Valley and Mrs. Smith's distinguished guests. Camy already had a time fighting the tears as he'd promised to love her with his affectionate gaze boring into the core of her being. The words may have been a pretense for Pastor Hammond and his wife, but she knew her sisters would be recanting the tale with timely sighs for months, possibly years, to come. She would. Too bad the story wouldn't be passed to her daughters as her own mother's wedding tale had been.

Of course, if they'd waited, there would have been no wedding, and she wouldn't now be Mrs. Duncan Murray.

"Are you ready to go to Mrs. Smith's?" His palm warmed the small of her back.

The urgency propelling her to seek out Mr. Weston no longer existed. Only the overwhelming possibility of losing her husband. "Yes, of course."

They gave their farewells to Pastor Hammond and his wife and thanked them for performing the service. Camy prayed Mrs. Hammond, plump with child, would decide to show up at the party even though it was far from fashionable. Selfishly, Camy wanted a friend there for support, as her sisters would most likely run interference with Levina and Mrs. Smith.

Once they arrived at Mrs. Smith's mansion on the north side of Rusa Valley, they were ushered into rooms on the upper floors in order to get ready for the party. Camy and her sisters on one end, Duncan on the other. No sooner had the maid slipped out the room than a rap of knuckles sounding on the door had her heart skittering to a halt. She cracked the door open and was met with a wide grin and twinkling green eyes the color of a patch of moss. Gone was his coat. Shirtsleeves rolled up, baring the sinewy muscles of his arms.

"Hi," he said, bracing his forearm on the frame of the door.

"Hi." Her lashes fell as her pulse raced and her knees wobbled.

Camy's head spun with a longing to be worthy of his sacrifice.

"Mr. and Mrs. Murray," Ellie chided, swinging the door wide. "There will be time enough for conversation later." Ellie grabbed her arm and dragged her back into the room, the door clicking in Duncan's face.

Ellie collapsed in one of the armchairs, upholstered in a claret velvet, and giggled. "I've never seen anyone so over-the-moon before."

"My mark is set high above the stars now." Mara swooned on the bed in a dramatic sigh, hand on her forehead.

"Honest, Ellie and Mara, I can't help it."

"I'm not talking about you, dear sister."

"Nope. He's been struck by a bolt of the *looooove* lightning."

Could it be? Had he fallen in love with her? Was that why he moved the wedding up two hours sooner? She gazed at the door, wondering if he stood on the other side waiting for her.

"Mara Jean, don't be so dramatic. I declare if Rusa Valley had a theater you'd be not only the talk of the county, but everyone's darling. Now," Ellie said, pushing to her feet. "Let's prepare your sister to meet her groom."

As Ellie fastened the last pearl button on their mother's gown, Mrs. Smith swept into the room. Her gray ringlets bounced at her shoulders as she came to an abrupt stop with her hand plastered to her chest.

"Dear child," Mrs. Smith said as Camy prepared herself for the insults surely to come her way. "I never thought to find you stunning. Look at you." She turned Camy in a circle. "The gown is far outdated, and your hair. Oh dear, I suppose we can't rid ourselves of the bandage on your shoulder, can we? Well, I guess there is nothing more to be done, since you were late in your arrival. Perhaps I have a shawl you can borrow. Mary, bring me my shawls."

Mrs. Smith called to her maid. Standing back, she rested her chin on her fist and clucked. "At least remove your spectacles, child." Before Camy could protest, Mrs. Smith had removed her spectacles and slipped them into her pocket. "Certainly you can see without them. We wouldn't want you to seem bookish and boring, not when you're the guest of honor."

"Mrs. Smith," Ellie said. "You wouldn't want Camy to fall down your stairs."

Knowing the futility of getting Mrs. Smith to change her mind, she gave her sister a sympathetic smile. At least she wouldn't see everyone staring at her if she did.

"Oh, poppycock." Mrs. Smith smoothed one of Camy's curls over her ear. "She'll be on the arm of her fiancé. By the bye, how did you ever convince such a handsome man to marry you? Rumor has it he's the one who shot you. I suppose men have married for stranger things than guilt."

Flinching, as if she'd been slapped on the face, Camy spun from the older woman and immediately whacked her knee on the corner of the bed.

"Child, do be careful. Now," she said, pausing. "Which of these best suits the occasion?"

"I don't need to cover my injury. Not when the entire town knows about it." Camy sat on the edge of the bed.

"Again, poppycock. Out of sight, out of mind. They'll forget all about it if they don't see it. The conversation needs to be about your upcoming nuptials, not how you coerced the man into marrying you."

Insult upon insult. How would she survive the evening? Fortunately Mrs. Smith didn't know they'd already married and Camy preferred to keep it that way, else the sugarcoated venom would, no doubt, be worse. Many times Camy smiled and nodded, or found a corner to hide rather than argue. She didn't want lectures from a woman who'd been less than teary-eyed when her husband perished from a heart attack. Camy didn't want to judge, but Mr. Smith had seemed nice enough, too jolly at times, but she couldn't imagine not mourning a man she'd been married to for as long as the two had been married. She couldn't imagine not mourning Duncan, and she'd been his wife less than two hours.

"Mrs. Smith," Camy said as she fortified her backbone. "Thank you for throwing us this party."

"Of course, of course. It's the least I can do. You poor dears, with no parents." She dabbed at her eyes. "I know I shouldn't, but I do pity you darlings. After all, the Good Book has commanded us to look after orphans."

Ellie's eyes narrowed and Mara's fist clenched at her side. No matter how intimidated Camy felt around the older woman, she couldn't hold her tongue. "And widows too. Perhaps we can find a charitable means to pity you as well, Mrs. Smith."

The *poor dear* quit flapping around like a duck, not that Camy could see much beyond shadows. She'd do about anything to have her spectacles, but had she been wearing them, she wouldn't have had the courage to say what she had to Mrs. Smith.

"Hmph," Mrs. Smith grunted as she turned toward the door.

"Mrs. S-Smith," Camy said, halting her. "You wouldn't want me to embarrass you by spilling punch on your carpet, would you?"

Camy imagined Mrs. Smith's face paled beneath her rouge. "You dare?"

"Of course not." Camy held out her hand. "However, I fear it's a risk you take if you don't return my spectacles posthaste."

Mrs. Smith deposited Camy's spectacles into her palm. The swift click of the door as it closed behind the woman cut off the angry swish of silk. Camy slid the wire rims into place, releasing the tension in her head from squinting.

"You've done it now. We'll never be invited to another one of her parties. How will I ever find a beau?" Mara fell into a fit of giggles. "I know, I'll ask the most handsome and richest eligible bachelors to shoot at me, and whoever hits the mark wins a bride."

"Don't be silly, Mrs. Smith wouldn't feel superior if

she didn't have anyone to demean, so of course she'll keep inviting us. Besides, she loves eating Camy's pies," Ellie said as she primped Camy's hair. "You are beautiful, Cameron. You're stunning in Mama's dress. Don't let Mrs. Smith's jealous insecurities tell you otherwise. Duncan Murray is one happy husband, and he wouldn't be if he married you out of guilt."

"I know. It still doesn't take the sting out of her words."

"Remember who you are," Ellie said. "You're a Sims by blood and a Murray by name. You have a heart filled with love and kindness, and you're loved by those who love you. And that, dear sister, is much more than being a Smith who lives in a mansion."

"Thank you, Ellie and Mara. I love you very much."

They joined in a group hug, and then Ellie started crying. "I am proud of you, Camy. I know marrying Duncan is a frightening thing, but you'll find your feet and we'll be here for you whenever you need us."

"Thank you for sacrificing so we can keep our home," Mara added.

"I thought you hated the farm." She hadn't considered marrying Duncan a sacrifice, even if theirs was only a marriage of convenience. She just prayed God would help them discover who had hurt Miller before anyone else came to harm.

"I used to, but with Duncan helping to do the chores, I don't mind it," Mara said, twirling a strand of hair around her finger.

"I'll admit, it is nice having a man help do the things we couldn't," Camy said as she stood. She shook out her gown and drew in a long breath as she adjusted her spectacles and opened the door. A new resolve came over her, a sense that all would be fine, right as rain as Duncan would say. She didn't know what the future would bring, but she was as ready for it as she'd ever be. "I think I'm ready to fetch my husband."

Ellie and Mara each gave her a hug, then swept down the stairs arm in arm, their heads bowed together in conversation. Camy slowed her pace as she neared Duncan's room. Staring at the white wainscoting door trimmed in powder blue, she willed her pulse to slow and raised her shaking hand to knock. She pressed her palm to her trembling stomach as she waited for Duncan to open his door.

"Hello, Mrs. Murray," Duncan said as he stepped out into the hallway.

"H-hcllo." All the bravado she had felt minutes before rushed to her toes, and she almost wished she'd allowed Mrs. Smith to keep possession of her spectacles. She'd thought Duncan handsome before in simple homespun garments, but now he stole the very breath from her, leaving her light-headed and at a loss for words. Hair slicked back from his brow. His jawline freshly shaven. Black trousers, a black frock coat and a vest nearly the exact color of her gown, he looked fashionable. Modern.

Mrs. Smith's words spun in her head. Mama's gown, hugging her curves in all the right places, thanks to Ellie's handiwork, paled in comparison. Nausea building in her stomach, she took a step back. "I—uh."

He captured her elbow, the warmth of his fingers sliding down her arm. Grasping her hand, he pulled her into his arms, wrapping them around her. Her cheek rested against the thudding of his heart, his chin atop her head.

"You look as though you're about to climb out a window." His deep timbre rumbled through her.

Trembling, she leaned back and gazed into his probing green eyes. "We d-don't suit."

The corners of his mouth turned upward. His eyes twinkled. "Why do you say that?"

"I'm a p-poor orphaned farm girl wearing her mother's outd-dated wedding gown."

"You're more beautiful than any I've laid eyes on, inside and out."

Her cheeks warmed at his compliment. "You should marry within your social ranks."

"But I'm already married." Winking, he lifted her left hand to his mouth and kissed the ring he'd placed on her finger a little over an hour before.

"Duncan," she said, turning out of his arms. "I'm being serious."

"As am I, sweetheart," he said, scooping her back into his embrace, his eyes searching hers. "And I intend to keep it that way, even if I have to give all my fortunes to charities to make you happy."

Certainly he joked, but she wondered just the same. "You would do that?"

The hum of conversation from the guests entering Mrs. Smith's home filtered up the stairs. Ellie's quiet "how do you dos" and Mara's giggles as they greeted individuals stirred her uneasiness. Soon they'd be called down. Soon she'd face Rusa Valley and the whispers of how she manipulated a brawny, handsome man with money enough to buy their entire town into marrying her. A man who coveted Sims Creek, enough to take on the burdens of the farm, and she, like one of the livestock, came with the property.

"For you."

Those two words tied her insides in a knot, just as they had done when he said he'd fight for her. Had he meant on her behalf, or had he meant for her? None of that mattered, as she couldn't remove Mrs. Smith's words from her thoughts. She had wanted to marry Duncan, had vowed to love him, to honor him, and she'd done so with everything in her. However, Duncan had seen their marriage as a business opportunity. Which was worse, being married for guilt or for business? "Mrs. Smith says you're only marrying me out of a sense of guilt. I guess I'm preying on your goodness."

Laughter burst from him. "If she knew me so well, she'd know I'm not easily swayed. Many a young lady has tried, and not one has succeeded."

"How many did you shoot?" She twisted her lips, knowing the truth. The other ladies might have tried to marry Duncan, while she didn't, as she hadn't been looking for, nor had she wanted, a husband, but the tactic worked nonetheless.

Sobering, he shook his head. "Only you, sweetheart, and I'm sorry for it, and yet I'm not. When Hamish first proposed I marry, I became enraged. He'd played me like no matchmaking mother I'd come across, luring me in with the promise of land full of vibrant green hills like my childhood home. He knew I didn't want to marry, that I emphatically planned to never marry. If you hadn't been injured, I never would have stuck around long enough to realize how well we're suited to each other."

"You're certain you wouldn't prefer a more refined lady?"

He took her face between his hands and searched her eyes. "Camy, I'm more than certain."

"Come along." Mrs Smith appeared in the hall. "Your guests are waiting." She raised her chin and descended the stairs.

"A moment, if you will," Duncan said as he returned to his room.

Camy stood at the top of the stairs, watching, as Mr. Weston appeared at the bottom step and took Mrs. Smith's arm. An image of Miller, beaten and left for dead, pressed into her mind, only it wasn't Miller at all but rather Duncan. Perhaps it wasn't too late to speak with Mr. Weston, but she knew that it was. She'd never forgive herself if anything happened to the man she loved. Never.

"Are you ready, Mrs. Murray?" he whispered in her ear. Looping his arm through hers, he sent a bevy of shivers down her spine. As if judging her trembling as hesitancy to spend time in the company of Rusa Valley, he said, "Another hour, and then we can go home."

Home. It had a nice ring to it, but she couldn't help wondering if they would survive the evening. Her overtaxed nerves were ready to see her in a fit of vapors because the man beside her, solely focused on her, didn't seem to care that somewhere someone had sought to hurt her through harming a friend. And if they did it once, they'd do it again, and this time, Camy feared, they wouldn't be as kind.

Chapter Twenty

Shock rocked Duncan back on his heels at the sight of Calvin Weston standing in Mrs. Smith's home. What was his business partner doing in Rusa Valley? Perhaps he should have met with his friend Deputy Nate Cooper instead of rushing headlong and marrying Camy. Not that he regretted marrying her, but the sight of Weston sent a chill into his bones.

Mrs. Smith rang a bell until everyone quieted. "May I introduce to you Miss Cameron Sims's fiancé, Mr. Duncan Murray?"

"Hold up there, missy," Hamish's raspy voice called as he pushed through the crowd. "They's married now." Hamish's toothless grin split his face, his white-gray beard bobbing as he chuckled. The guests gasped and whispered congratulations. Mrs. Smith's jaw dropped, and then her eyes narrowed to mere slits directed at Duncan's bride. Camy tensed. The chill in his bones turned frigid. "I's pleased to present to you Mr. and Mrs. Duncan Murray," Hamish said, holding up a glass of lemonade.

Duncan slipped his arm around Camy's waist, pulling her closer to him, shielding her like a hen would a chick. He glanced around the room, his gaze hard, daring anyone to dishonor his wife. "I'm honored and blessed to have Camy as my wife. The nuptials were spoken only an hour ago with Pastor Hammond and Camy's family as witnesses."

"He must have compromised her." Levina Smith's gold ringlets bobbed at her shoulders as her loud whisper echoed in his ears.

He firmed his hold as Camy tried to pull away. "I assure you that is not the case," he said to the crowd. Then he lowered his voice and looked into Levina's cold, calculating blue eyes as his wife's breaths became shallow and ragged, and he said, "I would ask you not to speak ill of my wife, as I have great affection for her. Now, if you'll excuse us, I would have a private word with my wife."

He guided her through a sea of suits and expensive gowns and noticed many of the folks weren't from Rusa Valley, but rather hobnobs he recognized from social gatherings in Topeka. Some had propositioned him for business deals, many of which he'd turned down. Several of the long faces greeting them as they passed through were those of mamas who'd tried to pawn their daughters on his bank account. Perhaps Weston's appearance at Mrs. Smith's gathering was nothing more than a coincidence. However, the niggling at the back of his neck told him otherwise.

Stepping out onto the porch, he tugged her along a cobblestone path lined with budding shrubs until they came to a raised limestone structure with a roof overlooking the river. He released her, giving her space to breathe.

"I should have been more prepared. I thought you would be among friends, not…" He didn't know what to say, given her earlier "poor orphaned farm girl" comment. He didn't see her as such, and didn't want her to think he did. He'd rather spend an hour arguing with her than playing niceties with a false smile and batting lashes. At least with Camy's expressive eyes he knew exactly where he stood with her. Most of the time.

"Rich city folks?" she tossed out, and then her shoulders sagged. "I'm sorry. Mrs. Smith's events are rarely pleasant, and even though I was surprised at her throwing an engagement party, I should have known she intended to impress your circle, not celebrate with Rusa Valley."

Leaning against a post, he drank in the sight of his wife. The setting sun made it seem as though strands of her hair were on fire. Her complexion glowed and her eyes were a deep gold, instead of the honeyed coffee. The affection bursting in his heart for her grew by the moment. He probably even loved her. He was quite certain he did. "Camy, I won't tolerate disrespect of my wife from anyone." His father had disrespected his mother in private and public. "Not even from myself."

One corner of her mouth lifted. "Th-thank you," she said, laughing. "I thought we would have to retrieve the smelling salts for poor Levina. Oh dear." She paled. "Mrs. Smith is not too happy about our nuptials. I'm certain she'd already had her sights set on you for one of her daughters, probably even Levina. Most assuredly, she had hoped for time to break our engagement."

He strode across the stones and swept a curl behind her ear. His gaze holding hers, he smiled. "Even if we weren't already married, that never would have happened, as I find I'd rather spend time beating you at chess than playing court to a spoiled young woman." Duncan caught sight of Nate Cooper standing at a distance and he tucked Camy's arm in his and walked her toward the house. He hated sending her in to face Mrs. Smith and the socialites without him. However, Duncan didn't want to subject her to any unsavory news concerning Miller's involvement in the attacks on her land. "I have business to tend to," he said, assisting her up the stairs. "I don't intend to be heavy-handed in our marriage, but I'm asking of you two things. Do not leave this house, and please stay away from Mrs. Smith's gentleman friend until I return."

She gave him a quizzical look, her mouth twisting as if she wanted to argue.

"Please," he said. "Trust me."

She nodded, then disappeared through the open door and a bevy of chatter and a haze of cigar smoke. Retracing his steps, Duncan found Nate hovering where he left him. "I hope you have good news for me, my friend."

Nate scrubbed his hand over his bearded chin. "I'm not sure what I have. I checked with the railroad committee about the property in question. Seems there was a recent request for a survey to be done."

Duncan crossed his arms in front of him wondering how it had passed by him without notice. "What for?"

"Coal beds."

"Hamish didn't mention coal," Duncan mused aloud. "Sure makes sense for someone greedy enough to go to great lengths to gain that property, especially with the railroad looking for a place to build." He mentally ran numbers in his head and calculated a raw estimate of what the railroad would pay if coal lay beneath the surface.

"The other thing, the day before you sent your message to me, Mrs. Williamson sent for the sheriff. Upon returning from the mercantile, she found two young men ransacking your room at the boardinghouse."

"I figured as much." Duncan told him about the three men tearing up the field, finding his pocket watch, the cigarettes and Miller's beaten body. In return, Nate told him about the two men Mrs. Williamson had described, both fitting Miller's friends. "I've only seen one man smoke this brand, and that's Weston."

Nate whistled between his teeth. "I didn't say anything, as I didn't think it mattered, but Weston requested the survey. There's some talk around town too. He owes a lot of money to some unsavory folks."

"Do you think it's possible these unsavory folks believed Miller worked for Weston?"

"I don't think so. These men wouldn't have bothered with a hired man, they'd come straight for Weston." Nate shifted his weight. "Do you think Weston could have been involved in Miller's beating? Our office has had several complaints of Weston roughing up the doves."

Duncan gave himself a mental kick for not seeing beyond Weston's facade. If Duncan ever took on another partner, he'd have him thoroughly investigated. "Weston is inside playing court to the hostess." He glanced toward the house, wondering how it all fit together. Wondering how his partner was involved.

Thankful he'd warned his wife to keep her distance from Weston.

"What are you thinking, Duncan?"

"I don't know. My gut tells me Weston is involved. I've never had reason to distrust him, but I kept my caution where he was concerned." Had Weston simply been seeking to purchase the land, or did he hire these young men to terrorize the Simses? He jammed his hands into his pockets. "I fear I'm no closer to any answers."

"I'm sorry. I wish I could have done more." Nate adjusted his hat and they began walking toward the house. "I never thought I'd say this, but congratulations on your bride. She's lovely."

"Thank you. I'm a blessed man," he said, longing to return to Camy's side.

Benjamin Northrop rode into the yard, his horse heaving as if he'd raced the beast across the county, and jumped to the ground.

"Northrop," Duncan called, catching his attention. "Is everything okay?"

The doctor lengthened his stride. "Miller woke up," he said in between hard breaths. "He'd gotten in trouble gambling."

"The mark on his cheek?" Duncan asked.

"Yes," Northrop said, pinching the bridge of his nose. "Said he'd been drinking one night near a year ago and bragged about how he'd be the richest man in the county once he got one of the Sims girls to marry him. He chased Camy thinking she'd be the easiest."

Duncan nearly laughed, knowing how easily she'd seen through Miller's ruse.

"We've known for years about the feud between

our families. My father bought land from Camy's father thinking he was purchasing Sims Creek, which belonged to Hamish, instead of what we own now. For years, Father has been obsessed with Sims Creek, especially given that he owns the land on the other side of Sims too. I broke things off with Ellie because of it. Miller thought if he could gain the land he'd make Father happy, and when he discovered a journal entry of my father's declaring a prospector had found coal on Sims land in Father's office, he tried to trap Camy into compromising situations. None of which worked."

Northrop shook his head and continued. "How Miller tells it, he'd become drunk after one of her rebuffs. He lost money he didn't have and promised Sims Creek once he married her. The fires weren't set by him, but he knew about them."

"Who did he owe money to?" Duncan asked, already knowing the answer.

"Mr. Weston. When Weston found out you were engaged to Camy, he threatened Miller if he didn't kidnap Camy and force her to marry him. You saw what happened."

"Weston is responsible for cutting up Miller?" Nate asked.

Northrop nodded. "I believe Miller is telling the truth. He said the two men who were with him on the field are Weston's nephews."

"Did you see them inside?" Nate looked through the open door.

"No, I didn't see them, but I also didn't get a good look at them when I chased them down. I'm not certain I would recognize them. However, if they're not in there, they're close by," Duncan responded as he climbed the steps. "Northrop, find Ellie and Mara and keep them with you. If you see Hamish tell him what's going on."

"Where are you going?" Benjamin asked, fast on his heels.

"To find my wife." Hopefully before it was too late. If Weston had been desperate enough to manipulate Miller into criminal activities and then leave him for dead, Duncan was afraid of what he'd do now the possibility of gaining Sims Creek was out of his hands. Fortunately all of his dealings with Weston were through the railroad and approved by the committee, giving the bounder no rights to Sims Creek.

As Camy wound her way through the party, smiling and nodding and stopping here and there to accept congratulations on her marriage, she saw Ellie helping serve dessert and Mara holding court among the young people. Her sisters had always loved social gatherings, even under Mrs. Smith's critical eye. Yet Camy needed a quiet corner and found one in Mrs. Smith's extravagant library, full of rarely used tomes. The waning daylight left the east-facing morning room in nothing more than shadows beneath the lanterns. Camy often sought out the peace and solitude of this room. She ran her fingers over the spines of the books, admiring their binding and gold-foiled letters. She'd longed to pull one from its position, to look inside and feel the paper and see the printed words, to smell the pages, but she never dared lest she disturbed the quietness of the room.

"There you are," Mrs. Smith said, sweeping in, her

dark blue skirts brushing against the doorway. "I have someone who would like to formally meet you."

Mr. Weston, dressed in a black frock suit and gray vest, came in behind her. Smoke from his cigarette danced into the air. Even though he wore a suit similar to Duncan's, he didn't look as distinguished or as handsome. Of course, he was a head shorter, and his shoulders weren't nearly as wide. His blond hair was slicked against his head, a stark difference to Duncan's chestnut curls, and the penciled mustache beneath his hawklike nose reminded her of a mangy coyote slinking around the farm last winter frothing at the mouth. How could she not have noticed the coyotelike demeanor when he'd approached her last year about Sims Creek?

"Of course, we've already met before," Mr. Weston said as he took her hand in his. She quickly pulled away when he leaned forward to kiss the back of her hand.

"Darling," Mrs. Smith purred, her blue eyes feigning kindness when in reality they were cold. The woman didn't like her plans to be usurped, and that was exactly what had happened when Duncan chose for them to marry when they did. "If you're going to be a successful wife in your husband's circles, you must learn not to be so rude to your betters."

Camy flinched as if she'd been slapped.

"My apologies, dear, but you should have known marrying above yourself would pose its challenges." Mrs. Smith pretended to inspect a spot on her dress as Mr. Weston's gaze roamed over Camy from head to toe and back again, sending a chill down her spine and a knot in her gut.

"Mrs. Smith," he said, never taking his eyes from Camy. "Would you mind giving us a moment?"

To Mrs. Smith's credit, she hesitated. Concern quickly replaced the facade of an uppity busybody. "Mr. Weston, I don't think it's proper."

Camy's insides roared in relief at Mrs. Smith's intervention. For all of her pomp, Camy believed a decent lady lay beneath the powder, rouge and sharp tongue. Perhaps, Camy thought, she should get to know her more, become her friend instead of judge her.

Mr. Weston glared at Mrs. Smith and said, "I promise not to ravage her in your home."

Mrs. Smith's blue eyes darted between Camy and Weston. She drew in a long breath and released it. Camy silently prayed Mrs. Smith would hold her ground. Camy knew the moment she relented. "Very well, then. I'll be outside the door if you have need of me."

Camy put the upholstered divan between them, the wood trim biting into her fingers.

"Truly I have no wish to cause you harm, Miss Sims."

"Murray, Mrs. Murray," she reminded him. The words solidifying in her heart. It felt good to know she had the covering of his name, no matter what anyone said about marrying above her social status.

"I suppose you no longer want to sell your property."

"I never did, Mr. Weston, as it was never mine to begin with, but rather my uncle's. And now it belongs to my husband." She realized then that all the stress and anxiety she'd experienced over the last months had left. The burden had disappeared with her knowing it was no longer hers to bear alone, that she had a husband with broad shoulders to share the burden.

He drew closer, his hand next to hers on the divan, his cigarette smoke tickling her nose as he puffed and released. The corner of his mouth turned upward into a smirk, and then he bit the inside of his cheek, his eyes hard, deadly. "I believe I can convince my business partner to come to some sort of agreement."

Camy felt her heart plummeting to her toes, uncertain of whom he spoke of, but something told her she didn't want to know. She looked him straight in the eye. "I don't understand."

"Don't you?" He puffed. "Your husband didn't tell you about me?"

Camy swallowed past the knot forming in her throat.

"I'm on the committee for the railroad, as is your husband, and of course, he happens to be an investor. I convince him of our need for money and he provides the funds."

Head spinning, she rocked back on her heels. "Mr. Henry?" She knew the man had claimed to be with the railroad before the attacks began happening at the farm. Her heart beat wildly in her chest as she waited for his answer.

"That would be my beloved nephew, an associate of mine."

Of Duncan's too? Did that mean he had something to do with Miller being left for dead? Her husband? *Trust me.*

"Excuse me." Camy started to run out the door.

"Mrs. Murray," he said, halting her. "I do get what I want."

She ran out of the library and bumped into Mrs. Smith. The concern etched in the lines of her face hadn't left. "Are you all right, Cameron?"

Camy shook her head and ran up the back stairs and to the room given to her to use for the evening. She slid against the closed door, crumpling into a heap of silk on the floor. How could she have been so foolish? After years of protecting her heart, after years of thinking that all men thought about was chasing two bits and nothing more, how could she have given her heart to the first handsome man who broke through her defenses? *Trust me.* "God, what did I do? I gave my heart to a man and he betrayed me. Betrayed my sisters. Miller." She sobbed, images of Miller lifeless and scarred ambushing her mind. "Poor Miller, and all because I fancied myself in love. How could I have married a man who would do something like that to another human being?"

Because he'd shown her kindness and tenderness. He'd wooed her by caring for the farm. Wooed her by challenging her at chess, reading scripture and praying. Wooed her with kisses. *Trust me.* She thought she knew him, knew his heart. Even though they'd had an understanding between them, a marriage in name only, she had still hoped... Her hopes fell, like a branch struck by lightning, to the ground. Blackened and charred.

She picked herself up off the floor and took off her mother's wedding gown, laid it on the bed and changed into the lavender one she'd been married in. Finding writing supplies in the desk, she left a note for her sisters and slipped off her wedding ring. She'd signed an agreement, even if Mr. Murray hadn't intended to keep his word. She was a Sims, and a Sims did, no matter what. Hamish had given him the land in exchange for her taking his name, but it didn't mean she had to keep it.

She laid the missive and the ring on top of her mama's wedding gown and then slipped out the door. She nearly tripped down the stairs as she rushed out the back door in her haste to get as far away from Duncan Murray as possible. The stables would offer a horse. She could have it returned. She came to an abrupt halt, halfway between the house and stables. Doubling over, she clasped her hand over her mouth to quiet her sobs and collapsed to the ground. She didn't even know how to ride a horse.

"God, why did Duncan have to be so kind and capture my heart?"

A small voice niggled in her head. *Because he is kind and his actions prove it.* "And worthy of my trust," she said to herself, knowing that even if Duncan hadn't revealed his connection to the railroad to her, his character should speak louder than Mr. Weston's accusations.

Drawing in several long breaths of air, she wiped her eyes and climbed to her feet. Her gown, wet and splotched with mud, hung heavy against the back of her legs, reminding her that a soiled gown didn't necessarily mean a ruined gown. Just like her heart, it might feel bruised, crumbling like clods of dirt, but it wasn't beyond repair, especially if the bruising was due to her own wayward thoughts.

Duncan deserved the opportunity to explain. She owed it to him, and she owed it to herself to move beyond her fear of rejection and give Duncan a chance, if he was willing to forgive her for doubting him. He deserved that she honor the vows spoken before Pastor Hammond, her family, and God.

With renewed determination to fight for Duncan as he'd promised to fight for her, she quickened her steps toward the man she loved. And she intended to let him know it.

Chapter Twenty-One

Duncan stormed into the house, his gaze roaming over the crowd, looking for the heart-shaped face he'd come to love framed by a crown of luxurious, burnished brown curls. He pushed to the center. Nate came alongside him, his keen eye sweeping through the room. "I don't see Weston."

"Where's my wife?" Duncan boomed. Every conversation abruptly halted; heads turned.

Ellie and Mara appeared from the parlor room. Benjamin, his hair sticking out at odd ends and dark circles making him look like he'd been in a brawl, stalked toward them, taking their arms and leading them to Duncan. "If it's all right with you, I'll take them to my father's."

"It's closer?" Duncan asked, then at Benjamin's nod, said, "I think that's wise."

Ellie pulled from Northrop's grasp, worry for her sister pressed lines into her brow, creasing the corners of her eyes. "I'm not going anywhere. What's going on? Where's Camy?"

Before he could answer, a scream sounded from

a hallway in the back part of the house. Duncan tore through the rooms. A maid knelt over Mrs. Smith, tears slipping from her eyes. Benjamin pushed through and checked the hostess's pulse and then glanced up at Duncan. "She seems to be fine. Does anyone have smelling salts?"

Mrs. Smith's lashes batted open and Benjamin helped her to the sofa in the library. "What happened?"

Confused, she looked around the room, then pressed her palm to her chest. "Oh dear, that awful man."

"Mr. Weston?" Duncan questioned.

"Yes, yes. He said he wanted to meet your bride, being your business partner and all."

Clenching his teeth, Duncan drew in slow, even breaths.

"He all but threw me out of the room, and then the poor dear ran out of here crying. I demanded answers…" She shivered. "She went up the back stairs."

Duncan left Ellie and Mara in Benjamin and Nate's care and took the stairs two at a time. He burst into her room. Camy's wedding dress was draped over the bed. The wedding ring he'd placed on her finger lay in the center of a folded piece of paper. The blood in his veins froze.

Clutching the ring in his fist, he unfolded the piece of paper. In heavy ink, and in the midst of the spattering of tears, he read, "My dearest Ellie and Mara, my sincere apologies for misplacing my trust and following my foolish heart. Love, Camy."

He collapsed on the bed, his emotions torn between relief that Weston hadn't taken her and grief that she'd left him. What had gone wrong to make her mistrust him? Had Weston somehow put doubts in her mind? Worse yet, caused her to believe Duncan was the one responsible for all her troubles? For Miller? He buried his face into his hands, the missive crinkling. He should have listened to his gut, should have kept her by his side. "I should have told her the truth, Lord."

"That ye should've. I warned ye, though, dinnae I?" Hamish's gravelly voice had Duncan looking up at him as he ambled into the room. "Maybe then ye wouldnae lost her."

Duncan squinted, fists clenched at his sides to keep from strangling the old man.

"Ye gonna sit there feelin' sorry for yerself or ye gonna go after my niece?"

The ring bit into his palm. "She doesn't want me."

"Did she say it?"

Duncan read the note to Hamish.

"Sounds like a lass in love sufferin' a broken heart."

"I didn't mean to break her heart."

"No, but someone did," Hamish said, scratching his head. "Best make it right."

Raking his fingers through his hair, Duncan said, "I asked her to trust me."

"I expect it's hard fer a girl to trust when so many folks has abandoned her."

"I didn't." He'd stayed when he could have left, and come back when he'd tried to leave. He'd made improvements to her home. *Their home*.

"No, but you didn't promise to stay either."

Springing from the bed, Duncan paced. "I promised to love her, cherish and honor her."

"Yep, you did, but does she ken those were more than words fer the preacher's ears?"

"For a crotchety old man you sure are wise." He smiled, knowing he'd promised to fight for her, and fight for her he would. Once he found her he'd make sure she knew the entire truth, not just Weston's version. He prayed she believed him, especially when he told her he loved her.

"Duncan," Nate said, standing in the hall, his hat crunched in his hands. "We have a problem."

Duncan dreaded hearing what his friend had to say.

"Well, whatcha got, boy? If it concerns my niece it concerns me."

Nate ignored Hamish and looked directly at Duncan. "Weston has your wife."

Duncan felt all the blood drain from his face and then return with a vengeance. "What makes you say that for certain?" He didn't want to waste time chasing shadows; he'd already spent too much time feeling sorry for himself when he should have been seeking out his wife to tell her what was in his heart.

"This," Nate said, holding out a scrawled note, "was brought in by one of Mrs. Smith's servants."

Duncan snagged the note and scanned over the lines. "A ransom note. He wants money in exchange for my wife, but he doesn't say how much, nor does it say where. I'll be a frog in boiling water if I sit around waiting for more instructions," he said as he pushed past Nate and Hamish and flew down the stairs to find Ellie arguing with Benjamin.

"Ellie, please, the man who harmed Miller now has Camy," Duncan said, forcing calm into his blood, knowing he wouldn't be any good to his wife if he didn't keep rational. "We know what Weston is capable of, but we have no idea what his intentions are for Camy. We can't track them down if we're keeping our attention on you. I need you and Mara to go with Benjamin until we find Weston, until I find my wife."

"The man who cut Miller up has Camy," Mara said. "You're woolly-headed to think I am sitting by darning socks like a proper lady." Her glare dared him to tell her no. "I can shoot."

"I know you can, Mara, which is exactly why you're needed at the Northrops'," he said, holding Ellie's gaze. "Dr. Northrop has fallen ill. Julius is caring for him and can't keep watch on Bella, and of course, Benjamin needs to get back to Miller." He pleaded to Ellie with his eyes.

"You'll send word?" Ellie asked, searching his face for answers.

"As soon as all is well," Duncan said, squeezing her hand in reassurance, and then he turned to the remaining group of people. "Will someone send for Pastor Hammond and ask him to pray for protection over my wife?"

Duncan bent his head toward Nate. "I left Heather Glenn at the farm. The Old Nag pulling the buckboard will do me no good, and Benjamin's horse was heaving when he came in."

"We have horses." Levina spoke quietly, almost so quietly that Duncan didn't hear her.

"Yes," Mrs. Smith piped up, still lounging on the divan, fanning herself. "Tell my groom to give you Sir Charles. He's our fastest runner, and if you need more horses, please, it's the least I can do."

"My thanks, Mrs. Smith." He scrubbed his palm over his face. "I need to go this one alone."

Alone somehow ended up including Hamish, Nate

and Pastor Hammond. Turned out the pastor had served with the Union as one of the best trackers this side of the Mississippi.

"Something's bothering me," Nate said as the four of them rode west away from Rusa Valley following tracks left by Weston and his nephews.

Duncan glanced at him, waiting for him to continue.

"Why do you think he left a ransom note and didn't tell you where to go?" Nate mused, as Hamish and the pastor dismounted their horses and checked for more tracks.

Duncan had been wondering the same thing. Weston delighted in power, which he wouldn't have behind bars, but perhaps he preferred the type of power where he controlled a man's neck by the noose. Like taking a man's wife and demanding a fortune. He thought back to the X carved in Northrop's face. "It's nothing more than a game to him." Duncan stared toward the setting sun. "If he thinks I'd do anything for my wife, he ups the ante by causing me to fret." He glanced at his friend. "I'd give all my wealth to save her, and he knows it. I made that clear at the party."

"The curse of the rich," Nate responded.

He'd hated his father's money, not because he thought being rich was accursed. He didn't care if he had money or not. He'd hated his father. "I've never considered it a curse. But then I've never cared for anyone the way I care for her." The way he loved her.

"Weston clearly realized that tonight, and your impromptu marriage took all possibility of gaining Sims Creek from his hands. If there's coal there, the railroad would have paid a handsome price." Nate shifted in his saddle.

"I hope he's intelligent enough to know that if he harms my wife, I won't pay a farthing."

He also prayed for self-control once he found them.

Hamish limped beside the pastor as they ambled back toward the horses and where Duncan and Nate were waiting. Hamish swept his hat off and smacked his leg. "Looks like they's headed to the farm. Now, I've been trying to work all this up in my cap, as I was telling Preacher here, and I can't imagine why all the sudden interest in Sims Creek and why would anyone go to such lengths to have it. There's parcels of land up and down the river folks is eager to sell. Why torment my nieces and cause me heart failure?"

Duncan furrowed his brow, wondering if the old man knew about the coal. If he did, he hadn't said a word. "Coal."

"Coal? There ain't no coal here. I thought I put that rumor to death years ago. Think I'd be spending my days in that there city if I thought there was coal? And I sure wouldnae gived it to ye to take my nieces off my hands." Resettling his hat on his head, Hamish climbed up onto his mule. "All be, ye hear that, Millie. Folks still seem to think there's coal at Sims Creek."

Hamish's chuckle echoed through the valley as they headed toward the farm.

Unfamiliar voices pierced through Camy's consciousness as she tried to open her heavy eyelids. They sounded angry and muffled.

"You imbeciles," Mr. Weston growled. "How is it Miller is here?"

Mr. Weston? Camy peeked through one eye. She recognized the bits and pieces of fabric dotting the chinking in Ellie's room. The curtains made from one of their older dresses. She glanced toward the light filtering through the cracked-open door. Weston paced near the bed where Miller lay in the other room. How had she come here? Last she remembered she'd been halfway to the stables to ride off, not that she could ride, but had quickly come to the realization that Duncan had never lied to her and had always kept his word to her. And she knew he wouldn't have harmed Miller. She hadn't even made it to Mrs. Smith's stables when she turned around to head back to the house, only to be grabbed from behind, a cloth doused with a sweet scent covering her nose and mouth. The moment before she slipped from consciousness, she'd seen Mr. Weston's smirk.

"You were supposed to dump him in the river. Who knows what he's told to whom?" Weston hollered. Flesh smacked against flesh.

"He's not even awake," a pitched voice argued.

"You fool, how do you know he hasn't been awake these past few days?"

Camy heard the cabin door open and slam shut.

"I'm sorry, uncle," came a different voice. "We were having some fun, and Miller disappeared. Someone must have found him and brought him here to Sims Creek."

"You mean you were drinking and dallying with the ladies at Rusa's saloon." Another smack. "Sorry won't keep you out of jail. You were given a job. I expected it to be done. Now go see if these guttersnipes have a wagon. We must leave before Murray figures out we've come this direction. And don't forget to load his trunk."

"But, uncle, we looked—"

"Looked? I should have searched his belongings myself. He's one of the wealthiest men in the country, and all you found was an old pocket watch? You didn't look well enough. Men like him don't keep all their coins in the bank. Now get the trunk and find a wagon and let's get out of here."

The door to the cabin opened and closed, and then footsteps clapped on the floorboards toward her room. Camy willed her breathing to slow as her door creaked open. Tobacco wafted in with Mr. Weston. "You have been a pain in my neck, missy. You should've convinced your uncle to sell when you had the chance. Now I fear my patience has long worn out, and I don't have the time to negotiate terms with your husband."

She heard the rustling of his clothes as he bent over her, felt the coolness of his dark shadow. She fought wrinkling her nose as he blew smoke into her face. He dug his fingers into her bandaged shoulder. Camy screamed in pain as she shot up. She clasped her palm against her shoulder. His deadly gaze chilled her.

"Now, then, we can discuss your demise," he said, pacing to the window. "As I recall, my boys threatened to dump you and your sisters in the river, but since they failed in doing so with your friend out there, I'm guessing that's no longer a possibility." He pulled long on his cigarette and blew out the smoke, then glanced over his shoulder. "The question burning in my mind is which would be more effective, killing you and letting your husband live with regrets, or allowing you to live with the burden of his murder knowing you could've prevented it. Of course," he said, the mattress dipping beneath his weight as he sat, his hand resting on her leg. "I could always kill you both."

"You won't get away with murdering either of us," she said through gritted teeth and the pain throbbing in her shoulder.

"No? After I take care of Miller, you and your husband, nobody would suspect me. And if they did, there would be no proof. Besides, I'll be headed to Mexico after your husband pays the ransom."

"You think to t-take his money and then k-kill him?" The sharp pain subsiding to a throb, she scooted away from him. "Mr. Murray and I are business partners, nothing more. Any ransom you've requested will certainly be ignored, as his keen financial sense will see that any money paid for a useless piece of land is senseless."

"For a woman who has remained one foot ahead of me, you sure are stupid." Standing, he tossed his cigarette to the floor and glared down at her. "I have it on good authority that your marriage is more than a business agreement."

"I don't know whose authority you're speaking of, but I can assure you our marriage is in name only. He wanted Sims Creek. I wanted to remain in my home with my sisters. The agreement is tucked away in the family Bible if you'd like to see it."

"Why do you suppose Duncan wanted this land?"

"B-because." The word slurred out of her mouth; she wondered how Mr. Weston would respond to her answer. "It reminds him of his childhood home."

His laughter burst like thunder, forming a knot of fear in her stomach. "What about the coal, darling?"

Confused, Camy furrowed her brow.

"Your uncle didn't tell you about the coal beds on this parcel of land?" Mr. Weston crossed his arms, a smug smile turned his mouth upward.

Her eyes narrowed.

"It makes Sims Creek worth quite a bit of money, as it'll be beneficial to the railroad when it comes through Rusa Valley."

"We're miles from Rusa Valley. Besides, if there's coal here and it's worth as much as you think, then why did Hamish give Sims Creek to Mr. Murray in exchange for nothing more than our marriage?"

"Because," Duncan's voice, low and threatening, growled from the doorway. Camy's heart leaped within her chest. Mr. Weston spun around, hand on the revolver belted at his waist. Duncan shook his head, his own revolver pointed at Mr. Weston's chest. "There isn't coal here, and your uncle knew I'd see you protected from weasels like Weston."

"And a fine job you've done, given that I was able to steal your wife from under your nose," Mr. Weston tossed out.

"That had nothing to do with my inability to protect her but rather her lack of heeding my wishes." He shifted his gaze from Mr. Weston to her. "I specifically told you to stay away from Mr. Weston, and not to leave Mrs. Smith's home."

Tears brimming on her lashes, she said, "I'm sorry. I should have trusted you. I did. I tried to come back."

Muscle ticking in his jaw and nostrils flaring, he nodded. "I know, sweetheart."

A man she didn't recognize wearing a shiny badge stepped beside Duncan. "Hamish and the pastor have the others tied up on the porch. You want me to take him?"

"Thanks, Nate."

After the deputy led Mr. Weston from the room, Duncan leaned against the door frame and stared at her with disappointment. His rumpled black frock suit matched her soiled lavender gown. She wanted to go to him, to wrap her arms around him and never let go, to tell him she loved him, but she feared she was too late. She angrily swiped at the tears streaming down her cheeks. "I'm sorry, Mr. Murray, for any inconvenience I have caused you."

Straightening, he crossed his arms, bracing his legs shoulder width apart. "We need to renegotiate the terms of our marriage."

Staring at her hands folded in her lap, she drew in a shuddering breath. She should have trusted him. If she did, her heart wouldn't be breaking. "I understand."

"No, I don't think you do," he drawled. "First, you will no longer call me Mr. Murray. Duncan, my love, darling or any other endearment you can think of, but no more Mr. Murray. I am your husband, and whether you like it or not we spoke vows before God and your family. I expect you to honor those vows, just as I promise to do the same."

She released the breath she'd been holding, happy to get a second chance.

"Second, obedience," he said, and then mumbled beneath his breath when Mara and Ellie flew past him. Her sisters bombarded her with hugs. "Can any of you heed instructions? I told you I would send word when all was well."

"Only when it suits us," Ellie said, dismissing him with the wave of her hand. "We couldn't wait."

"Poor Benjamin didn't have a chance when we—including Bella—threatened to come on our own."

Ellie released Camy and glanced over her. "Your shoulder is bleeding again. We'll see to it once you and your husband finish talking. Come along, Mara," Ellie said, grabbing Mara's hand and pulling her out of the room.

Duncan gazed out the window. Camy went to him and placed her hand on his arm. "Do you regret our marriage?"

After two rises and falls of his chest, he turned toward her. His eyes shone with tears. "How could I regret marrying the woman I love?"

Air caught in her lungs. He—he loved her? A bevy of flutters took root in her chest.

"I've never been so scared in all my life, Camy." He pulled her into his arms and molded her to him and then leaned back. "I told you I don't intend to be heavy-handed. When I request something from you, it's for good reason. Do not disobey me like that again, please?"

Camy drew her lip between her teeth. "As long as it's within reason."

Smiling, he shook his head. "I can live with that for now."

"Was there a third thing you wanted to negotiate?"

"Hmm, I require this every day until death parts us, sweetheart," he said, bending his head and kissing her.

Epilogue

May 1867
Rusa Valley's Spring Run

Camy sat on the quilt drinking in the sight of her husband as he lifted his arms overhead and stretched. Benjamin elbowed him in the ribs and, pointing at Deputy Nate, laughed. After Weston and his nephews were apprehended, the county had decided Rusa Valley needed a jail and a permanent deputy. Poor Nate had more than he bargained for when he took the job. He spent more time dodging the wide-eyed younger ladies, including Levina and her friends, than he did keeping the peace.

Pastor Hammond knelt beside his wife and gave her a kiss, his hand affectionately rubbing her belly. "How's Little Hammond doing? Oh," he said, smiling. "He's ready to race."

Mrs. Hammond playfully swatted his hand and said, "What makes you think our child is a he, Pastor?"

"He's feisty."

"And girls cannot be feisty?" Mara said with a hand on her hip.

Hammond laughed. "That is my cue to leave. Pray for me," he said, kissing his wife on the cheek.

"Are you not running this spring, Mara?" Mrs. Smith, with her big floppy hat decked with every color of ribbon and flowers known to man, reclined next to Mrs. Hammond.

Mara sighed and looked longingly at the men lining up. "I'm nearly eighteen now. Time to be through with childish games and act a lady."

Bella Northrop giggled, hand to chest, feigning as if her head were in the clouds, and batted her lashes. "Deputy Nate."

"Bella!" Mara stalked away, Bella following after her.

"Well," Mrs. Smith said, "if I was a few years younger, I suppose I'd daydream about a handsome deputy too. By the bye, has anyone heard how Dr. Northrop's father is doing?"

"Pastor says he's improving. Having his sons caring for him, he should be on his feet in no time," Mrs. Hammond said.

"Is Benjamin taking over all his patients, then?" Mrs. Smith asked.

Camy glanced at Ellie, who stared longingly toward Benjamin, sipping her lemonade as Mrs. Hammond responded. "Benjamin and Julius have been discussing what to do. Julius would like to open a pharmacy, but Benjamin isn't set on remaining in Rusa much longer."

Camy didn't blame him. She couldn't imagine living in the same town loving Duncan, knowing she could never be with him. It would break her heart. Every day. As she quite imagined Benjamin's did. Ellie loved him; she just couldn't forgive him for the aches he'd caused her, but Camy prayed they'd figure it out. But considering her sister had left Rusa after Camy's marriage to Duncan, only returning yesterday for Rusa's spring picnic, she feared it was too late.

"Miller stopped at the church before service this morning," Mrs. Hammond said as she arched her back and rubbed her belly. "He looks well. He's not ready to see folks yet, but I'm sure he will soon. He did ask my husband, once again, to send his apologies for any trouble he's caused you ladies."

Camy had long forgiven him, as she understood the need to feel loved and wanted, something the elder Northrop had failed to instill in his youngest son.

Duncan, along with the rest of Rusa Valley's men, lined up across a white line. Uncle Hamish, who had oddly stayed around to help Duncan build a larger house overlooking the river, shifted his weight back and forth with his revolver pointed toward the sky. The men leaned forward, their arms back, waiting for the shot.

Duncan glanced back at her and Camy blew him a kiss. He unfurled from his stance and started toward her.

"Oh!" Mrs. Hammond moaned, her hand flying to her heavily pregnant belly. "Oh my!"

"Oh dear!" chimed Mrs. Smith.

Ellie spilled her lemonade as she scrambled toward

Pastor Hammond's wife. "Oh. Baby! Camy, get the reverend and Dr. Northrop."

Camy jumped to her feet, her husband's brow furrowing in concern as she ran toward them. "Ben! Pastor Hammond! Baby!"

Hamish cocked the hammer back and Duncan tackled Benjamin and Hammond just as the shot sounded. He laughed as they looked up at him in shock. Hammond sprang to his feet and sprinted toward his wife, Benjamin quick on his heels.

Duncan lengthened his strides, meeting Camy with a twinkle in his eye that sent her heart into a series of flips. "Hello, my love."

"Hello," he said, taking her in his arms. "So we're having a baby?"

She swatted his arm and danced away from him. "Don't be silly. The Hammonds are having a baby today." The corner of her mouth turned upward as she walked backward, keeping one step out of his reach as he stalked toward her. "I think we need to renegotiate the terms of our marriage."

He narrowed his eyes. "I've given you everything I have, including my heart. What more do I have to negotiate with?"

"We *are* having a baby."

He came to an abrupt stop, jaw dropping. "What did you say, Mrs. Murray?"

"That's Camy, sweetheart, darling, mother of my child or any other endearment you may choose."

Before she could say another word, he swept her into his arms and spun her around before setting her on her feet and kissing her. He drew back, his gaze holding hers, his palm warming the small of her back. "I love you, Cameron Murray, mother of my child."

She melted against him. "And I love you, Duncan Murray, father of my child."

* * * * *

If you enjoyed THE NEGOTIATED MARRIAGE, look for these other books by Christina Rich:

THE GUARDIAN'S PROMISE
THE WARRIOR'S VOW
CAPTIVE ON THE HIGH SEAS

Dear Reader,

I hope you enjoyed Camy and Duncan's story as much as I enjoyed writing it. Rusa Valley is a fictional town based off many of those lingering small towns that once burst with life as the railroad pushed through.

As a native Kansan I love the places where the gentle rolling hills meet the Flint Hills. I love the secluded rivers canopied by the trees. And I loved stepping into my own backyard to bring pieces of my childhood into Camy and Duncan's story as well as bringing in my own ancestry. Several of my ancestors came to Kansas after the war, some following the iron road for work while others sought to make a life of farming. Several of them married and raised their families in this beautiful state.

I look forward to writing more stories set in Rusa Valley.

I love to hear from readers. You can find more about me and my writing at *www.threefoldstrand.com* or on Facebook, AuthorChristinaRich.

Blessings,
Christina

REQUEST YOUR FREE BOOKS!

2 FREE INSPIRATIONAL NOVELS
PLUS 2 *FREE* MYSTERY GIFTS

Love Inspired® **HISTORICAL**

YES! Please send me 2 FREE Love Inspired® Historical novels and my 2 FREE mystery gifts (gifts are worth about $10). After receiving them, if I don't wish to receive any more books, I can return the shipping statement marked "cancel." If I don't cancel, I will receive 4 brand-new novels every month and be billed just $4.99 per book in the U.S. or $5.49 per book in Canada. That's a saving of at least 17% off the cover price. It's quite a bargain! Shipping and handling is just 50¢ per book in the U.S. and 75¢ per book in Canada.* I understand that accepting the 2 free books and gifts places me under no obligation to buy anything. I can always return a shipment and cancel at any time. Even if I never buy another book, the two free books and gifts are mine to keep forever.

102/302 IDN GH6Z

Name _____ (PLEASE PRINT) _____

Address _____ Apt. # _____

City _____ State/Prov. _____ Zip/Postal Code _____

Signature (if under 18, a parent or guardian must sign) _____

Mail to the Reader Service:
IN U.S.A.: P.O. Box 1867, Buffalo, NY 14240-1867
IN CANADA: P.O. Box 609, Fort Erie, Ontario L2A 5X3

Want to try two free books from another series?
Call 1-800-873-8635 or visit www.ReaderService.com.

* Terms and prices subject to change without notice. Prices do not include applicable taxes. Sales tax applicable in N.Y. Canadian residents will be charged applicable taxes. Offer not valid in Quebec. This offer is limited to one order per household. Not valid for current subscribers to Love Inspired Historical books. All orders subject to credit approval. Credit or debit balances in a customer's account(s) may be offset by any other outstanding balance owed by or to the customer. Please allow 4 to 6 weeks for delivery. Offer available while quantities last.

Your Privacy—The Reader Service is committed to protecting your privacy. Our Privacy Policy is available online at www.ReaderService.com or upon request from the Reader Service.

We make a portion of our mailing list available to reputable third parties that offer products we believe may interest you. If you prefer that we not exchange your name with third parties, or if you wish to clarify or modify your communication preferences, please visit us at www.ReaderService.com/consumerchoice or write to us at Reader Service Preference Service, P.O. Box 9062, Buffalo, NY 14240-9062. Include your complete name and address.

LIH15

*Finding a husband is the only way Josephine Dooly
can protect herself against her scheming uncle,
so she answers a mail-order-bride ad.
But when she arrives and discovers her groom-to-be
didn't place the ad himself, can she convince
Thomas Young to marry her in name only?*

*Read on for a sneak preview of
PONY EXPRESS CHRISTMAS BRIDE
by Rhonda Gibson, available December 2016
from Love Inspired Historical!*

"You have spunk, Josephine Dooly. I've never heard of a woman riding the Pony Express. And now here I find you outside when you know it could be dangerous."

Josephine turned her gaze back on him. Had she misheard him a few moments ago? The warmth in his laugh drew her like a kitten to fresh milk. Was she so used to her uncle treating her like a child that she expected Thomas to treat her the same way? She searched his face. "You aren't angry with me."

"No, I'm not. I am concerned that you take risks but I am not your keeper. You can come and go as you wish." He pushed away from the well. "I came by to tell you that tomorrow we'll go into town and get married, if you still wish to do so."

Josephine exhaled. "I do."

He nodded. "Can I walk you back inside?"

A longing to stay out in the fresh air battled with wanting to please him and go inside. The cold air nipped